THE VENICE DOUBLE

THE VENICE DOUBLE

A GRANTCHESTER "DUKE" DUCAINE THRILLER

JESSE DEROY

UNION
SQUARE
& CO.
NEW YORK

UNION SQUARE & CO.
NEW YORK

This is a work of fiction. Names, characters, businesses, events, and incidents are the products of the author's imagination. Any resemblance to actual persons, living or dead, or actual events is purely coincidental.

Cover design by Faceout Studio, Tim Green
Cover images by Shutterstock.com/Terrace Studio (Mask); Getty Images/Gina Pricope (Door)

Union Square & Co.
Hachette Book Group
1290 Avenue of the Americas, New York, NY 10104
unionsquareandco.com
@unionsqandco

First Edition: January 2026

Union Square & Co. is an imprint of Grand Central Publishing, a division of Hachette Book Group, Inc. The Union Square & Co. name and logo are registered trademarks of Hachette Book Group, Inc.

Union Square & Co. books may be purchased in bulk for business, educational, or promotional use. For information, please contact your local bookseller or the Hachette Book Group Special Markets Department at special.markets@hbgusa.com.

Library of Congress Cataloging-in-Publication Data has been applied for.

ISBNs: 978-1-4549-5562-7 (paperback), 978-1-4549-5563-4 (ebook),
978-1-6686-5492-7 (audiobook)

Printed in Canada

MRQ-L

10 9 8 7 6 5 4 3 2 1

For my brother

1

DAD AND I WERE IN FLORIDA trying to kill a man named Janus.

But first, we had to find him.

A little more than two years ago, I'd made a colossal mistake. As a result, I'd taken a bullet to the chest, my dad got arrested, and my sister, Ginny, got tossed off a sixth-floor balcony.

I healed up fine, but Dad drew an eight-to-twelve in federal prison, and Ginny ended up in a coma.

About four months ago, broke and desperate—I was on the verge of losing my thumbs because of a gambling problem—I'd done a job that earned me enough money to erase my debt and, more importantly, came with a Get Out of Jail Free card for my dad. Not just early release, but a full pardon. Never mind that it was my fault in the first place that he'd been sent to prison, me getting him an actual pardon was a miracle. Jesus turning water into wine. Except it was a bitter vintage; I hadn't been able to get a miracle for my sister.

Which is why our dad and Aunt Paulie were able to convince me, as Ginny's healthcare power of attorney, to let her go under the knife. Highly experimental surgery, uncharted territory. Her autonomic nervous system and her swallow reflex worked, which meant Ginny was able to breathe on her own, but that was about it. Two years since my screwup had gotten her hurt, and there'd been no change to her state of consciousness despite every other medical intervention I had authorized.

What was there to lose by trying an experimental operation?

Everything.

Of the eighteen patients who'd undergone the surgery before Ginny, half of them had left the operating room as cold bodies. Or as the doctor had put it, "gone with the angels," which I thought was a weird thing for an MD with a PhD to say, but our surgeon's spirituality didn't seem to faze Dad or Paulie.

"Who cares," Dad said. "And it's not like being dead makes any of them worse off."

"Real sentimental of you," I'd said.

Aunt Paulie, who was a fixer, a fence, and a shot caller—if you worked on the West Coast, you paid her toll one way or another—had to have a couple of her goons break us up.

Once we were sitting down again, like reasonable adults, Paulie cut through the argument: "We're choosing between a small chance and no chance at all."

She was right. It wasn't much of choice.

The surgery had been three weeks ago. Ginny had survived—"the angels were looking after her," the doctor told us—and gone through the step-down units at the hospital. She was back in her private care facility. As expected, Ginny was still in a coma; between the swelling from the surgery and the new cocktail of drugs being pumped into her, we'd know if the procedure was successful sometime between week four and eight. Past week eight, and that would be an answer in and of itself.

Nothing I could do but wait.

And go hunting.

Two years ago, after I'd recovered from being shot, I'd gone after all the people who'd crossed us, leaving a trail of bodies behind me before finally hitting a literal dead end even though I still had two more people on my list: Janus, who'd set everything up and then betrayed me and Ginny, as well as the unnamed client who'd commissioned the Paris Job and ordered Janus to commit the betrayal.

The job I'd done four months ago, the one that saved my thumbs and sprung Dad from prison, had extra bonuses stacked on top: The first bonus was that I found and killed that client from two years ago, a Russian billionaire named Volkov. But the second bonus was that I'd gotten a lead on the double-crossing Janus.

Which was great, but the problem was that the Volkov Job was, in a lot of ways, a boondoggle. In the process of trying to extricate myself from the whole fiasco, I'd inadvertently stolen an item of supposedly incalculable value from the safe of a CIA black site in Germany, broken into the Los Angeles offices of the FBI, shot a couple of people who needed shooting, killed Volkov, sunk his yacht, and generally caused a bunch of havoc. As part of the debacle, a freelance hit squad trying to send me a message waltzed through Paulie's office, murdered three of her men, and beat her almost to death; her right arm was still in a cast, the deep scar near her hairline was just starting to look reasonable, and the slight limp would probably never go away.

It wasn't like the Volkov Job had been quiet and subtle; at the exact same time I'd gotten a fix on Janus, I'd essentially lit a bonfire he couldn't ignore. The aptly named two-faced fixer was going to be looking over his shoulder. We had to be cautious in our approach, so we didn't scare him off. Which meant a lot of sitting around, watching. It wasn't a lot different than waiting for the doctor to come out and tell us if Ginny had made it through the surgery or not.

I checked my phone again. Nothing.

Dad said, "Relax, Captain ADD. It's not like the more you look at that screen the more likely it is that Ginny comes out of her coma. It's only been three weeks."

I thought about smacking him. I decided against it. We'd been in Florida nearly a week. Waiting. So far, getting a sighting on Janus had been like chasing a whisper in the wind.

"Plenty of *other* people I'd be *willing* to kill if we don't find Janus soon," I muttered under my breath.

"You're in a mood," Dad said.

He didn't need to add *again.*

"I can't wait to get out of here."

Thankfully, Dad didn't respond.

Things had been hit-or-miss with the two of us. I'd taken him on an over-the-top vacation to Hawaii to celebrate his release. That had been fun, but working together now, without Ginny as a buffer, we were finding a lot of places we chafed. He'd raised me and my sister to be the greatest thieves in the world, but greatness came with a cost. As charming as Dad could be when he wanted, he was also an awful lot like one of those abusive sports dads determined to shape their kid into the next Michael Jordan or Serena Williams. Except with shooting and safecracking, what Ginny called bloody knuckles and brainteasers.

Dad and I had so far spent today the exact same way we'd spent every day the whole time we'd been in Florida: camped out at a strip mall. All the businesses on the strip had that same hollowed-out feeling of serving only the temporary needs of sun-starved tourists. Seven days in a row, the same thing: morning in the coffee shop, lunch at the sandwich shop next door, then, two doors down from that—we skipped the ice cream parlor—we moved to a rooftop bar after lunch. There was nothing to recommend any of the businesses except that they existed, and that they had a good view of the marina across the street where Paulie thought we might find our quarry.

Water, water everywhere, and not a drop of that piece of shit, Janus.

I was tired of being patient.

In the parking lot, below the bar, a man walking through took the last bite of his ice cream cone, crumpled up the piece of paper that held the cone, and dropped the paper onto the ground. I thought about taking a potshot at him. Even if he hadn't been littering, he was wearing one of those "FBI: Female Body Inspector" T-shirts. That alone was probably enough to deserve a bullet.

A panel van pulled into the marina parking lot. Dad and I both perked up, but the driver entered the office with a package and then left empty-handed. Otherwise, it was sporadic movement: boats coming in for fuel, the occasional owner leaving or arriving, a maintenance man repairing the dock at one of the boat slips.

But no Janus.

Dad and I took slow sips of our beers, watching, waiting.

I had a 9mm pistol under my shirt and a knife in my pocket. Both weapons were functional, not fancy. Tools, not jewels. Designed with one purpose in mind. But when I finally got to Janus, I wanted to use my hands.

2

WE WERE EACH ON OUR THIRD BEER when I went to the bathroom. The upside of our camouflage—the waiters didn't care how long we lingered in the slow hours of the afternoon as long as we kept telling them to keep the change—was that I always had a ready excuse to slip away from Dad for a few minutes. After I washed my hands, I gave Ginny's care home a call. If I'd called from the table, Dad would have either rolled his eyes or made a comment about "watched pots." I wasn't in the mood for it. Maybe Dad had a point, but checking in on Ginny's status was *something*, even if I got the same answer every time I called: no change.

The floor nurse picked up. He'd just finished a check: no change.

I was waiting for Janus. I was waiting for Ginny. No change, no change, no change. I thought I was going to explode.

I put my phone away and headed up the stairwell. I had to get back to waiting.

But when I came out to the rooftop, Dad was standing next to our table. He had his phone pinched between his ear and his shoulder. He was peeling bills off a roll. He looked shaken.

Even though I'd literally hung up from talking with Ginny's reassuring nurse, I had a sudden lurch in my stomach.

He walked toward me, still on the phone. I mouthed Ginny's name, but he shook his head and then motioned for me to follow him. I realized as he passed me that he wasn't upset or scared; he wasn't shaken, he was serious. The languid look we'd both adopted to stay under the radar while we worked surveillance had been replaced by utter focus.

"Got it," he said. "No. On our way now... No... No... Yeah, I'll call her."

He stayed on the phone as we made our way downstairs and out back to where we were parked. He handed me the rental car keys, made a few more cryptic comments to the other end of the conversation, and then hung up.

"Airport," he said. "Stop at Slurry's along the way to ask him to hold the gear."

"But what about—"

"Questions along the way. Phone call first."

I took a quick look at the map on my phone to remind myself how to get to Slurry's. Fortunately, his place was on the way to the airport. Slurry was a long-time acquaintance of my dad's. He was a leathery old man who'd been retired from the active part of the trade for at least two decades. Despite pushing nearly ninety, however, he still dabbled in supplying material to fellow travelers. He was the one who'd sold us our pistols and my knife, all clean, all tested, all untraceable. If we were going to the airport, our choices were to either ditch the weapons or leave them somewhere safe. It made sense to ask Slurry to hold them for us.

Fortunately, we'd already planned to switch hotels. We had checked out this morning. The small amount of clothing we'd brought with us—a single carry-on each, nothing more—was already in the car.

Dad's call must have gone to voicemail, because he said, "It's me, give me a call," before hanging up.

"Now are you going to tell me what the fire is? I thought we were going to stay here until the job was done."

I didn't want it to be done. I needed it to be done. Whatever happened with Ginny's surgery, Janus was a box that needed to be checked. Or rather, a rectangular box that needed to be filled and put six feet under.

Dad said, "It's been two years since the Paris Job. Janus will keep. Helen"—Helen MacDonald, my dad's partner in crime, and my mentor slash surrogate grandmother—"called Paulie, Paulie called me. I left a message with Helen."

"And?"

"And an old friend called in a chit. Look, it was a quick call. I don't have all the details, but Paulie said move, so we're moving."

"We?"

A long, long pause.

I waited. I was getting good at waiting.

Finally, he added, "Paulie said that Helen told her, and I quote, 'bring the kid.' "

"Gee, since y'all are asking so nice."

"Don't be a brat."

"Where are we going?"

"Rome."

"Rome?"

"Yeah. And I know. Paulie is figuring out the passport thing."

"Who's bankrolling?"

"Each their own," he said. "I don't even know if this is a paid gig for you. You'll have to talk to Paulie about it."

"Basically, I got voluntold to go do some job with an old buddy of yours, I may or may not be getting paid, and I've got to cover my own expenses."

"Yeah, but you get to go to Italy. It could be worse."

3

DAD PUT THE CALL ON SPEAKER SO I could tell Paulie where she could find my passport in my apartment. Also, she wanted to know how I was covering my tickets, and I had to ask her to front me the money since I didn't have enough space on any of my credit cards.

I'd been paid well for the Volkov Job, but that had been four months ago and I'd treated it like Monopoly money. I'd had to pay tax on it—everything about the Volkov Job had been complicated, including how I'd gotten paid—and then I'd fallen back into my old pattern of profligate spending. Cash had run like water from a broken main: After deducting Uncle Sam's cut, paying the state of California its share, retiring my gambling debts, catching up on my delinquent rent, prepaying the next six months at my landlord's insistence, taking my dad on the month-long high-end Hawaiian vacation, and covering the costs of our hunt for Janus, I was close to broke again. Worse. My credit cards were still cranked out.

"As my *Aunt* Paulie," I said, "I'm asking you to do this for me, to front me the money, as my *Aunt* Paulie. As a personal matter. Not professional."

"How are you out of money already, Duke? All right, yes. I'll buy you a ticket, but you're a moron," she said. "No vig, but don't expect a glamorous trip on my dime. Knox, take me off speaker."

Which was fine, because I needed to focus on dealing with the traffic. Florida drivers, it turns out, are as bad as drivers everywhere else. And 80 percent of drivers everywhere think they are above average.

Dad was still on the phone when we got to Slurry's. An unremarkable 1970s ranch house in a tract of cookie-cutter ranch houses. It was well-maintained, with a postage stamp of zoysia grass that looked recently mowed. The neighborhood was a mix of old-timers and first-time home buyers, and a few of the homes showed the signs of children: bikes dropped haphazardly on lawns, basketball hoops installed on driveways, and swing sets peekabooing from backyards.

Slurry answered the door before I had a chance to ring a second time. He offered me a beer, but I declined and then presented him with the weapons instead. He reared back like I'd pulled out a pair of rattlesnakes instead of the pistols he'd sold us, but calmed down as soon as I told him they hadn't been used, we didn't want a refund, and all I needed him to do was hold on to them until we were back. When I offered him five hundred bucks as a "convenience fee"—which put my "kill Janus" fund at close to zero dollars—his attitude changed from belligerence to resigned annoyance. I told him I figured it would be a couple weeks at most.

He took the money, both pistols, the extra ammunition and magazines, and the knife, and nodded in a noncommittal way, as if he didn't much care who I killed, let alone when I got around to it.

Which suited my murderous mood fine, because when I got back to the car, Dad told me the travel arrangements, and it was all I could do not to throw a tantrum.

Now that I'd had fifteen minutes to wrap my head around leaving Janus for another time, I was almost happy to have a break and the chance to do something—anything!—that was more interesting than sitting in a strip mall and letting my butt go numb. That wasn't what set me off.

And I wasn't angry because I'd been voluntold to help Helen, Paulie, and Dad pull off some heist on behalf of a random old friend of my dad's. Nor was I upset that my dad, my aunt, and the woman

I thought of as a grandmother, all owed a "drop everything" favor to that same random old dude they'd worked with in the past, and this was the first I was hearing about it. I wasn't even annoyed about the absurd itinerary: Miami west to Los Angeles—Paulie was going to meet us at the airport with our passports—and then immediately east, direct to Rome, twenty hours of travel, give or take.

Heck, I wasn't even mad that I had to fly in economy!

What I was furious about was that I had to sit in economy *while Dad and Paulie sat in business class*! They were going to be drinking sparkling wine, eating seared scallops, and sleeping on their lie-flat seats. Meanwhile, I was going to spend most of the next twenty hours in the middle seat, wedged between a college student who probably smelled like stale weed, and somebody's grandpa who wanted to talk politics.

Being a high-end, international thief was usually more glamorous than this.

I was so busy feeling sorry for myself that I almost missed it when Dad said the name.

"Wait. Did you say *Nando*? Nando's the one calling in a favor?"

"Aren't you listening? Of course this is for Nando."

I wondered if I could ask him to hold the steering wheel while I choked him in frustration. What was it with parents explaining like 10 percent of something and then making you feel like an idiot for not magically knowing the other 90 percent of it? Whenever Dad, Paulie, and Helen talked old times, they'd tell the same stories over and over again. The Kingsford Job. The Berlin Magnet. The Gold Standard. The Broken Axle Heist. That sort of thing.

I *loved* hearing the old stories, particularly the ones where Mom made an appearance, but the old folks were constantly aghast that I didn't remember some random detail about some random person *that they'd never told me existed.*

Except Nando wasn't some random guy.

4

NANDO WAS AN INVETERATE CON MAN. Almost every word out of his mouth was a lie. He claimed, differently at different times, to be a French chemist, a British barrister, a former Navy SEAL and Vietnam War veteran, the heir to a Texas oil fortune, a one-time professional wrestler, and distantly related to Frank Sinatra, and during at least one job, he managed to pull off a convincing act as a Norwegian diplomat.

Nando liked to say that he could trace his *true* ancestry back nearly a thousand years, to Afonso Henriques, the first king of Portugal, and that even though everybody called him Nando, his *real* name was Ferdinando Marcos Ricardo De la Mora III. His name and his heritage, like everything else in his life, were probably an invention. But the reality was beside the point; Nando was fully capable of acting like royal blood coursed through his veins.

He was a terrible driver and useless with a gun, but if you put a deck of cards in his hands, he could do a rum punch shuffle or the Moscow two-step so smoothly that even a seasoned pit boss wouldn't spot it. His hands looked ordinary, but he could tie a knot in a puff of smoke. He'd taught me and Ginny how to dip a wallet so you could strip the cash without even taking it out of a mark's pocket, and as a teacher, he had an almost inexhaustible supply of good humor.

He was funny, profane, deeply intelligent, and intensely loyal. He was a polyglot who spoke seven languages like he was native born, and another eight or nine with near fluency, and he could slip in and out of different skins as easily as changing a shirt. He could make a mark say thank you for the privilege of getting skinned. The joke was that Nando was so charming that when the grim reaper comes looking, Nando will talk his way out of it.

He was also the ex-husband of Helen MacDonald.

I thought of Helen as my surrogate grandmother, but if she was that to me, Dad was more like her kid brother. She was about a dozen years older than him, and they started working together when my dad was in his early twenties. Dad's dad had been a crook himself, but my paternal grandfather was more of a mechanic. Helen was the one who showed Dad how to be an artist.

They worked separately plenty and would often go off on their own for months, or even years at a time, but Dad and Helen were a natural pair. Right about the same time my mom and my dad met and fell in love, Helen and Nando connected. The two of them getting married meant that, for all intents and purposes, Nando became family.

When Helen and Dad swapped old war stories, to hear them tell it, those early years of the two of them, and then the two of them plus Nando, working together as a team, Paulie sometimes rounding out the string, with Mom along as nothing more than a tourist, well, those were the best years of their lives.

I loved hearing about that time, even if it usually took Dad a while to remember to do the perfunctory, "Best years of our lives *before* we had kids, okay?"

And then, two things happened when I was seven. The first is that my mom was killed by a drunk driver. The second is that only a few weeks later, Helen and Nando split up.

It's impossible for me to separate those two things and apportion it out. Perhaps in different circumstances, him leaving wouldn't have hurt so badly. Nando would just have been an adult I remembered with fondness. But I was devastated by my mom's death; I have no idea how much of that made it worse that Nando was suddenly no longer a regular presence in my life.

I'd worshipped Nando with the fervor that only a young boy can muster. I know that my dad loved me—loves me—but he was intent on transforming me and Ginny into the greatest thieves who ever lived, and even with my mother's civilizing influence, he could be a hard, hard man. Aggressive and passive-aggressive, sometimes at the same time. Controlling. Moody. He motivated me through fear, pushing, prodding, nothing I did ever good enough for him, especially not compared to Ginny.

Nando, though, was completely unreserved with me and Ginny. He was always ready to make me smile with a joke, a magic trick, a warm hand on my shoulder. If he ever got tired of having me follow him around like a puppy, I never knew it.

Him and Helen splitting up didn't mean he was completely out of our lives. I saw him maybe a half dozen times after that, usually for a few weeks at a stretch, when he'd bring us in on a job or vice versa. Sometimes, during those "after" jobs, there was a certain tightness in the interactions between Dad, Helen, and Nando that I, even in my youth, could see, but I didn't care. Having Nando around was like Christmas come early.

The last time I'd seen him was right around when I turned sixteen.

It was a job in Panama City. We hit a mobster for a ton of cash. It had been the full crew: Helen and Nando as a couple, me and Ginny as their nephew and niece and spoiled brat wards, and Paulie—making a rare reappearance in the field from the executive suite—and Dad as employees, secretary and body man respectively.

But what made the job even more fun for me is that when it was all done, we met back in Los Angeles to cut the take, and Nando gave me a birthday present: a completely restored 1966 MG coupe in jet black.

A grand gesture, though Nando was prone to grand gestures. He'd almost certainly conned somebody out of it, despite us coming off a particularly rich score, but stealing it was part of what made it so slick. To a sixteen-year-old boy who already idolized Nando, that MG made him the coolest person in existence.

It infuriated my dad, though. He had some strict rules about staying under the radar at home. Traveling was different—we went first class all the way, staying in luxury resorts and eating at Michelin-starred restaurants, my sense of the world impossibly skewed from the beginning—but it was still important to be discreet. Even more so in Los Angeles. For himself, when we were in California, Dad cycled through a series of BMWs, Mercedes, and Audis. Wealthy, but not ostentatious. Still, he wasn't about to make Nando take the MG back. Ginny ending up borrowing the car and totaling it a few months later—an entirely different story—and left me with what Dad thought was an appropriate car for a sixteen-year-old, a gently used Honda Civic. By that time, Nando had exited our lives once again.

I thought I might see him one more time. But after a while, vague rumors got back to us. We heard he was in Barcelona, and then Ecuador, somewhere in Peru or in Ottawa. Two different people said Bangkok. We heard a job had gone wrong, something to do with a kid, or maybe it was an old flame, or it might have been payback for a different job.

A few more years and during the rare times I *did* think about him, it was with a sense of loss.

And now, nearly a decade and a half later, here he was, back from the dead, asking for help.

5

I WAS FUMING AS I DROVE.

"Why didn't you lead off by telling me this was for Nando? You only said it was somebody you, Helen, and Paulie all owed a favor."

I could almost hear my dad roll his eyes at me as he responded. "Who else could it be? We're redoing the same job we pulled thirty years ago, of course it's Nando. And for some reason, Helen thinks we need 'the kid' to help us out. Nando, Rome. It's not complicated. Keep up."

"Wait. What? What do you mean we're 'redoing' it?"

"Remember the thing we did in Venice?"

"The thing you . . . ? Do I *remember* the thing you did in Venice? You said Rome, now you're saying Venice?"

"The original job was in Venice. We're flying to Rome. Not complicated."

"No. I don't *remember* the thing you did in Venice. It was before I was born." But even as I spoke, it came back to me. "Something to do with a book? No, not a book. Like a scrap of paper, except . . . I remember you guys making a joke about it. Music? An original composition? No, a musical score. Nando had a dumb joke that was like, it was 'the only time the score was an *actual* score,' right? Wait, was it Puccini? From *Tosca*?"

He made a gesture to me, to the air, to the car in the lane next to us. It didn't matter. What mattered was his clear frustration and annoyance that he had to deign to explain any of it to me.

"*Tosca*. Good god, I don't understand how you can be such a philistine. Yes, Puccini, but *Tosca*? Please," he said, with the scorn that only a brilliant autodidact can muster for people who clearly should just know things. He cleared his throat, and then, in melodious Italian, said, "*Che gelida manina, se la lasci riscaldar.*"

"*La Bohème?*"

"Duh. Yes, *La Bohème*. Rodolfo sings it to Mimì. How do you not know this? You've seen *La Bohème* at least twice. In Sydney when you were a teenager, and then before that, when you were little, with your mother, at La Fenice."

It was one of those sense memories. As soon as he said it, it came back fully. Not anything about *La Bohème* itself, but Venice. I would have been four or five years old. Venice in winter. A pastry at a café. Shivering in a gondola. The lights, the water, the cold air outside, but warm, inside, in my mother's lap as we sat at the opera, me asking her why she was so sad, and her explaining to me that sometimes you can weep at the beauty of the world.

"I remember it," I said. Though if I'd been fully honest, I would have added that all I remembered about seeing *La Bohème* in Venice was my mother. And in Sydney, I'd watched most of *La Bohème* through the slowly fluttering eyelids of a teenager fighting off slumber; what I knew of *La Bohème* was mostly from seeing *Rent*. Opera was Dad's thing. He'd dragged me along enough times that I had at least a passing exposure to Puccini's biggest hits: I'd barely stayed awake through *La Bohème*, had slept my way through half of *Tosca*, and had, for a period of several weeks in my early twenties, been sleeping with a mezzo-soprano who was performing in *Madame Butterfly*.

"*Che gelida manina, se la lasci riscaldar*," he said again. "One of the greatest love stories ever told. Such an extraordinary thing to see the words written in Puccini's own hand. A blank piece of paper given meaning. Remember? Not that it was the complete score, of course. Simply a sketchleaf. But arguably the inspiration for the entire score. Nando joked that if we said it was a score instead of a sketchleaf, then we could refer to the job as the Venice Score Score. Which, well, jokes aside, *that* would have been a dumb name, I'll give you that, but your mom called it the Venice Double, and that stuck. You know how she liked to do that, label them all?"

"She did?"

"It always made Nando laugh when your mom did that. Fun job, boring story."

"What job?"

"What job do you think we're talking about? The Venice Double. Did Nando ever tell you the full story?"

A pickup truck doing at least thirty miles over the limit came barreling up behind me, switching lanes at the last possible second before rocketing past me on the left and then swerving across three lanes to pass a small sedan that was trundling along at a speed too slow for the pickup's liking. I doubted the driver of the truck was listening to Puccini.

The Venice Double.

I could almost hear Nando's baritone voice.

Those few times I saw him again after he and Helen split up were always raucous reunions. Lots of drinking and reminiscing as the grown-ups cut up old scores. It was always talk, talk, talk about the old times, from before when Nando and Helen split.

Ginny and I were kept clear of the booze, but we got to listen.

I could never get enough of it.

I remembered only bits and pieces about the Venice Double. They'd pulled the heist when Mom was pregnant with Ginny. "A contract job for a wealthy Italian scion named... Giovanni Something?

"Malanari," he said. "Giovanni Malanari. Short version is Giovanni wanted to give the Puccini score to his brother for a wedding present. The score was being held in a kind of opera museum. The job was a breeze, but it was kind of an odd duck because Giovanni gave it to his brother and new sister-in-law, but couldn't tell them the truth. As far as anybody in the world knows—except for us and Giovanni—the real version is still in the opera museum, and the one Giovanni's brother had was just an exquisite copy commissioned as a gift."

"Okay, but what does it mean that we're 'redoing' the job, then?"

"According to Paulie, I guess Nando wants us to put the real one back in the museum."

"What's the rush?"

He gave me a look that made me embarrassed to have asked the question. Whatever it was, Paulie wasn't going to blab it over the phone.

"And you don't know why we're going to Rome instead of Venice either?" I said.

"Relax. If it's *anything* like the first version of the Venice Double, it's basically a family reunion. I mean, I know Helen's not actually... well, and it's not the same without Mom, and Ginny, of course, but..." Dad said. He was flailing around trying to explain, and finally he ended with, "You know what I mean. It's Nando."

Which was as close as he could get to saying that for him, the job didn't matter. For him, it was going to be a kind of vacation.

Some families play golf together; our family stole shit together.

We were quiet for a few seconds as I navigated a tricky exit off the highway, threading my way between two tractor trailers.

Then I said, "I thought Nando was... How old *is* he?"

Dad snorted. "You make it sound like he's ancient. He's maybe ten years older than Helen. And she's only twelve years older than me."

Dad had crossed his mid-fifties, which meant Nando was probably...

"He's in his early eighties? And he wants to work a job?"

"Nando's retired, not dead, *kid*. And this heist is... Like I said, more of a family reunion or a vacation than a job. Now, last chance for questions," he said, gesturing to the rental car sign, "at least until we have privacy again."

I had a *lot* of questions: Was this Nando's job or Giovanni's? What had made Giovanni Malanari change his mind and want the Puccini scrap returned? Nobody but Giovanni knew that museum held the copy instead of the original, or that he'd given his brother the stolen original rather than a copy. Even if Giovanni had changed his mind, it had been thirty years, so what was the sudden rush?

But there were also a lot of things that weren't questions. Things I wanted to say to Dad. Like how I resented being treated like a kid, as if he could snap his fingers and make me dance.

And I wanted to tell him *he* wasn't young anymore. Dad had only spent two years in prison when it should have been eight to twelve, but two years was still two years. He'd never get those years back. But if Dad wasn't young anymore, then Nando was ancient, and I worried about working with him. No matter how much of a light lift Dad thought this job was going to be, as he'd always said, this isn't an old man's game.

Time moves in only one direction.

But sometimes, I thought, remembering Nando's booming voice beckoning me grandly, history repeats itself.

6

I FUTZED AROUND ON MY PHONE during the flight to California. I was bored out of my mind by the time we touched down at LAX and wished I'd had a thriller to read, but as I pulled my carry-on down from the overhead bin, I suddenly realized that the first thing I was going to have to do when we landed in Italy was go shopping. February during a heat wave in Florida was different than February in Rome. The heaviest piece of clothing I had with me was a hoodie. I should have asked Paulie to grab me some more appropriate clothes when she got my passport.

She was waiting for us as we came off the plane, passports in hand. She hustled us to the correct terminal. We got to our gate as they were getting ready to close the doors.

I spent the first hour at the back of the plane, stewing. Though I wasn't sure how much of that was from being in economy and how much of it was from how little I knew about what was happening beyond what I remembered plus Dad's basic sketch of the original Venice Double. But once I stopped feeling sorry for myself, the trip was uneventful: We went up and down to California, and then up and down to Italy, landing in Rome late morning, with the sun bathing the city in light.

I've traveled a lot. Los Angeles was always my home base. As a kid, we were on the road at least half the year, sometimes nine months, once for two years in a row. A lot of places I went to once, maybe twice, and never felt the need to go back. Not because I didn't like them—London is a great city, and so is Memphis, and I would highly recommend visiting both for different reasons—but whatever that itch was for me to see them in the first place, it was scratched. Happy to go back, but don't need to. And there's always somewhere else. It's a big world, and I'm not tired of it. But the thing that makes it so worthwhile to explore, for me, is that there's somewhere for me to go back to between explorations. A home. Going back to Los Angeles is going home, but there are also some places I visit that have a feeling to them that is also a little bit like going home.

Rome was not one of those cities for me.

Everybody likes Rome, and I get it. It's the city of the Caesars, the Eternal City. It was one of the essential stops for a gentleman on a Grand Tour in the seventeenth and eighteenth century, and that hasn't changed much for the modern traveler; if you haven't been to Rome, there's a gap. If you know how to avoid the tourist stuff, the food is mind-blowing—I had a slice of pizza the last time I was there from this little hole-in-the-wall place that was one of the best things I've ever eaten—there's cool art and culture, and there is ancient shit *everywhere.*

When I say Ginny and I spent a lot of time training, it wasn't all "how to be a thief" stuff. Homeschooling was part of our training, and it was *rigorous.*

In all honesty, I had no idea how rigorous it was until we went to college. Part of the deal my mom made with my dad was about education. Because she'd gone to school for a teaching degree, it made sense for her to homeschool us until we were old enough to go to college. But that *was* the deal: We were going to college in case we *didn't* follow in his footsteps. She wanted us to have choices, and she took our education seriously.

After her death, like everything else to do with the two of us, Dad immediately turned it into a competition. He had Ginny and I constantly making bets about who could read more books, or memorize pi to the most digits, or solve a cube the fastest. Winner gets a prize.

Dad himself was mostly a self-taught intellectual—he made me and Ginny learn the word *autodidact* when we were young enough to sound cute instead of obnoxious when we slipped it into a sentence—and as somebody who'd wished he'd had the chance for a classical education, Dad was on board with making sure we learned about everything. He was also a big believer in getting help from experts. For enough money you could get very good, very discreet tutoring from people who were some of the best in the world in their respective fields.

Ginny and I were precocious students when we wanted to be. If we weren't interested, however, it was rough weather. One tutor, Neil, tried to teach us Greek *and* our place, which we didn't like, and Dad ended up having to add an extra ten grand to his severance package as an apology for our behavior when we ran him off.

It was either ten grand or kill Neil and dump the body in the ocean, Dad said at the time. Which I just realized I had always thought was a joke but was not.

But when Dad wasn't bringing in old buddies to teach us to handle weapons or crack ciphers or defeat a Dewey Double Dial safe with our eyes closed, professional coaches for MMA and acrobatics and eye-hand and rock climbing and rigging, he brought in tutors, and we learned our math and read our books. And every time we'd go to a new city, a good portion of our books would be for localized learning. The history of a city or a country, the history of the culture and the art—how else were we supposed to know what to steal?—and politics, and usually we'd have to learn at least enough of the language to do reading in translation. When I was fourteen or so, we spent nearly six months in Rome. I've seen all the ancient shit in Rome! I know all about it!

But... I love Italy. The country. Not Rome, the city. I want to go to Tuscany and stay in the valley below Montepulciano, in that sun-bleached house we rented for a spring, so Ginny and I can stagger back down from the city, drunk from wine and moonlight. I want to eat seafood at La Cambusa and look out over the beach in Positano, maybe charter the same boat we'd used to take us to Capri when Ginny was dating that redhead from Kansas. I wanted to hike the Cinque Terre again, with the same quick stop in Corniglia to fill our pockets with diamonds like we did when Ginny and I were teenagers.

And wanted to go to Venice. If Rome was one essential stop for a traveler on the Grand Tour, then Venice was the other, and for my money, Venice blew Rome out of the water.

Why couldn't I have been there for the original job, the Venice Double, the one Mom had named? I'd been to Venice probably a dozen times, but I'd never worked there. Sure, Rome was fine, but Venice? The alleys, the bridges, the canals, the mystery, the history, the allure of a city that is one with the ocean? To be there not as a tourist, but as a man with a job, even if the job had been as simple as the original Venice Double was supposed to be, that would have been something to remember. No wonder Nando had said it was the most fun he'd ever had. And no wonder repeating the job was something he was willing to come out of retirement for. And no wonder, too, that Dad was treating this like a vacation. I was thinking about Venice in the same way.

I know that I was romanticizing Venice. On the wrong day, Venice can be a literal shit show. Recognizing, of course, that I was a tourist myself, the fact that Venice was both floating and sinking at the same time meant that with too many tourists at the wrong time, it could be a hellscape. I wasn't sure that anybody even lived in Venice anymore; maybe everybody was a tourist.

But it wasn't only that early memory sitting in my mother's lap as we watched *La Bohème*. I'd never worked a job there, and I'd never gone on my own, but every time I'd been back in Venice, the city had opened its arms to me. I'd gone only when brought or invited by somebody else, nervous to come on my own in case the delicate magic of the city was taken from me.

But I suppose I was born at the wrong time: Dad, Helen, Nando, and Paulie had pulled the Venice Double before I was even born, Mom along for the ride, and now, instead of going to Venice and getting to stalk the alleys, to watch the moonlight play off the water, to steal something written by Puccini's own hand, I didn't know what I was supposed to be doing.

Playing cleanup, I suppose? Maybe unpaid? On my own dime?

So, nothing against Rome, but when we landed, mostly all I wanted to see was lunch and a shower.

7

AS SOON AS THE WHEELS HIT THE TARMAC, I called Ginny's care home. With the time change, it was two in the morning in Los Angeles. The night floor nurse was a guy named George who had the grizzled look of a lifelong alcoholic. Except that he'd told me that he'd never touched a drop. He was just somebody who had been hung up on the sharp edges of life once too often. Yet, when I talked with him, he never sounded anything less than delighted to be alive.

"No change, Duke. At least nothing to worry about."

"What's that mean?"

"Well... Don't want to get your hopes up. You met Daisy yet?"

I had not. She'd only been there a few weeks. A newly minted certified nursing assistant, young enough, George said, that he wasn't even sure she could legally drink. Eager. Optimistic. Like a golden retriever puppy.

"Get to it, George."

"She thought maybe... But Nurse Crusty was on duty. You know how she is."

I did. Nurse Crusty—her last name was Curtsy, but the nickname fit—was unpleasant, but she was also diligent to a fault. I'd complained about her attitude to George in the past, but he'd told me that if he ever had a medical emergency, he hoped somebody like Crusty attended to him.

According to George, after the new kid had rushed excitedly to the nursing station, Crusty had done a full workup.

"False alarm, Duke. Sorry. We would have called. It's barely been three weeks, and you know, the doctor said four weeks on the early side of hoping for anything, but really week four through eight is what matters, right?"

I thanked him, hung up, and then waited as patiently as I could for the young and the old seated ahead of me on the flight to gather up the personal items they required to make it through being stuck in a metal tube for twelve hours. I didn't have to worry about business class blocking me, as they had their own entrance and exit on the plane. Wouldn't want them having to mix with the hoi polloi.

Not that I was still bitter.

As I expected, Paulie and Dad were waiting for me outside the jet bridge. What I had not expected, however, was for them to be accompanied by a woman.

As I approached, she strode forward with her hand out, and in British-accented English with the lightest flavoring of Italian said, "Mr. Ducaine, my name is Richa. I work for Giovanni, and I am here to facilitate matters."

Richa looked like her family had come to Italy from South Asia. Maybe India or Pakistan. She had her hair pulled back into a ponytail. Tall, only an inch or two shorter than me. I'd guess her at five foot ten. I would have said she had the look of a runner, but her posture said former dancer, and when she stepped toward me to shake my hand, I couldn't stop myself from sizing her up.

For professional reasons.

For instance, her earrings. A diamond stud in each ear, about two carats apiece. And I would have bet dollars to donuts that they were real, organic diamonds, rather than paste or lab grown, because the watch she was wearing *was* real. I recognized the black dial Jaeger-LeCoultre Master Compressor at first glance. It was expensive, maybe ten grand, but beautiful; this woman was making a statement. I didn't need to hold it to know it was authentic.

But I *wanted* to hold it, so in the process of shaking her hand, while I introduced myself in Italian—"Ciao, sono Duca."—I touched her left elbow and then slipped the Jaeger-LeCoultre off her wrist and into my pocket.

I could almost see her updating the file she had on me. Prefers "Duke" to Grantchester. For some reason, the image I had in my head was of her working on an old-fashioned manual typewriter, replacing the previous card she had for me, "Grantchester Ducaine: The Help," with one labeled, "Grantchester 'Duke' Ducaine: Thief. Handsome."

Okay. The handsome thing was just me hoping.

"Welcome to Rome, Duke. You may give me back my watch when we reach the car, but for now, follow me," she said, turning on her heel. "Time is precious."

8

I WAS A HALF STEP BEHIND Dad and Paulie at following Richa's orders. Probably the jet lag. Definitely not surprised that she'd caught me slipping off her watch.

She wove through the shifting crowds of leisure and business travelers, advancing with purpose. We weren't exactly running, but we were moving fast.

"Here," Aunt Paulie said, shoving her roller bag at me.

"Sure, happy to take your bag," I muttered. Let's be real, though: The reason she couldn't manage her own suitcase and that her arm was in a cast was because she was still recovering from the absolute beatdown she'd gotten as part of my screwup with the Volkov Job a few months ago.

But even if that hadn't been my fault, I didn't *really* mind carrying her bag. It felt pretty good to get moving after the back-to-back flights. I don't know that hustling through the airport qualified as exercise, but it seemed like I wasn't going to get a chance to start my Italian morning with the kind of workout I was used to and needed.

I'd been pushing myself across the board since the accident with Ginny. Even I was self-aware enough to recognize it was a coping mechanism. But it also meant I was the fittest I'd ever been in my life. There were two upsides to working out so hard: The first was that I could eat whatever I wanted. One of these days, the metabolic cliff would fall out from under my feet, but until that happened, I was going to take advantage of being young and athletic. I ate cheeseburgers and drank beer when I felt like it. The other advantage of working out so hard, however, and one I was vain enough to be aware of, was how it made me look: I was a shade under six feet, and right now, I was packing two hundred and ten pounds with about 11 percent body fat. I'd been surfing a lot, too, and even though it was a bit shaggy, my hair had caught the sun. Last time I'd seen her, Meg had told me I looked like a "stone cold fox."

Meg.

Meg and I were currently in the "off again" phase of our on-again-off-again romantic relationship. I was half in love with her, but it was clear to both of us that we had too much baggage to make things work. We'd spent all day together in the waiting room at the hospital on the day of Ginny's surgery—Meg had been Ginny's friend first, and since the accident, Meg and I had become close to best friends—and when Ginny had made it through the operation, we'd celebrated together. And afterward, she'd made it clear to me that I didn't have any kind of a claim to her. But that somebody else might. Soon.

In other words, she might have found something serious enough that there'd be no "on again" in my relationship with Meg anymore. Good luck with your love life, Duke.

Richa turned down a corridor and pushed through an unmarked door. "Passports," she said over her shoulder.

An immigration official was waiting for us, accompanied by a man in a suit who had the look of an executive, maybe the airport manager. We barely slowed down long enough for the *chunk, chunk, chunk* of having our passports stamped. The man in the suit told Richa that if there was anything else he could do to help Signore Malanari, to please be sure to—

But Richa didn't bother waiting for him to finish speaking before she ushered us out of the room and back into the hustle and bustle of the main terminal.

"With me, please," she said. "There are two cars waiting. Paulie and Knox, you will ride in the front car, with Helen." They nodded, both a little out of breath.

"Duke, you and I will ride in the second car."

She pushed through a door to the outside, and suddenly we were in the early-morning daylight. She'd gotten us out of the airport in under five minutes.

She wasn't breathing hard at all.

9

TWO LUXURY SEDANS WERE PARKED at the curb. Both cars were a dark blue that verged on black, sleek, and so elegant that they were almost invisible. A pair of men—one short, one tall, both wearing dark, smart, well-tailored casual clothing—stood chatting by the back car. Their outfits functioned as camouflage against the car: like shadow on shadow. But if you knew what you were looking for, you could see the telltale bulges: both men were strapped.

As soon as they saw Richa, they moved toward us, hands extended to take suitcases.

Watching the men was interesting. An AP Royal Oak on one guy's wrist, a Seamaster on the other guy's. Expensive clothes. Expensive cars. They carried pistols, but they weren't gangsters or cops. Neither one had the right kind of predatory instinct for them to be of any use with their guns or in any way functional as bodyguards. They were drivers, but they weren't only drivers—that seemed clear too. They came along with Richa. Giovanni's crew. But the guns didn't make sense. These guys were civilians all the way.

Huh.

Helen was also waiting. She was leaning against the front car, wearing a cream trench coat and sipping from a to-go cup of coffee, looking in the other direction.

When she turned and saw me, she beamed. She stepped right past Paulie and Dad, her arms wide open, enveloping me. "Darling," she said, kissing me on my right cheek and then my left. "You look fantastic. Meg said you'd been training more than normal, and it shows. Oh, your hair. You need to get a better haircut, dear."

"Meg? When did you talk to Meg?" I said. I'd been giving myself haircuts for the last two years, to save some cash, and I was overdue.

"Meg and I talked a few days ago. Now, there's no time at all to waste. I've spent all night on it and made no progress, but I'm sure you'll be able to figure it out. Everything else for the rest of the job will be simple, but I could use your help on this one. We'll be there in fifteen minutes. Richa will explain everything to you along the way, and once you're done, we'll have time for a proper catch-up. Oh, that hair. But you look terrific otherwise. Healthy."

And with that, she disappeared into the front car before I had the chance to ask what the heck she'd spent all night working on to no avail, and how was I supposed to figure it out, and, more importantly, when was it that she and Meg became people who talked to each other? I wasn't sure how I felt about the woman who was functionally my surrogate grandmother being in contact with my on-again, off-again but probably, maybe, off-forever girlfriend.

But that was going to be for another time, because we were still moving with haste.

I slid into the back seat of the second car and said to Richa, "Are we late for lunch?"

She said, "Helen told me you fancied yourself a comedian. She also said you'd be able to open a Nimsik Elite."

The trunk slammed, and I glanced back to see the driver coming around.

"You can talk in front of him," Richa said as the man got in. "The other driver is Bosco. This one is Fio."

Fio reached back to shake my hand, and then turned and followed the other car into the flow of traffic, moving aggressively but with a mastery that let me relax. He might not be somebody I could trust to have my back with a gun, but he was competent enough that he wouldn't accidently shoot me in the back.

I said, "I can talk, or I can *talk*?"

Up front, Fio's eyes flickered to the mirror. I felt pleased with myself. That had been a reaction to what I'd phrased and how I'd phrased it. Twenty bucks said Fio had a heavier accent than Richa but spoke English nearly as well.

"You can talk," Fio said.

Richa said, "All the staff is multilingual. Now, can you or can you not open a Nimsik Elite?"

Interesting. I liked Richa already. I said, "Yeah, assuming a Nimsik Elite is a safe, I can open it. But have I ever even heard of a Nimsik Elite? No. And I thought the gig was in Venice. I still don't know why we're in Rome. What's going on?"

"Duke. You have fifteen minutes. If you cannot open this safe now, here, in Rome, then everything else becomes much more difficult, and what needs to be done in Venice may no longer matter."

"Why can't we do all this in Venice? Whatever it is."

"It is a Nimsik Elite. You must open it. *Now*. Focus on what is at hand. Nimsik Elite. Questions later."

"But . . . Venice?"

"The safe."

I took out my phone and started trying to find schematics. "N-I-M-S-I-K?" I said, spelling the word out.

"Yes," Richa said. "And there is a slight complication beyond simply the lack of time."

"What?" But I already suspected what she was going to say.

"In Venice, it does not matter if the intrusion is discovered after the fact as long as it is thought simply to be a small lapse in security. It would be better if it was not discovered at all, but if it is, there will be no way to connect it to the reason behind your visit. But here, in Rome, when you open this safe, it must not be known that you opened it. It is important to Giovanni that there be no question of anything inappropriate happening here in Rome. You understand?"

"Of course," I said resignedly. "I have to open a safe I've never heard of without leaving a trace. Why not?"

10

FOUR MONTHS AGO, I'D BEEN HIRED to break into a safe... without leaving a trace. It was technically impossible, but with the help of a jerry-rigged argon-filled tent, a modified robo-dialer, and me being generally fantastic, I was able to get it open in a way that was completely undetectable.

But, let's say, mistakes were made. No need to dwell on the Volkov Job; I was supposed to be focused on the Nimsik Elite right now. That being said, the American Castle Galaxy Nine had been a beautiful safe.

"Quick question," I said, "how much time do I have?"

"Fifteen minutes."

"No, Helen already said we'd be there in fifteen minutes. I mean, how much time will I get with the safe?"

"Also fifteen minutes," Richa said.

"Oh. Fun."

She did not appear to think it was fun. So far, Richa was a serious woman, but that hadn't stopped me from thinking I liked her.

I looked back at my phone. Okay. Helen said she spent all night on it and didn't get anywhere. And now I had fifteen minutes to prepare, fifteen minutes to do the job. No problem.

Maybe.

My first stab at getting the schematics for a Nimsik Elite did not work out. The fact that I'd never even heard of a Nimsik Elite was either an excellent sign, or a terrible one. I was hoping that my lack of knowledge was a good thing: If it was a crackerjack box, then the reason I'd never heard of it was because there was no point learning about it. There were dozens and dozens of brands of safes that were perfectly good. Nothing wrong with any of them, but somebody like me could open one with a popsicle.

Your garden-variety safe that you can buy for your home will do its job most of the time. Bolt it to the wall or the floor and make sure you don't use a dumb combo, and you'll slow down anybody but a true pro for long enough that amateurs usually move on. But a basic box ain't stopping a pro. And it isn't even slowing *me* down. The problem is, even as I searched for plans for the Nimsik Elite, I realized that if it was an easy pop, Helen could have done it without my help.

Helen was like a grandmother, but she'd also been my mentor, and before that, Dad's mentor and regular partner in crime. My real grandfather—my dad's dad—was a criminal, too, but he hadn't been able to offer the kind of polish Helen did. He was more of a heavy-hitter type of professional. Strictly blue collar. The last of a dying breed, making a living with big, brutal heists in a day of declining dollar bills. A couple of times a year, he'd steal some money, usually killing a few people in the process, and the rest of the time he either swam in the pool or drank. He'd raised Dad to follow the same path, and it was only when Dad met Helen that he saw how much more was out there.

If Dad had been born to crime, Helen snuck in the side door. She'd been the kind of scholarship girl who knew how to adopt the camouflage of wealth despite not coming from it herself. Dad was nineteen when he and Helen first did a job together, and she taught him the difference between being a laborer and a craftsman, and how a little extra polish and attention to infiltrating the worlds of the hyper-rich could add a zero to the take. She was a dozen years older than my dad, and her hair had gone gray early, but I never forgot that she was as good at her job as any of us.

Meg, who aside from being my . . . well, whatever we were to each other, she was also my MMA coach. She worked part-time at a gym, mostly training pros, and she treated me like one of them. She said the way Dad was trained compared to how I was brought up was like the difference between pros back in the day and pro athletes now. Old-school players chain-smoking cigarettes and drinking beer on the sideline instead of traveling with hyperbaric chambers and personal nutritionists.

The point being, maybe I was the franchise player, the next generation, but Helen was a pretty good player herself back in the day, and she kept up. Sure, you could see her age on her, and there were some things she clung to that felt a little fussy at times, but she could *play*. Maybe not an all-star anymore, but she'd still be a starter for a few more years. If the Nimsik Elite was a safe that I could open with a wave of my hand, then she'd have opened it already without me.

I hunted through a few different repositories of information about safes and vaults, looking for a rabbit hole to dive down, and after a few false starts, managed to get a basic set of prints.

Uh-oh.

Me never having heard of a Nimsik Elite was not good. It was not going to be a crackerjack box.

Fifteen minutes to open it was going to be a problem.

"How much time do we have until we're there?" I asked.

"I could tell you, if you gave me my watch back," Richa said.

The edge in her voice had a hint of playfulness.

"I was hoping you'd forget," I said. I fished her watch out of my pocket.

"Doubtful. The staff is paid generously, but the watches are annual presents and have sentimental value for all of us."

"I have a *lot* of questions."

"So do I, but the only question that matters for now is can you open the safe?"

"When will we get there?"

"About nine minutes."

"Ask me again in eight minutes," I said, and started studying the Nimsik Elite in earnest.

11

A SAFE IS A BOX WITH A DOOR IN IT. THAT'S IT.

They've gotten more and more complicated over the years, but the basic concept hasn't changed. There's always been a need to keep stuff secure. The first "safe" was probably a bunch of rocks that Mr. Caveman piled on top of his favorite club to keep it out of the hands of Caveman Junior. But safes, as we think of them, have been around for a long, long time; mechanical locks are more than six thousand years old.

Modern safes use a lot of tricks to make them more resistant to being opened. The type of metal the box is made from matters. As does the thickness. And whether it comes in layers or alternates with other materials. For instance, a drill-resistant safe might sandwich three types of metal together that have different properties so that they will bind up a drill bit. It won't stop you, but it *will* slow you down. Same with corrosives and explosives: there's always a way. Time might be an issue, but anything made by man can be sundered by man.

Except.

Of course I couldn't sunder it. I had to open and close it as politely as possible.

"Where's the safe? Bank, store, office, what?"

"Do you know how to open it?"

"You keep asking that, and I keep telling you I'm working on it, but I need you to answer some questions for me," I said, looking back at my phone. You could call it hacking—I was exploiting a privilege execution flaw—but basically I'd gotten into Nimsik's internal computer systems and just needed to find the right engineering plans. "I can figure out the safe and talk to you at the same time."

"The safe is in Auldhilda's house."

I looked up. "Who's Auldhilda?"

She appeared surprised. "You don't know?"

"I know basically nothing other than like thirty years ago they"—I waved toward the car in front of us—"helped steal an original Puccini score from an opera museum and replaced it with an exact duplicate. And that for some reason Giovanni gave the original to his brother but told him it was actually the duplicate. Oh, and that we're supposed to be 'redoing' the job."

Richa gave a curt nod that seemed to indicate I understood enough.

"Other than that, well," I said, "I was sitting at a bar in Florida less than twenty-four hours ago, and now I'm in the back of a car headed somewhere in Rome and I've got, what, eight minutes to figure out how to break into a safe I've never heard of, so if you could fill in some gaps, that would be helpful. I need to know the situation. Guards? Alarms? What do you know about this safe, and what do I need to know?"

I had to give Richa credit for her professionalism. She didn't bother wasting time with dumb questions. She started talking as I looked back down at my phone.

"Once we arrive, you will have fifteen minutes undisturbed to open and close the safe. Maybe two or three minutes longer, but that I cannot promise. I apologize," she said. "There are things that we cannot control.

"There are no guards currently in the house, beyond those controlled by Giovanni, and they will not approach you and you will likely not even see them. The alarm system will be turned off. Inside the safe, there will be several items, but you are looking for a framed piece of paper. It will likely be resting on a rectangular box for a necklace. It should be easy to identify: The paper is approximately the size of a large magazine. With the frame, that is. The paper itself is not much larger than a photograph. Several words in Italian, musical notations, Puccini's signature. That is what is in the safe, and you will swap a counterfeit in its place."

"No," I said, "wouldn't it be the other way around? Aren't we bringing the original to the museum, putting it back, and taking away the counterfeit from *there*?"

"That will be next," Richa said. "But Auldhilda was married to Giovanni's brother, Giancarlo."

"Was?"

"Giancarlo died last year. Cancer. The original Puccini sketch-leaf was a wedding gift from Giovanni to Giancarlo and his bride, Auldhilda."

"And she didn't know either? That it was the real one?"

"Correct," Richa said. "But the Nimsik—"

"I told you, I can do both things at the same time," I said, tapping my way through a different subdirectory of engineering files in Nimsik's computers. "But I don't get why Giovanni didn't just buy the real thing from the museum, or make a suitable donation so he could get a 'lifetime' loan of it for his brother? Why'd he want it stolen in the first place? What's the point if he couldn't even tell his brother it was the real one?"

"As to why he did not purchase it, you are familiar with the idea of 'ownerless' art because of the Nazis?"

I noticed that her language seemed to shift in formality depending on what she was talking about. It was charming. Well. It would have been charming if we weren't talking about Nazis.

"Yeah," I said. "The Nazis looted art and property when they weren't busy murdering millions of Jews. Dad said the Puccini score was one of those, but..."

She was shaking her head. "As with many things, it is complicated. Giovanni himself is a good man, but his grandparents were heavily implicated in fascist activity during the war, and they were the ones who had originally... acquired the score."

"Ah," I said. "Basically, Giovanni didn't want to stir up publicity and remind people that his grandparents were Nazis."

"Essentially, yes."

"But I still don't get why Giovanni gave his brother the original but pretended he was gifting a reproduction?"

"I do not excuse Giovanni's grandparents, and neither does he, but again, Giovanni is a good man," she said rather primly. "As to why he wished to give the original to Giancarlo and Auldhilda despite not being able to tell them it was not in fact a reproduction? I will leave it to him to explain why he engaged in the original folly."

"Folly?" I glanced up quickly and then went back to navigating my way through the Nimsik corporate database: I'd found a promising link for the internals of the safe. "Is that what we're calling stealing things now?"

"Actually, Giovanni calls it a 'crime of the heart.' He says that the only thing he did that was wrong was to deny—at first, only—that his sister-in-law and brother were truly in love. But that is for later. For now, the safe."

Arguably, I thought, there were some other things Giovanni did wrong. For example, he did, in fact, commission a crime, and it was hard to argue that stealing a piece of art looted by the Nazis for any reason *other* than to return it to the heirs of the original owner was kind of a douche move. Frankly, if you were aligned with the Nazis on anything, you were a douche. But I'd learned a long time ago that people of immense wealth didn't have a problem justifying their actions; when it came down to it, the answer of why they did anything was always essentially the same: because they wanted to.

But that was also for another time, and Dad had a general rule about Nazis, which was that the only thing better than a dead Nazi was two dead Nazis, so I was going to assume that Giovanni was not like his grandparents and—

Bingo!

My whole life had been built around making me and Ginny the best thieves in the world, and in the aftermath of my screwup two years ago, I'd decided that the only way to punish myself properly was to walk away from what we'd done—what *I'd* done—and instead walk the straight and narrow. Nearly two years of that, and then, when I'd taken the Volkov Job a few months ago, it had been like I'd been dead and was revived.

It felt so *good* to be back in it. Because of times like this.

No, not Richa. I mean figuring out how to pull off a heist: I'd found the schematics, complete builds for the safe, the entire design plans and internals. Neatly labeled too. Easy for me to click through.

"Found what I was looking for," I said.

"The safe?"

"Yeah. Told you I could do two things at once. Wait, but if—what was her name, the widow?"

"Auldhilda."

"If Auldhilda thinks the Puccini score that she has is just a copy, why did she put it in a safe?"

"On Saturday night, Auldhilda will be performing for the first time since her wedding."

"Hold up," I said. "You're going to need to give me some broad strokes here."

"Broad strokes?"

"Like an outline. Nobody's explained anything to me. I barely know anything about the original job let alone what's happening right now."

12

RICHA SPOKE FAST.

Before Auldhilda met Giovanni's brother, she was an opera singer. Mildly famous, good enough to get leading roles, but not quite at the level where she was truly a star. Which didn't stop Giancarlo, an opera fan, from becoming besotted when he saw her in *La Bohème.* Her last public performance had been the night of her wedding to Giancarlo—which was also the same night Nando and Dad and the crew pulled off the heist back in the day—and this coming Saturday was going to be Auldhilda's first time performing in public again since she'd taken the Malanari name. A reprise of her performance from thirty years ago.

"She's singing a whole opera?"

"Only a single song," Richa said. "It's a duet. There will be other singers there for other songs, but no, not a complete opera."

It was an annual benefit for La Casa del Libretto, the opera society, museum, and event space that Giovanni and Giancarlo's fascist grandparents had helped to start soon after the war. Auldhilda had decided to wear a very, very expensive necklace for her performance, Richa said, and that necklace was currently in the Nimsik in Auldhilda's house. Given the value of the necklace—high seven figures—the insurer required a secure guard to take it directly from the Nimsik in Auldhilda's house to Venice, and to deliver it directly to Auldhilda, on-site, at the gala, and then take it back as soon as the night wrapped up, so that it wouldn't be a target for thieves.

"Like us?" I said. "But that only explains why the necklace is in the safe, not the Puccini score. She thinks the sketchleaf is just a copy, right, so why bother locking it up?"

Richa clicked her tongue. "She has made things much more difficult because of this. This was an unexpected problem to have her place it in the safe. The gift has been hanging in their library for ages. And of course, because she and Giancarlo had always believed it to be an exquisite replica, but a replica nonetheless, and therefore only of sentimental value, it was not even alarmed. Until a few days ago, it had been, oh, how did Nando say it? Yes, ripe for the picking."

"But?"

"As part of the celebration of her husband, Auldhilda has made a large donation to La Casa del Libretto. They will be renaming the museum portion of the building in Giancarlo's honor. Auldhilda has asked them to install, as part of a permanent display honoring her donation, the wedding present Giovanni gave her and his brother. Because the courier is picking up the necklace already, out of pure convenience, she put the Puccini score in the safe with her jewelry. It is simple bad luck and poor timing. The courier will take both the 'copy' of the score and the necklace."

"You've got my head spinning," I joked.

A smile bloomed on her face. She seemed delighted. Maybe she was sick of her standard job as Giovanni's assistant or whatever she was? She said, "Nando has assured me that the job itself is simple, and that no one will get hurt, but it does not feel so simple, does it? I can explain more after you open the safe, but does that answer your questions for now?"

"Barely," I said, "but I have a different question. The courier service is coming now, right?"

"Yes. As I said, fifteen minutes after we arrive. And we will arrive shortly. You are running out of time."

"I'm working on it," I said. And I was. With access to the schematics, I was starting to understand what I was going to be dealing with. "But Auldhilda's at home, waiting for the courier so she can open the safe, right? How am I supposed to—"

"No," Richa said. "She will be arriving with them. Or just before. As I said, you should have fifteen minutes, but not much longer. If it is helpful, you should know that while it is essential for you to be done with the safe by the time Auldhilda and the courier service arrives so as not to raise suspicion, Auldhilda is aware that Giovanni may be entertaining guests in her house, so it is not a concern if you happen to meet her."

"We're supposed to be Giovanni's guests in Auldhilda's house?"

"Correct. Auldhilda is only in Rome for the day. She has been wintering in southeast Asia. Giovanni is currently between properties in Rome, so he has been using Gian—Auldhilda's. But you may be in the house as well. Auldhilda has met Nando on several occasions. They are not close, and Auldhilda is not a woman who is likely to remember his name, but she will recognize him as an old friend of Giovanni's. Nando has instructed me to tell you 'Panama City.' He said you would know what that means. Do you understand 'Panama City'?"

"Yeah. That's our legend," I said.

"Legend?"

"Nando's supposed to be an old friend of Giovanni's, right?" She nodded. "Okay, so she doesn't know who he *really* is, right? So whatever Auldhilda knows about him, that's his legend. A cover story. A disguise. And he needs to stay consistent, so he's telling us to play the Panama City script. Which means that's the identity he must have been playing when he first met Giovanni, but I wouldn't know that, so he says Panama City, which I *do* know."

"I see," she said. "An identity, like you are in a play. And Panama City was a . . . ?"

"It was a complicated job. Helen, Dad, Ginny, Paulie, me. It was a while ago, but we all had our parts. It's all pretend."

"Except it is not an act with Nando and Giovanni," she said.

"Sure," I said, almost as if I believed Nando wasn't working some sort of angle on Giovanni. "They're old friends."

13

AS WE'D BEEN TALKING, I'd been thinking about the safe.

Nimsik was a small company. Korean. Based in Daegu. Pretty much the only thing I knew about Daegu was that it was South Korea's fourth or fifth largest city.

Nimsik's standard safes for consumer purchase were mostly designed to be mounted in walls. You know the kind: swing open a painting and voilà! A safe! High quality, probably two or three times the cost of a standard wall safe, but worth it: A thief who stumbled upon one unprepared wasn't opening it with a crowbar or a well-timed smile. Nando, unless he'd seriously leveled up his safecracking skills, wouldn't have been able to dial a Nimsik Wall Sentry in less than an hour, but both Dad and Helen could have done it in five minutes, and I was willing to bet I could do one in less than sixty seconds.

Of course, I wasn't trying to open a Nimsik Wall Sentry. I was trying to open a Nimsik Elite.

The Nimsik Elite was a bespoke model. Custom made. Larger than a wall safe, designed to be bolted to the floor or the wall. The box consisted of multiple layers of metals of different hardness designed to constrict and bind, all sandwiched between armored plates. Even if I'd been able to drill it, I would have needed more than fifteen minutes for that. I was going to have to dial my way in.

Dial mechanisms all work more or less the same way: You spin a knob on the front of the safe, and doing so turns wheels or disks inside the door. The difference between a combination padlock you put on your shed and the combination lock for a safe isn't that big from a conceptual standpoint. Four turns to the right, three to the left, all that sort of stuff. All that happens when you enter a combination is that gears turn until a bunch of stuff aligns so that there is a gap to move the bolt out of the way—or release the hasp for a padlock—so that you can open the door.

A safe is a box with a lock. You could work an old safe with a stethoscope or any other listening device; the click, click, click as you turned the dial would give you the occasional clack that indicated you'd hit one of the combo numbers. Alternately, with a little practice, you could feel your way through it, the clack vibrating through your fingertips. If you dropped me back in time a hundred years, there wouldn't have been a safe in existence that would have slowed me down for longer than it takes to drink a cup of coffee. Almost all good modern safes, however, have some sort of incorporated technology designed to dampen the feedback. Call it two cups of coffee.

But the Nimsik Elite, at least according to the documentation I could find online, presented a special problem. It had a physical dial, but the dial was not physically connected to the internal wheels. It used a floating electromagnet system: Essentially, the dial that I would turn had a powerful electromagnet attached that could interact with the internal wheels. When you dialed the correct combination and then turned the unlocker on the face of the safe, the electromagnet turned on and spun the internal wheels into alignment and shot the bolt home. But there wasn't going to be any feedback for me to work off.

I looked out the window, thinking about the Nimsik. None of the mechanical tricks I could think of worked with the electromagnetic coupling system. Again, easy if I could drill it, but to do it quickly and without leaving a mark?

It made me nostalgic for a good old smash and grab.

Traffic was surprisingly light. I hadn't been paying attention to where we were driving to, so I didn't know if it was our route or if we'd caught the lull before the lunchtime rush in Rome—if that was even a thing—but either way, I only had...

"Two minutes," Richa said.

We passed a heavy, blocky building that looked like it had been built in the 1970s. Just past that, I could see a larger modern hospital. An ambulance slowly eased itself into traffic in front of us, lights off, in no particular hurry. I wondered if the passenger it had ferried to the hospital most recently had survived, if they'd been in a car accident, or had slipped in the shower or fallen down the stairs, or maybe it was a false alarm, a panic attack masquerading as a heart attack...

Holy crap.

"Stop the car!"

14

FIO REACTED IMMEDIATELY, pulling over to the curb. Good reflexes. Good driver. Steady. If the other guy, Bosco, was the same material, those two could be of use. Not with a gun—I had to ask about that—but as general manpower. Sometimes you needed a dude who could run errands with basic competence, or dig a ditch, or paint a wall.

As I opened the door, Richa called out.

"Wait! Where are you going?"

"I'll be back in less than one minute. Open the trunk."

"But—"

"Richa, I can explain, or I can get the safe open."

"Go."

I went.

I slipped around the side to where the ambulance entrance was. There were three ambulances stacked up, but no sense of urgency. I saw three EMTs—two women and a man—chatting and drinking coffee. One of them was smoking. They were huddled together against the cold, and with the first two emergency vehicles working like a screen, blocking me from their view, they didn't pay me any attention.

I was already unscrewing the pen I had in my pocket.

It was, of course, an actual pen, but broken down to its component parts, it was also a set of lockpicks. A lousy pair of lockpicks, but all I had to do was open the door to an ambulance, not rob Fort Knox. I hummed a little of Beethoven's Ninth to myself as I worked the lock, thinking of the actual Fort Knox—the United States Bullion Depository—a white whale my grandpop had fantasized over, hence my dad's name, Knox. Paulie and Dad and Helen had thrown their own harpoon at Fort Knox—spoiler: they missed—back in the day. Ginny and I had talked about it occasionally, one of those "someday" kind of things.

The ambulance unlocked with an audible click before I got three measures into humming Beethoven. I hummed four more measures in the time it took me to find what I wanted and then close the ambulance up after myself.

I walked casually back to the car even though I was shivering by then. I was bathed in morning sunlight that didn't do much to cut the chill; I had weather whiplash, a February Florida heat wave to seventy and serene in Los Angeles to Rome and the switch to Celsius. Four degrees felt cold. But I didn't rush, because I figured that appearing inconspicuous was more important than saving the ten seconds hustling would have gained me; getting caught robbing an ambulance seemed dumb.

I dropped my borrowed item into the trunk. I closed the lid and then got into the back seat with Richa again.

Fio started driving as soon as I closed the door. Richa was looking at her watch. She bit her lip.

"The first car has arrived. They will be waiting inside, by the safe, ready to assist you."

"Tell somebody to get me an extension cord, heavy-duty if possible, and a pair of wire strippers or a knife."

"Anything else?"

"Yeah. I'm freezing. I'm going to need some warmer clothes while I'm here."

"Give me your clothing sizes and I will arrange for it," she said, raising her phone up to her ear.

There was a thought nagging at me, but I couldn't quite catch it. When I didn't respond beyond telling her my size, she started giving instructions over her phone. To Bosco, I assumed, though what the hell did I know? Now, the bigger thing I had to worry about was—

Pacemakers.

"Hey, Richa?"

Richa told the person on the phone to hold on.

"Anybody in there with a pacemaker? Or with any metal in their body, you know, like replacement knee, that kind of thing? You know. Old people stuff." Richa raised an eyebrow at me. "Helen and Nando," I continued. "They need to get out of there."

"Out of the villa?"

"In another room, at least. A couple of rooms away. Just in case."

She rattled it off in Italian, hung up, and turned to me. "Just in case?"

I would have pointed out to her that, had I been given slightly more notice, I might have had a chance to figure out a more elegant solution, but that was exactly the thing that would wind up my dad into a lecture machine: "You've got to make do with what you've got," and "The most important tool is your brain," and "You can't expect everything to be easy," blah, blah, blah.

Also, we'd arrived.

15

TO CALL IT A VILLA DID IT A DISSERVICE: It was a compound. Giovanni Malanari's wealth was measured by where he ranked on Italy's richest people list, and even though this was only Giovanni's brother's place—or, rather, his brother's widow's—and in the scheme of rich dudes with a ruler in a measuring contest, I've seen bigger, it was still impressive. One look, and my first thought was, *yeah, I'd for sure rob that.*

The villa was walled all the way around the property. A solid wood gate that opened inward when Fio punched in a code. Inside, there was a small guardhouse to the immediate right. No. Correct that, a caretaker's house. A cottage. Maybe six hundred square feet.

No visible security.

Catching my interest in the caretaker's cottage, Richa said, "The bulk of Auldhilda's staff went straight from Vietnam to Venice. Her Rome house is kept with a skeleton staff while she is traveling, and they have all been excused for the day. The only staff today are me, Fio, Bosco, and Giovanni's personal chef, Pérez. You may also speak in front of Pérez. You may act as if we are alone."

"Until Auldhilda and the guards arrive?"

Richa cursed in Italian. "Yes. Unfortunately, that will be sooner than we expected."

The first car, the one Dad, Helen, and Paulie had gone in, was already parked in front of the villa, empty.

"How early?" I asked. "How much time do I have?"

"They will be five minutes early. Auldhilda will now arrive in ten minutes. The courier is directly behind her."

"That's bad. Did you get Helen and Nando out of the way?"

"Just in case? Yes. Paulie and your father wait with the safe. Helen and Nando are in the guest kitchen."

"The *guest* kitchen?"

She didn't understand my real question, because she said, "It is far from the library."

We pulled to a stop behind the first car.

"Fine. The *guest* kitchen. Fio, get the bag I snagged from the ambulance and bring it up," I said, opening my door and sliding out of the car. "Richa, come on. Take me to the safe. Let's go. Ten minutes?"

"Nine, now."

As soon as we entered the building, the outside world fell completely away. The villa itself occupied that sort of odd middle ground you could find in cities like Rome. Ancient by American standards, but when compared to places like the Colosseum and the Pantheon, practically brand spanking new by Italian standards. The building had been cleaned with a power washer recently, returning the stone close to white. It could have been built five hundred years or five days ago.

But inside, the tension between the past and today was fully evident; the stone walls had been a monument to permanency on the outside, but on the inside, they were unyielding. Even with carte blanche to spend money—the designer had chosen expensively—there was only so much you could do to warm the place up. The entranceway was flanked on one side by a great room with a hearth, and a formal dining room on the other. They looked like somebody had given a designer a free hand, and they'd leaned fully into the *Extra Fancy Homes and Gardens* vibe. Perfectly tasteful, tastefully lacking in any kind of personality. Even the one hint of whimsy—a swirl of red fabric as an art installation around the dining room's chandelier—felt mechanical.

Through the entrance, and down a long hallway. Paulie called to us. I jogged to where she was, and then entered a grand library. This was more like it: fourteen-foot floor-to-ceiling bookshelves with a rolling ladder, around all four walls, with space carved out only for the door, a bank of windows complete with a reading nook, and a fireplace big enough to roast a goat in. A grand piano. And holy crap, I had no idea how much that stereo system was worth. Whoa. Another time, I'd want to linger in the room, put on some music, pick out a book, and grab a drink: There was a grouping of padded chairs, a writing desk with an appropriate chair, a couple of lounge chairs, a bar cart with liquor and glasses, everything to indicate that this was a space meant to be used, to be relaxed in. It was furnished and decorated in what I liked to think of as "European updated classic," which meant that everything looked like it belonged.

Which was why the Nimsik Elite looked so odd, lurking in one corner. It was matte black, dark enough that it seemed to sink into itself, and announced itself as nothing other than absolutely modern. As I approached, I noted that the corners were rounded, that there were no sharp edges anywhere.

Dad was standing in front of the Nimsik. He looked annoyed.

"Might as well not bother," he said, offering the kind, thoughtful paternal encouragement I relied on. "Helen spent all night trying to dial it and didn't get anywhere. Everything else is going to be easy, but I'm assuming you've heard Auldhilda's going to be early?"

Richa looked at her phone. "Eight minutes."

"Not a lot of time," Paulie said, "but you can do it, right?"

Dad scoffed. "In eight minutes? No way."

"Thanks for the vote of confidence, Dad," I said.

I was aiming for jocular poise, but my voice came out with a little squeak when I said *Dad*, like I was a teenager again. Not that I wasn't feeling solid—I was sure, at least in concept, that my idea would work—but there was something I knew I was forgetting. I'd missed a step somewhere.

"Just being honest," he said.

"Super helpful."

16

PAULIE PULLED MY DAD'S ELBOW. "Hey, Knox, how about you come over here so I can show you the *stop being an asshole for a few minutes* part of the library?"

They took a couple steps away and started jawing at each other as they stood by the bar cart, Paulie flapping her broken arm like a wing. That left me and Richa standing in front of the safe. I rolled my eyes, smiling, and Richa snickered. It turned warm. What you might call a moment.

"Your father is not an optimistic person, is he?"

"Not when it comes to me."

"But I am. You *will* open it. Again, all you have to do is remove the original and replace it with the copy."

"And this is a *different* copy from the one that's in the safe in Venice?"

"Correct," Richa said.

"Uh, not to be a pain here, but where is the new reproduction?"

She looked at her watch. "It is with Giovanni. He is supposed to be here, but there is traffic. No traffic for Auldhilda, traffic for Giovanni. As I said, this is not how we planned."

"Well, I've still got to get the safe open too."

She turned earnest. "Helen has said that you are supposed to be the best in the world at this. You will open it," she said firmly. "And then you will make the swap and close it before Auldhilda arrives in... seven minutes now. It would be best if we were not even in the room. I understand it is not *much* time, but it is enough, yes?"

"Yes," I said. Maybe I didn't have *much* time to talk with Richa, but I had enough time to talk with her for now, because until the Wonder Twins, Bosco and Fio, came in with the gear, talking with Richa—a smart, attractive woman who wasn't wearing a wedding ring—seemed more fun than staring at the Nimsik Elite and wondering if I was going to electrocute myself while trying to pull this swap.

She didn't say anything, but we were both smiling at each other in a way that made me think—despite the time pressure to get the Nimsik open—my dad wasn't entirely wrong about this job ending up being at least kind of fun for me.

Ginny and I, as an inside joke, used to call these kinds of situations—when one of us met somebody and had that instant spark—"the genie in a bottle" moment. It's from one of our science tutors, who showed us the experiment: Essentially, you drop a catalyst into an Erlenmeyer flask filled with hydrogen peroxide, and right away you start to see steam.

In other words, immediate and obvious chemistry at work.

"How can I help?" Richa asked.

"Can't do anything until we get gear. And, speaking of which, assuming I *can* get the Nimsik open—"

"You can," she said, arching an eyebrow.

And after a few seconds that steam gets thicker and stronger, as the catalyst accelerates. The Erlenmeyer flask starts to fill, the vapor heavy enough now to look like smoke. Undeniable chemistry.

"Maybe when we're done, you can explain a little more about why we're doing all this," I said. "How about over a cup of coffee?"

"Perhaps, once you have succeeded in opening the safe," Richa said.

"Perhaps?"

She smiled. "Perhaps a glass of wine instead?"

And once the Erlenmeyer flask fills, the steam billows out of the mouth of the flask like a puff of smoke, and the genie is out of the bottle.

Did asking her for coffee make me the person who grants the wishes, or the person holding the lamp? And did it matter that she'd countered with a glass of wine? I'd figure it out later. For now, I had other concerns.

Chemistry. It's some weird stuff.

It was only few seconds, but it felt like it was only me and Richa standing there, a bubble of time in the middle of this mad rush to open a safe as part of a job.

And Dad, from where he stood with Paulie at the bar cart, popped the bubble neatly.

"Fine, *maybe* you'll get it open," he said. "I bet Ginny would have already had it open, though."

Before I could respond, Fio came rushing through the door with the kit I'd stolen from the ambulance, and right behind him was Bosco, holding a toolbox and an extension cord.

17

THE TOOLBOX DIDN'T HAVE A PAIR of proper, gauged, professional wire strippers, but that didn't matter; the wire stripper built into the pair of pliers was good enough. I handed it to Dad and told him to cut off the female end of the extension cord, split it so that I had four or five feet of reach, and trim the rubber coating off so I had six-inch-long bare wire leads on the neutral and hot wires.

Dad eyed the kit Fio had brought me. "Is that a defibrillator?"

"Yep."

"Is this going to work?"

"Maybe," I said.

"We're going to run out of time."

I pointed at the extension cord. He nodded and started operating.

Paulie asked what she could do. I eyed her arm, still in a cast, and told her that the best thing she could do was make sure Nando and Helen stayed in the "guest kitchen" until we were done. I wasn't sure that I needed her to babysit, but it was better that Helen and Nando didn't come wandering in at the wrong time. Like I'd said. Just in case. The truth was I had no idea if I was overreacting with my "pacemaker and metal" warning. Heck, maybe I was under-reacting. My solution for getting into the Nimsik Elite was, if I do say so myself, rather brilliant from an idea perspective, but I would have felt a lot better about it if I'd had the proper amount of time to double-check my work. There was always something that got missed when . . .

Ah, crud.

At the college I went to, there was supposed to be an outdoor skating rink, but the story was that the plans had indicated feet instead of inches, and the cooling coils were buried like useless treasure. And there were plenty of stories of engineers forgetting to convert from metric to imperial or vice versa, all mistakes that could have been caught with a little extra time.

I was an idiot.

If Ginny and I had taken this job together, we could have made this seem elegant. We would have run the proper calculations on voltage and amperage, built our own self-contained device, and when it was time, it would have looked easy. Which was what I would have preferred. I wanted Richa to think that I was a magician, a miracle worker, Duke just strolling in, snapping his fingers, and the safe would roll over and play dead. That's what I wanted Richa to see.

Instead, I might snap my fingers and nothing whatsoever would happen. Which might be the best case of all the bad options, because the worst-case failure was going to be that instead of the safe rolling over and playing dead, one of us was going to get dead for real. I'd forgotten a thing so elementally simple that the scale of my sheer stupidity was almost enough to have me literally smack myself in the forehead: Electricity in the United States is 120 volts and 60 hertz, and in Italy it was 230 volts and 50 hertz.

Trust me, it doesn't matter if you can't tell the difference between volts and amps and hertz and watts, this was a problem. It was like the difference between pounds and kilograms. Except with electricity. Forget pacemakers. There was a reasonable chance somebody in this room was going to end up fried. I looked at Dad. Maybe I'd get lucky.

I must have been muttering, because Richa asked if there was a problem.

"Send the dream team out front."

"The dream team?"

"Bosco and Fio. To help Giovanni when he gets here, or to try to slow down Auldhilda. Or both. I might need more time. What's the clock?"

"Clock?"

"How much time do I have left?"

"Three minutes."

18

I STARTED TRYING TO FIGURE OUT the defibrillator. I was going to have to hope I could step it down to a low enough level of output that I didn't blow anything up, while keeping it high enough that it still did what I needed. I'd had the math worked out in my head for if I was in the US, but plugging in to an Italian outlet changed the numbers.

The disconnect between the Nimsik Elite's physical dial and the internal wheels that kept the door bolted shut only "talked" to each other through an electromagnetic charge: When everything was aligned properly, you could slide the unlocker, which completed the circuit, and sent power to the internal magnets, which then spun the wheels so that *they* aligned, and rotated a different set of magnets forward that then retracted the bolts. It was wildly overcomplicated, and equally overpriced, like a fancy watch that had more moving pieces and complications than it needed, so the person who wore it could brag about it. But in this case, it was functional, because it made it almost impossible to simply dial the safe by feel: that image of the safecracker kneeling next to the box, his ear pressed close to the metal, moving one click at a time, until a sly whisper of a grin means he's got it open.

But I thought there was a reasonable chance I could shock it open.

I figured there was a 50 percent chance it works, and a 50 percent chance I permanently bork it and they need to cut the safe open. And a 50 percent chance I electrocute myself. Plus, a 50 percent chance

I blow out all the power in the villa. And I knew that wasn't proper math, but with my belated remembrance of the difference in electrical systems, calling my math "back of the envelope," in terms of the charge I was aiming for, was a generous description.

Oh well. At least I'd figured out how to set the defibrillator.

I wished Ginny was there to make a dumb joke about being "shocked" if this worked.

Richa said, "Giovanni is arriving shortly. He is one hundred and twelve seconds ahead of Auldhilda and the security team, and he has the reproduction with him."

"There's no way this is going to work," Dad said.

He'd finished stripping the insulator off the ends of the extension cord. Now it had a plug that could go into the wall on one end, and on the other end, there were two bare wires.

Instead of answering or defending myself—he had thirty-plus years of history here and the chance to talk with Paulie on the plane and Helen in the car, and all I had was a couple of snatched minutes with Richa while I was trying to figure out this beast—I returned my attention to the Nimsik Elite.

There was an unexpected problem.

"Now what?" Dad said.

"Nowhere to attach the leads," I said. The Nimsik's rounded edges, its almost futuristic smoothness, and the extraordinary tight tolerance of the door within its frame all meant that...

"Unless... Dad?"

He looked at me. He looked at the safe. He looked at the bare wires on the end of the extension cord in his hands. He looked at the outlet in the wall. He looked back at the bare wires on the end of the extension cord. I could see him figure it out: Somebody got the job of plugging the cord in... and somebody had to touch the bare wires to the safe. They'd be holding the insulated part of the cable, but still.

"No."

"Dad."

"No way."

"It's probably fine."

"Absolutely not."

Richa took the extension cord from my dad. "Giovanni has arrived. I will do whatever it is that you require, Duke." She stared at me. "I trust you." And then she looked at my dad and back to me. "The two of you will have to settle your differences later, because now, we are out of time."

An extension cord contains three separate wires: a ground wire, a neutral wire, and a hot wire. Dad had left the ground wire ensheathed in rubber, but the hot and neutral wires were exposed at the ends.

"On the corners, please. Make sure you're not touching the safe."

Richa held the extension cord on the insulated rubber, spread her arms wide, and then carefully touched the bare metal to the safe, keeping her body held back.

Dad took the plug and waited next to the outlet.

I'd overridden the internal controls on the defibrillator—this didn't fall within the realm of "intended use" for the tool—and took a paddle in each hand.

"On three," I said.

Richa looked terrified.

"Hey. I've got this, okay? We'll be laughing about this over drinks tonight."

"Perhaps," she said, and despite her fear, she winked. It took me a second to remember to start my count.

"One."

Richa closed her eyes as I placed the paddles on the Nimsik Elite's door, on either side of the dial.

"Two."

I started to squeeze the trigger on the paddles. Dad's hand hovered in front of the outlet.

"Three."

A bolt of lightning.

19

RICHA'S FACE WAS ONLY A FEW INCHES from mine. She was staring into my eyes.

"Hey," I said, my voice full of sleep. There was a buzzing taste on my tongue. The bed was hard, uncomfortable. I realized I had a headache. How much had I had to drink?

Dad's face suddenly appeared beside Richa's.

"Good," he said, "you're not dead."

The room spun around a couple of times, then came to a stop.

I was neither hungover nor in a bed. Instead, I was lying on my back on the floor of the library. Dad and Richa were kneeling beside me. They moved back as I struggled to my feet.

I thought about throwing up. Then I thought, if I did throw up, my head might fall off my body. I touched my neck to make sure everything was properly attached.

"How long was I out?"

"Only a few seconds," Dad said. "No big deal."

I blinked tightly a few times. There was a ghost of white in the corner of my vision that was already fading, a high-pitched hum in my right ear that seemed to be winding down, and as near as I could tell, my heart was loping along at a calm, consistent fifty beats per minute, my standard resting rate. If my heart had stopped, it had started right back up.

I was fine. Calm as a cucumber. No. Cool as a cucumber. But I was fine. Maybe a bit wobbly.

I started to reach for the safe.

"Whoa!"

I looked at Dad. He pointed to the leads on the extension cord. Richa had let go, but the cord was still plugged in to the wall and both bare ends were haphazardly touching the metal skin of the safe. Sheepishly, Dad unplugged the extension cord.

I reached for the safe again, a little more slowly this time—I wouldn't have said I was scared to touch it, but I wasn't sure I was up for getting electrocuted again—and turned the unlocker.

I was greeted by the thunk of the first one, and then a second bolt. Holy crap. It worked! Turns out forgetting to convert from United States electrical standards to Italian standards was no big deal. Though I did have a weird taste in my mouth.

I opened the door of the Nimsik Elite as Giovanni Malanari came bounding into the library, with a waxed canvas satchel under his arm.

He was graceful. Fit, lean. I'd guess his personal trainer kept him on a tightly guided balance of movement, muscle, and cardio. He had complete control over his body, and it came across as confidence. He was wearing a pair of hand-tooled leather sneakers and dark olive-colored slacks. He'd pushed the sleeves of his black cashmere sweater up his forearms. Even though it was more accurate to say that his gray hair still had streaks of dark in it rather than that his hair was dark with streaks of silver, Giovanni looked like he was in his early fifties rather than the mid-sixties I knew him to be.

Before either one of us could say anything, Richa, looking at her phone, cut in: "Auldhilda has arrived. The courier is directly behind her. Two men. Fio and Bosco are taking their time moving their cars out of the way, but you better hurry."

Giovanni gave a slight dip of his head as he proffered the waxed canvas satchel, like I was an actual titled duke and he was a marquess.

I nodded back, took the bag, and turned to the Nimsik.

The safe was neatly organized. On the bottom two-thirds, the shelves were relatively full, with seven or eight green leather boxes of different sizes. The quality and finish on the boxes themselves would have made me assume big money even if there wasn't a leather valet on one of the shelves that held two matching watches, a man's and a woman's—each worth low seven figures—and a short stack of twenty-euro notes that, at a quick guess, I'd say consisted of thirty or forty thousand in cash. If I'd been there to clean it out, even after taking the standard buzz cut from fencing everything, it would be a decent haul for quick work. If you didn't count the part where I zapped myself.

But eyes on the prize. The top shelf had a single royal blue necklace box, and on top of that, conveniently located for my pilfering pleasure, the original Puccini score.

My target was no larger or thicker than a medium-sized laptop computer. The frame was wood, a mess of baroque over-ornamentation, covered in gilt, a scrolling cacophony of carved-out curlicues that stood in stark contrast to the unassuming piece of paper beneath the glass. All this fuss, and the score itself was a modest, unadorned scrap, slightly faded with age, three neatly scalloped edges with the fourth ragged from tearing, with nothing more than a little ink splashed across the page: "*Che gelida manina, se la lasci riscaldar.*" A lot of fuss over a few words and a couple of notes, I thought.

I opened the satchel and pulled out the forgery. It was sheathed in a large padded envelope. I took it out from its protective cover. With a quick inspection, they seemed identical, from the wear-through of the gold on the upper right corner showing the grain of the wood beneath, to the tiny smudge of dirt across the bottom edge of the paper, where Puccini might have dragged the butt of his hand as he wrote.

But one was real, and the other wasn't, and that made all the difference. On one piece of paper, Puccini himself had marked the first few notes, the first few words—*Che gelida manina, se la lasci riscaldar*—and on the other piece of paper, another anonymous hand had done the work. Some forger bent over a drafting table, meticulously recreating the small expenditure of ink offered by Puccini: a single dip of the nib of the pen for the words, another dip for the music. It was a static representation of a stroke of genius, and yet, despite the true beauty coming in the performance of the opera itself, only one of these was a treasure, and the other, despite appearing to be the same, was made worthless because it had not been created by the hand of Puccini.

Well, maybe not worthless. The frame itself of the forgery could probably be sold for a couple hundred bucks. But regardless, I had to admit that I kind of dug the idea of putting the original back so that it could be returned to the legal heirs, and I know that's kind of hypocritical, but there are crimes and there are *crimes*, and I don't know how else to put it.

Fio came sprinting into the room. "She is out of the car!"

Dad was busy gathering up the scraps from the extension cord and tidying up the toolbox. Richa and Giovanni were frantically fanning the air with magazines they'd taken from a side table, trying to dissipate the last vestiges of the odor that had come from my grand experiment. Richa put her magazine down and picked up an errant scrap of rubber from the floor while Fio grabbed the defibrillator and hurried out after Dad.

I carefully took the original out of the safe with my free hand and swapped it for Giovanni's fake. Then I tucked the original into the protective sheath, put that into the waxed canvas satchel, and handed the bag to Richa. Finally, I closed the door of the Nimsik Elite, locked it, and spun the dial to reset it.

Before I could so much as say a "howdy do" to Giovanni, Richa tugged my arm, pulling me out of the library, leaving Giovanni alone to wait for his bereaved sister-in-law.

20

THE DISTANT SOUND OF A WOMAN TALKING drifted past me as I turned the corner with Richa.

"I think my fingertips are tingling," I said.

"Are you okay?"

"I'm good," I said. I mean, I was probably fine. I'd only zapped myself unconscious for a few seconds, how bad could it be? It hadn't even left a mark! "I'm going to stop here for a few seconds, though."

"I will arrange for a doctor," Richa said firmly.

She was looking down at me, because, evidently, I was sitting on the floor for some reason.

"No. No. Just . . . give me a minute."

She hovered, and then paced. She opened the satchel and then the padded pouch, looked at the framed piece of paper. I'd swapped it for what was, at anything other than a purely scientific level, functionally a perfectly identical item, and yet, somehow, the look on her face made me feel like it had been an impressive accomplishment.

She put it back away and sat down on the other side of the hallway, across from me.

"That was clever," she said. "But also stupid. You could have been killed."

I had a mild ringing in my left ear. I rubbed at it, but it didn't seem to do anything. "Win some, lose some. More time would have been nice, but it worked. That's all that matters."

"Is it?"

"Isn't it?"

I had my feet flat on the floor, knees bent, and my hands resting lightly on my knees. I closed my eyes for a few seconds. I opened my eyes up again. She was staring back, the concern on her face enough to force me to smile.

"I'm okay. Just catching my breath," I said.

She considered me. "You said earlier, in the car, that you know almost nothing. And yet you risked killing yourself to open the safe."

I shrugged. "And didn't you say that this whole thing was, how did you say Giovanni put it, 'a crime of the heart'? Maybe I'm a sucker for romance."

She tilted her head slightly and bit her lip. There was a hint of mischief in her eyes. "Then you will like Venice."

"Venice is a dream."

A slow blink, a smile, and if I'd been sitting closer to her, I got the feeling she might have kissed me, but instead, she said, "You only feel like that because you are still dreaming from the time you spent unconscious. And I think you are not such the person for romance that you claim to be."

"What makes you say that?"

"Because I know how much Giovanni is paying you. You are not doing this for love. You are doing this for money. This is a job for you," she said, as she stood up, but there wasn't any sting in her words. She meant it as a compliment. I was a professional. "Now, are you feeling better? If so, we can join the others, and Nando can explain to you what the plan is for Venice. I know you must have many questions."

I had so many questions. Including how much exactly was Giovanni paying me, because nobody had bothered mentioning that in the last—I looked at my watch. Well. Crap. My watch was toast. I unstrapped it from my wrist. There was a slight scorch mark in the shape of the case on the top of my wrist, a perfect, faint circle. I showed Richa the watch, but she focused on my wrist.

"You're burned," she said.

"I'm fine," I said, stuffing the dead watch into my pocket. I was bummed. It was a Baume Moon Phase with a blue lacquered dial, and as the name suggested, a cool tracker showing where we were in terms of waxing and waning. I'd dropped a grand for it while I was in Hawaii, a reward to myself for the Volkov Job, and my first attempt at restocking my empty larder; I'd had to sell almost every watch I'd owned to cover my gambling debts in the aftermath of my disastrous outing with Ginny two years ago. Unfortunately, for the same reasons I was still cutting my own hair—i.e., I'm terrible with money—I was no longer able to buy a replacement. Though judging by the way Giovanni treated his staff, I figured I'd make out okay by the time it was over.

"It's not a bad burn," I added. "Nothing to worry about... Shame about the watch, though. Listen, give me a hand up off the floor. I'm not sure I can stand up on my own."

She turned serious. "I insist that you see a doctor."

"Just kidding. I'm just kidding, Richa."

I climbed to my feet. That was the easy part. No harder than jogging up Pikes Peak a couple of times. No, the hard part was making it look easy for Richa's benefit.

She appeared skeptical.

"Don't worry," I said, "but you're right. It was stupid of me."

"You could have said no."

"Sure," I said. "But I didn't. Now, what I need is a cup of coffee and some lunch."

And maybe a week in bed and a massage and a shower and a new watch and a couple million bucks in cash?

I expected her to turn briskly so I could follow her, but instead, she stared at me. Maybe she was waiting for me to collapse, but whatever it was, her brown eyes softened again. "Are you sure you do not need to see a doctor?"

"I'm sure."

"Let us get some coffee now, then." She began to walk, and as she did, she tossed the words over her shoulder: "*Perhaps* later, a glass of wine."

Evidently, I looked healthy enough that we could go back to flirting. Though I wasn't joking about wanting a cup of coffee. Even with sleeping on the plane, I was wildly out of whack, and I was committed to the idea of blaming it on jet lag rather than on my failed attempt to electrocute myself.

I followed Richa.

Okay, maybe I needed to sit back down, because I could feel myself wobbling a bit. I bounced off one of the walls, and Richa glanced back at me, but I gave her a thumbs-up.

We went down a flight of stairs and into a modern addition. Glass and steel in the shadow of stone, the transition abrupt for my taste.

A ping of Richa's phone. She looked and then stopped abruptly. "I need to return to the library," she said.

"Problem?"

"Yes. Sorry, no," she corrected herself, as she tapped with her thumbs. "Not with the safe. With the transfer. There are documents that I need to assist with. Auldhilda's assistant should have arranged everything, but she is already in Venice and not good at her job and... It doesn't matter. Your father, the rest of them, they should be in there. The guest kitchen is ahead."

"Want me to hold on to that?"

She patted the satchel. "No. I will keep it with me. Nobody will look inside. It would not occur to Auldhilda to be suspicious of me. I'll bring it to Venice. I'm sorry that I can't join you for lunch now. Or," she said, smiling, "for coffee."

"Rain check?"

"On the train."

"We're taking the train to Venice?"

"Yes. Giovanni will meet us there, but the rest of us will be taking the train after lunch."

"Coffee on the train, then?"

"Of course."

"A glass of wine in Venice?"

A smile. "Perhaps."

21

THEN SHE WAS GONE, AND I WAS BY MYSELF.

Alone in the hallway, but not alone: a baritone speaking in the cadence of a punchline delivered, and then a peel of laughter spilling down the hall. The siren sound lured me forward until I could see into the kitchen. It was big enough to play Frisbee in but looked like it had been plucked from the pages of an architecture magazine. Perfectly modern with clean edges and lines, an acre of countertop, counter seating as well as a banquette table, and behind cabinets painted in a riot of colors, I assumed, all the usual appliances, but fancier. There was also an entire glass-fronted bar cabinet, next to a floor-to-ceiling wine fridge. It was a showpiece kitchen, the kind of place that got a full-page photo in architectural magazines.

The "guest" kitchen.

Rich people.

If normal people understood the sheer scale of inequity, how much wealth was hoarded by so few, there would be riots and guillotines. Or, at the least, higher taxes with no loopholes for the 1 percent.

I hung back in the hallway: The corridor split off near the entrance to the kitchen, giving me a sheltered, shadowed vantage from where I could watch without being seen. But it wasn't the kitchen I was interested in.

I hadn't seen Nando since I was sixteen, but I recognized him immediately. He was *noticeably* older than the last time, somewhere in his eighties now, even if he looked only mid-seventies. But he'd changed. That was for sure. The last time I'd seen him, I'd thought he was old, but now I was old enough to realize that he'd still been in his working years. That had been a while ago, though. His glorious salt-and-pepper pompadour had thinned and turned completely silver, and it was clear he'd lost some of the physical grace he'd always used to his advantage when working. But he could still flash energy.

Nando had just gotten up from a counter stool. He was in profile to me, and he picked up his highball glass. Paulie sat next to him. Helen on the other side of the counter. Dad at the banquette table.

Nando was finishing a story about how a couple of sharps had mistaken him for a mark and tried to fleece him in a poker game when he was first starting out, a story I remembered him telling at least a few times when I was young. He was shaking one hand in the air for proper comic effect, and he was rewarded with another burst of laughter even though he hadn't come to the punchline of the story. I stayed, lurking in my shadow, waiting for it:

"But the best part," Nando said, pausing to take a sip of his sparkling water, his hand trembling slightly, "is that when I pulled the straight flush, the only way they could have called me on it was to show the cards they'd hidden in their sleeves."

He was rewarded with the desired chuckles and laughter, and then they were all talking at the same time, with and over each other, a cacophony of happy memories, the warmth of old friends and family seeing each other after a long absence, Helen and Nando telling each other the remnants of the same story at the same time, my dad and my aunt both deep into terrible impressions of my grandfather, and then the four of them coming back together, all shouting and joyfully yelling over each other.

I waited for a lull and then stepped out of the darkness and into the guest kitchen.

"Nando," I said.

I spoke his name like a benediction, less of a greeting and more of an acknowledgment of what he'd meant to me when I'd been a child. And like a benediction, it brought a hush to the room. "I heard you were de—"

His face lit up at the sight of me. His smile was as infectious as ever.

I thought my face was going to crack when I smiled back at him. It might have been the first time I'd smiled in days.

"Been a long time, kiddo," he said.

22

WE ALL MOVED TO THE BANQUETTE TABLE.

Nando pressed a button near the light switches. A few seconds later, Bosco came trotting in, looking eager to please. Evidently, in addition to the "real" kitchen in the main part of the house, and the guest kitchen that we were currently in, there was also a professional kitchen in the basement where Giovanni's personal chef was stationed on loan and currently making us lunch. Bosco apologized, said Auldhilda's staff was in Venice so service might take longer than normal—which was hilarious, because it had been almost instantaneous between when Nando pushed the button and Bosco showed up—and then he took our drink orders and scampered back out.

We spent several minutes on how Nando couldn't believe I was the same kid he used to know, how long it had been, how good it was to see me, to see all of us, looking good there, Helen, maybe we're not as young as we used to be, but looking good, can't believe we're all going to work together again, just like old times, and how lucky it was that it was *this* job, one of the easiest and most fun we'd ever done, what a kick it was to get to do it a second time, and now, tell me, Duke, could you truly have given me a heart attack with your little trick with that safe?

He was using his American voice, rather than what I'd always thought of as his natural accent, a mongrel mix of romance languages laid on top of a lightly British foundation, though it was hard to tell what was "natural" for a polyglot chameleon like Nando.

Helen touched the top of my hand with her fingertips. "Are you all right?"

"He's fine," Dad said. "Got it open. Not the most elegant thing you've ever seen. Would have been better if he'd had Ginny to help him, but he got it open. No need to whine about it, right?"

"Sure," I said. I still had a residual tingling feeling in my fingers and toes, a sort of sparkling numbness that was easing up. It made me think a little bit of screwing around with Life Savers candy with Ginny, trying to see a spark when we bit into them in the dark; if the guest kitchen had been dark enough, I wondered if there would be little lights dancing on the surface of my skin. I took a deep breath. All in all, I felt... okay. At least I wasn't going to fall over anymore.

Bosco returned with a tray: espressos for me and Paulie; a beer for Dad; a glass of white wine for Helen; a new glass of sparkling ice water with a wedge of lemon for Nando.

Nando cleared his throat, and I saw a deep sadness in his eyes. "I'm sorry to hear about your sister. I loved that girl, which is no surprise. Everybody loved Ginny, right? But don't worry. She'll get through. Hey, all we do is beat the odds, huh? That's not ever going to change, right?"

He picked up his glass. The ice clinked and the slice of lemon bobbed as he held it up to the sky, toasting Ginny. We clicked glasses and cups. Nando took a sip and looked down at the floor for a second.

I had a bit of trouble swallowing.

That part of him hadn't changed either. He might have been a liar, but you could *feel* that it was true: He'd loved Ginny, and he'd loved me, and he still loved Ginny, and he still loved me. He was a con man, and he could slip on a new skin with the snap of his fingers, but the part where we'd been like family? *That* part had never been an act.

23

DAD BROKE THE SILENCE. "Tell him about Venice."

Paulie chimed in. "It's a gala. Black-tie. Total hassle."

Richa hadn't mentioned black-tie. I should have known. I guess I needed a tuxedo?

Nando, who was taking another sip of his water, scoffed. "A hassle? You're delighted. It will give you an excuse to put on a fancy gown and dance with Giovanni in the shadows, the same as at Giancarlo's wedding."

I looked at my aunt. It might have been a trick of the light, but I thought she was blushing.

Paulie wiggled the arm that was in the cast. "I'm not exactly in fighting shape, thanks to Duke here. Signore Malanari will have to dance with himself."

"Even with a broken arm, I bet he'd be happy to dance with you again," Nando said.

"Charles"—Paulie's husband, who would have been my favorite uncle even if he wasn't my only uncle—"keeps my dance card full," Paulie said, with a leer, and she and Nando and Helen and Dad all cackled.

I hated galas. I looked good in a tuxedo—most men look good in a well-cut tuxedo—but trying to pull off a heist in the middle of festivities isn't the camouflage it seems. Sure, you can disappear into the crowd, slink alongside the waiters, bring in gear with the catering deliveries, but more people meant more people to stumble upon you while you're in the middle of something nefarious. Much easier to sneak in under the cover of darkness when the place is empty, open a safe, and be gone while everybody is none the wiser.

"Why can't we do it before the gala?" I asked. "We've got the original now, right? What else do we need?"

Nando gave me a toothy smile. "Saturday night is soon enough. The moon waits for no man, Duke."

The actual expression, as far as I knew, was "time and tide wait for no man," but Nando seemed sure of himself, so I asked, "What's that mean?"

He said, "It means that despite the years that have passed, and despite the fact that we shall be doing this at night, there's nothing new under the sun."

Which, in no way, answered my question.

"It means," Dad said, "when we did the job the first time, we did it the right way, and nothing meaningful has changed about the job, so why change things up? The only difference is that instead of doing the job during Giancarlo and Auldhilda's enormous wedding at La Casa del Libretto, we're doing it during an enormous party. And that you're tagging along. The job's in forty-eight hours."

It was lunchtime on Thursday, so it was a bit more than forty-eight hours, but I didn't want to quibble. And I decided not to react to the "tagging along" comment. I started to ask another question, but Paulie said, "It means the Venice Double is *the* Venice Double. We're going to do it again. Pretty cool."

"Don't worry, Duke," Helen said. "It's a fine plan."

"Yeah, but—"

"It means no worries, kiddo," Nando said. "It means we're retracing our steps. It's a new take on a classic. All we need is a star-studded cast and we'll be a hit. Everybody loves a good revival."

It wasn't that different from how I'd described using the Panama City legend to Richa, stepping into character, but the difference was that the way Nando said it, he might as well have pinched my cheek and told me it was real. He sounded like me psyching myself up earlier with Richa when I was about to try to open the Nimsik, like he was working himself up into character, trying to con himself into being ready. It felt different on the other side of it, though, listening to him be so clever. *The moon waits for no man, there's nothing new under the sun*, words that sounded like they might be profound but didn't mean anything. Deflections rather than answers. I didn't like it.

I didn't like that the grown-ups didn't seem open to questions. I didn't like that the grown-ups thought this was some sort of "greatest hits" tour, that they thought we could revisit a job they'd done more than three decades ago and do it the same without any worries. I didn't like that the grown-ups were acting like this was all a harmless game.

And I really, really didn't like that I was thinking of them as the "grown-ups."

I wasn't a kid. I hadn't been in a long time, and yet, suddenly, I was being treated like one. Every question got a patronizing answer. Nando, Dad, Helen, and Paulie had all essentially patted me on the head and told me not to worry, there weren't any monsters under the bed.

I looked at Helen. "Was this all you needed me for? Just the Nimsik? Because if you're running the same play you did however many years ago, it doesn't sound like you need me in Venice."

"Give me a break, Duke," Dad said. "Don't worry. There's plenty for everybody."

"Knox," Helen scolded. She turned to me. "No. When I called Paulie, I didn't know I couldn't open the Nimsik. I can't believe I spent all night on it, and you waltzed in with almost no preparation and suddenly that infernal contraption was a piggybank."

If it had been Dad or even Paulie, I would have sarcastically made a joke about how you can access the internet on planes nowadays, and a heads-up would have been nice, a chance to do some proper research on the Nimsik, that maybe I waltzed in with almost no preparation, but if I *had* been given time, I probably could have opened it without nearly turning myself into an electric eel.

But it was Helen.

Sometimes you make allowances.

She rubbed at her eyes, and for the first time I noticed that she looked tired. Gorgeous, elegant, with the poise and grace of a woman who was comfortable with her age. But tired.

"You worked on it all night? How long did you give it?"

She laughed. "How long was the flight?"

Nando tapped the table. "We do, in fact, need you for Venice, Duke. I was the one who told Helen to make sure you came along. Removing the original from Auldhilda's safe, well, that was unexpected. But we do need you in Venice. We can't do Venice without you." He looked at me directly, and he did that trick of his of softening every feature of his face, including his eyes, so that his attention was fully focused on me: "But if you weren't here, in Rome, today, now, if you hadn't been able to open the safe, then it's possible we wouldn't have even had the chance to do our little dance in Venice at all. We should say it. Well done, Duke. Well done. The whole charade would have come down without you."

Paulie and Helen agreed.

Dad sipped his beer.

"Thanks," I said. "But I still don't understand why you need me for Venice if it's the same job and you've got the old crew back together."

"Well," Nando said, with a wry little grin, "perhaps it's not as simple as I made it sound. But don't worry. We have until Saturday night to figure it out, though I suppose the real test will be when you're in front of it."

"What he means," Helen said, "is that *you* have until Saturday night to figure it out."

"Figure *what* out?"

She sighed. "There's a Frankensafe."

24

FRANKENSAFES ARE A NIGHTMARE.

As the portmanteau implies, a Frankensafe is a mash-up, a monster safe made of bits and pieces of other safes. And yeah, yeah, yeah, I know Frankenstein was the scientist, and it's Frankenstein's monster.

The problem with a Frankensafe is that you had no idea what you were dealing with until you were already in the middle of trying to open it. Take the Nimsik Elite, for example. If I'd walked into the library and been confronted with a metal box with a dial on the front, there would have been no way for me to immediately divine the internal components and realize that it used an electromagnetic mechanism to work the dial. Sure, I would have figured it out eventually, but certainly not in the time allotted, and probably only after I'd opened it up using a drill or some other brute force method. But, because it was a standardized build, once I was able to access the plans, I could figure it out, and figure it out quickly enough—electrocution elements aside—without too much trouble.

That wasn't to say you couldn't open a Frankensafe quickly. Much of the time, the reason a safe was a hodgepodge of components was because the owner of the safe wanted to stay cheap when it needed service, using old components or things that fit "well enough" rather than doing things properly or upgrading as necessary. Sometimes, though, it was also a case that a manufacturer created replacement components that didn't quite match the original.

Take a Graham Starmaster, for instance. First manufactured in the 1930s and continuing through the beginning of the Korean War. At the time, it was considered a good, moderately priced, professional safe. The kind you'd find in a jewelry store in Joliet or a pawnshop in Pasadena. Reasonably well made, tough enough to stop an amateur. And tools were different back then, so even a pro in the 1950s would need a couple of hours to open a Starmaster.

The problem with them was that after about twenty years of daily use, the Starmaster's locking mechanism—basically, think of how a deadbolt connected to a door shoots into a metal bracket in the doorframe so you can't open the door—started to fail. If you tipped the safe onto its right side, the bolt slid open. But there was nothing wrong with the box itself, so given the cost of a new safe, most shopkeepers who owned a Starmaster ended up simply getting the locking mechanism replaced. There were about a dozen different locking mechanisms that worked as replacements, even if they didn't match perfectly to the same specs as the original. The law of unintended consequences, however, was that because the replacement pieces never quite fit exactly—again, think of Frankenstein's monster all stitched together—it suddenly became what I thought of as a "noisy" safe. You could literally take a water glass and do that old trick of putting it against the door to amplify the sounds and dial it open.

But the flip side of that were safes like the one we ran into when we were doing a job in Buenos Aires about a decade ago. It was a corporate espionage gig, and we'd been expecting a standard Lichterm Silver. In fact, because it was a job with a tight window, we'd purchased a used Lichterm Silver, taken off the interior door panel, and studied the mechanicals. In theory, with me and Ginny working together, we should have been able to open it in less than five minutes. Except when we got to the day, the Lichterm Silver had been

Frankensafed into a completely different beast: Somebody had literally replaced the entire door of the safe with one from the Lichterm Gold Standard, and they'd replaced one of the internal dials plus the relocker with pieces from a GridKing 2000. We didn't realize it until we'd already triggered the relocking mechanism, and at that point, there was no way for us to get in with the tools we'd brought. We had to skedaddle and come back the next night. Long story short, Frankensafes were usually easy to open once you knew what you were up against, but you never knew what you are up against until you were in the middle of trying to open it.

"What do we know about it?" I asked Helen, hoping I'd at least have a starting place.

She turned to Nando, who looked abashed.

"Well," he said, "your father can tell you about the first and second vaults, but the safe itself is new, and—"

"Whoa, whoa, whoa. There's a *second* vault?"

Nando furrowed his brow. "Well, yes. Of course. Where do you think the safe is? They are like nesting Russian dolls."

I was pretty sure my eye was twitching. "La Casa del Libretto has a vault, and inside that vault is another vault. And inside of that, there's a safe?"

"A Frankensafe, dear," Helen said, putting her hand on top of mine and giving a little squeeze. "Therein lies the rub. It's a single dial. That's all we know. There's no reasonable way to get an in-person look ahead of time, which is why Nando insisted you come with Knox. I *think* I could manage if I wasn't otherwise engaged, though it might take me too long. I couldn't open the Nimsik, and I had overnight for that one. But you'll have three or four minutes, which, for you, should be plenty on a single dial." Her eyes darted to Dad and then back to me, without saying the obvious: Dad was even slower than she was at opening a safe.

"But everything else? Well, the vaults are the same as the original job, how we get in and get out is the same. There's nothing new. Even Auldhilda's performing the same song she did at her wedding, though, of course, she doesn't know about what we're doing in the same way she didn't the first time either."

"This is weird," I said. "It's some crazy rush to get here, and now that I got the Nimsik open, all of a sudden everybody's relaxed about the whole thing."

Nando said, "Why wouldn't we be? It's like you're not even listening. This is going to be fun. We're doing the same job. Except for the Frankensafe, of course, but that means you get to be here. I'm not sure why we're even talking about it. It's all set. It'll feel familiar, like riding a bike."

"I mean, I guess," I said with a little laugh, trying to keep it light. "But you know I wasn't there, right?"

"Of course, but you must know about..." Helen turned and addressed my dad and Paulie. "Didn't you tell him anything about the original job on the flight over?"

Paulie scratched at her cast, and Dad crossed his arms.

He said, "We were in a hurry. It's fine. He'll be fine."

Easy for him to say. He wasn't the one who'd almost electrocuted himself.

But instead of telling him that and risk getting accused of being a baby again, I said, "Maybe the best thing to do would be to start from the beginning."

25

BY NOW, BOSCO HAD RETURNED with Fio in tow, carrying more drinks—another espresso plus a glass of water for me, another beer for Dad, and what I realized was not ice water, but rather a gin and tonic for Nando—as well as a light lunch consisting of a bowl of fresh berries and melon, an arugula and lobster salad, and a platter of sandwiches.

They put the food and drinks on the banquette, and then Bosco took plates, silverware, and napkins from the kitchen drawers, while Fio pulled a bottle of prosecco from the wine fridge, opened it, and poured glasses for Helen and Paulie.

Nando gestured for a glass of sparkling as well, and then started from the beginning as Dad got up to fill a plate.

"So, for this to make sense, you've got to understand that Giovanni and I are friends. We've known each other for nearly forty years, well before any of this happened with the Puccini score. In fact, I was invited to Giovanni's wedding." Nando paused, looking expectantly at Helen.

She sighed. "Which one?"

"All of them," Nando said. "What? It proves he's a romantic, doesn't it? Though, to be fair, I should mention that he and..." He looked over at Fio and Bosco, but they were both on their way out of the room. He looked back and continued. "Well, what I meant to say is that he and his most recent wife, whose name eludes me, got divorced a few months ago. Which means that I do not need to learn her name, and, perhaps, more importantly, Paulie, Giovanni is single."

I did *not* like that. He was well aware of Paulie's marriage to Uncle Charles, and I wasn't pleased with his suggestion.

Neither was Paulie. She raised her broken arm reflexively, as if she might club him with her cast, and she said his name with a knife-edged tone.

"I know, I know," he said in that butter-melting way of his so that Paulie instantly forgave his cheek. "But the point is, Giovanni and I are friends. We see the world alike in a lot of ways. Now, his brother, Giancarlo, that kid had a whole different way of looking at things. If it wasn't opera, or once he met her, his wife, it might as well not have existed."

Helen snorted. "Kid? Giancarlo was *sixty-three*, Nando."

"Which is young to die. He was still a kid."

It made me take a closer look. The thin skin on the backs of his hands, his neck, the slight dullness in his eyes, his hair, the little stoop on his shoulders. It was like the longer I saw him the more I saw through the smoke and mirrors, the bones under the flesh on his face. He was old. To Nando, sixty-three was still a kid. I wasn't sure what that made me in his eyes.

"I don't mean Giancarlo was a kid in a bad way," he continued, "but you know what I mean. He had that kind of aura. Giovanni and I, we are romantics, but we live in the world around us. That was not Giancarlo." He snagged half of a sandwich, took a bite, and chewed while he talked to me.

"He was like... Duke, do you remember that time we were all in, I don't know, Mexico or Costa Rica or somewhere, living in that house on the beach for a few months prepping for a job? You couldn't have been more than five or six. Not sure if you remember that."

When he said, "Mexico or Costa Rica," I wanted to point out to him that those weren't interchangeable countries, even though I understood that this multilingual, cosmopolitan, shape-shifter of a man had a pretty good grasp on that basic concept, but then suddenly the memory came back to me:

An effortless rolling wave, like a metronome, somewhere between a foot to two feet high, wave after wave after wave. Mom with the blue swimsuit with flowers. Dahlias. Dad putting me on his back on his longboard, then standing chest deep and holding the board and launching me so I could learn to pop up on my own. Building a fire on the beach with Ginny, giggling when the tide woke us up, the water licking at our feet. Helen and Nando playing cards with me and Ginny on the porch of our rental. Nando grabbing masks and snorkels and—

"Stingrays."

"Exactly."

When Dad and Mom and Helen went scuba diving, Nando, who said diving made him feel claustrophobic, would take me and Ginny snorkeling. One of the days, Ginny got spooked by a stingray. It wasn't a big deal. I don't even remember that part of the story beyond having heard it over and over again. But Ginny got scared, for some reason, by seeing a stingray, and the story goes that I said to her that she shouldn't be frightened and stingrays were lonely because they were the only birds in the water.

Evidently, because of the way that stingrays swim by flapping their "wings," I was under the impression that stingrays were birds that had somehow gotten lost and were stuck underwater—give me a break, I was six—but from then on, that's what we said when somebody was out of place. Like instead of fish out of water, we'd say stingray.

"Wait," I said. "A fish out of water. A stingray. And I thought a stingray was a bird. Fish out of water, bird in the water. I just got that!"

Dad covered his face with his hands. "Oh my god. You're a moron."

"I was six!"

"You haven't been six in a *long* time!"

"The point," Paulie broke in, "is that Giovanni's brother was his own weird dude. Nice guy, but the one time I met him, yeah, it was like he was flying in water. Or whatever."

Nando frowned. "No. Not whatever. It matters. It was important to Giovanni that he protect his brother, and he feels he must continue to protect Auldhilda now that his brother is gone. She must not find out that she and Giancarlo have had the original for all these years. That is essential."

"Plus," Helen said, "you know of the question of it being looted art?"

I nodded. "I asked Richa why he couldn't just have gone to the heirs and offered them a ton of money to sign a quitclaim or something, and then convince his opera society to sell it to him, but she didn't go into it beyond the looted art part of it."

Helen nodded. "There was a lot of media about the score and the lawsuit from the heirs at the time, but because La Casa del Libretto was considered the owner, Giovanni had been able to keep his name out of the press and avoid reminding anybody that his grandparents were Nazi sympathizers."

Before I had a chance to ask a follow-up, Nando said, "You need to think more romantically. When Giovanni realized he couldn't buy the real thing for his brother, he commissioned an exact replica. It was what the scrap of paper *represented*: Giancarlo and Auldhilda falling in love. It was a very thoughtful gift, and Giovanni's brother and Auldhilda were delighted when he told them that he was doing this."

"Okay," I said, "that begs the obvious question. Why steal the original, then? If the reproduction 'delighted' Giancarlo and Auldhilda, why would Giovanni risk it?"

"Well," Nando said dismissively, "it wasn't a risky job. But as to why Giovanni wished to go ahead with it, as I have said, he is a true romantic. A reproduction may have been enough for Giancarlo and Auldhilda, but the closer it came to the wedding, the more it began to feel as if it was *not* enough for Giovanni. Even if he was the only one who knew, he wanted them to have the actual piece of paper that Puccini had written on as a marker of their love."

"That's..."

"It's romantic," Nando said.

"I was going to say nuts. Billionaires are nuts." I shook my head.

Dad was amused, though I suspected he was laughing *at* rather than *with* me. "I thought I taught you to stop asking those kinds of questions a long time ago. Trying to figure out why entitled people who are richer than god do *anything* is a fool's errand. The answer is always the same: because they can."

"And this whole time," I said, "Giancarlo and Auldhilda had the real thing and thought it was a fake."

26

I WAS STILL SKEPTICAL. "It seems like a lot of risk for nothing."

"Practically no risk at all," Nando said cavalierly. "Aren't you listening? It's the kind of job you do for fun, not because of the payoff. Nothing's changed. There's no chance of anybody getting hurt, no reason to say no."

"Easy for you to say," Helen said. "You're not the one who has to fake a medical emergency." She gave me a wink. "When we did the job the first time, in order to make the distraction as big as possible, I threw a drink in Nando's face, accused another woman of trying to seduce my husband, and then started a brawl. It was fantastic. The nice thing about the intervening years is that anybody who remembers that will be even more likely to stare this time. Unfortunately, now that we're past our prime, accusing Nando of being a scoundrel is a bit harder to sell. I have to resort to other measures. No, Nando, it's not *entirely* safe. It hurts like hell to take a fall at my age, even when I'm doing it on purpose."

He looked at her, and holy mother of god, did I suddenly understand why she let down her defenses for him. You can't fake that kind of response. Or, if he was faking it, he was absolutely as good of a con man as he thought he was: "I'm so sorry. I didn't even . . . We can do an ease-down. I'll knock a table over or yell, make a commotion myself. You don't need to pratfall. I hear you. Lots of options. Don't worry." And then he called her the equivalent of "darling" in about eight different languages.

"How about we call it at the event," Helen said. "You know same as me that it depends on the crowd. Quiet room, a good ease-down never fails, because you get that quiet ripple of people starting to buzz and it kind of grows until nobody can ignore it, but a loud room, and you need a sudden, visual cue, plus sound, maybe a crash. I'll take some dishes with me. Like that first time, in Quebec City."

"Oui." He said it seductively, like it was a three-syllable word.

I could have dropped a bomb, and they wouldn't have noticed anybody else was in the room with them.

And suddenly, I got pissed off with Nando.

He couldn't help himself.

He was always a rascal. Sure, he'd held a gun. When he was younger, he could hold his own in a fight according to Dad. And he wasn't above resorting to threats of violence. But mostly, Nando seemed to get a kick out of the con. I don't even know if he cared how much he took off a sucker, but if a sucker was willing to be took, Nando went for it. I remember a story Dad told about the two of them getting braced by a cop, and not only did Nando talk them out of it, when he shook the detective's hand at the end, he lifted the guy's badge. Ballsy, sure, and a story that killed, except, it was stupid as anything, because it turned from a forgettable, throwaway encounter into an instant BOLO. Only, the rest of the job was quick and smooth, and it was a remote enough place that it was a one-off visit—like, maybe the Falkland Islands, or somewhere in Argentina, that neck of the woods?—so nothing ever came of it.

"I said, why'd you do it, he looks at me"—Dad would always do the two fingers to his eyes thing, back and forth between him and his audience, to show that Nando was totally serious—"and he says, 'because.' And I'm like, 'because what?' And he says, 'because.' And this goes on for like an hour, me asking why'd you do it, him saying because. And we're about to kill each other when I suddenly realize, that's his answer to why he does anything. Because. Because he felt like it. And that, my friends, was when Nando taught me how to properly say the word *sybarite*."

Which, yeah, he made me look it up. It means pursuing a life of luxury and leisure.

Nando saw something he wanted, and if he could take it, he would take it.

The prick was trying to seduce Helen.

27

HELEN WAS STARING INTO HIS EYES like she was a mark afraid that she wouldn't have time to take the bait.

"Hey, I have a question," I said, interrupting the intimacy.

My question was did he have to break Helen's heart again? Wasn't it enough that he left her after my mom died, and then again, every single other time we'd all gotten back together to work as a group. Sure, maybe he'd hang around for a few weeks, even a couple of months, but there was always one day when he'd pull a French exit. And sometimes that meant Helen would get weird and pack up herself after a while, and other times, she seemed perfectly fine in the aftermath, but either way, it was like Nando couldn't help himself. He could make Helen fall in love with him whenever he wanted to. And right now, he wanted to. Why? Because.

Why was I upset? Because this wasn't some job off the tip of South America. Helen wasn't some mark who thought she was getting one over on somebody else and who deserved a good fleecing. Because he was conning her. I mean, maybe not in what he was saying to her. But in the *way* he was talking to her. That was the "I love you and I'm going to stay around, for real, baby" voice, the one that said, "don't worry, this time will be different. I'm changed. This won't be like those other times I broke your heart." All that he was missing was the grand gesture.

Just like Nando to think that stealing a piece of paper to give to somebody who thinks it's just a copy is romantic, because it was the sort of grand gesture he loved. Steal something just for the fun of it.

They were all looking at me now. I said, "Yeah. So, my question. What about security. You said there's no real risk, but the place is a museum, right? Wouldn't they have guards? Plus, it's public knowledge that Giovanni's going to be there, and this is a big money thing. You can't tell me that isn't going to be armed security."

Nando said, "There is Auldhilda's necklace and many other women who will be there wearing jewelry as well, perhaps not as famous nor as expensive as Auldhilda's, but expensive enough to attract people like us. And yet, that's the best part. Even with all of that, there's no risk of getting hurt. Helen's role excepted, of course. So yes, there will be armed security, but you do not have to worry about them."

"Why not?" I asked.

"Thumb on the scale, my friend, thumb on the scale."

Oh. That smarmy son of a bitch. He was all but putting his arm around Helen. Thumb on the scale. I wondered if he'd done whatever this trick was the same way the first time, or if it was different enough back then that the fancy folks could have done without security.

"Giovanni's guys," I said. "That's how you're doing it, isn't it? Fio and Bosco? They're already strapped. They're going to be the armed security instead of rent-a-cops?"

"Oh, you are the *worst*!" Dad slapped the table.

"Au contraire," Paulie said. "It's not his fault you made a dumb bet. Duke, you are, once again, serving as your own proof positive of why you are my favorite. Equally with your sister, of course."

"Of course," I said, "but I feel like Dad's saying I'm an idiot, and you're saying I'm right, and..."

Dad huffed. "She said you'd ask about security and figure out the answer before Nando explained it, and I said you wouldn't even know to ask."

"Sorry." I hoped he'd bet enough that it hurt to lose.

Helen said, "There will be a handful of unarmed guards inside as well, and they won't be ours, but they're really more staff than guards. Nothing to worry about. But yes, it's been arranged that Giovanni's men will replace the normal security team. We didn't have to worry about armed guards at all back when we did the job the first time! It was such a different world before 9/11. And none of the rest of the staffing will be an issue."

I turned back to Nando. "I've got another question. If the score is locked up, how'd you get a perfect replica made?"

Helen said, "Because of the exhibition, dear. A few years before the first job, Giancarlo had financed the staging of a new version of *La Bohème*. The sketchleaf was the centerpiece of an exhibition at La Casa del Libretto to celebrate the commissioning of the piece; it was supposed to symbolize the moment when Puccini truly created *La Bohème* as we know it. The museum published a book to accompany the exhibition, and the sketchleaf was profoundly well photographed. It was all quite a success for La Casa del Libretto and Giovanni said he'd never seen his brother happier."

"The forger worked off the photos from the book?" I asked.

Nando let out what I could only describe as a giggle. "The forger *was* the photographer. It wasn't planned. Just a coincidence that he was hired to document the score for the book."

"But the exhibition, and in particular the score, got a lot of press," Helen said, "which is how the legal heirs got involved. They accused La Casa del Libretto of harboring looted artifacts, but nobody connected the dots to Giovanni's grandparents donating it in the first place. Anyway, the lawyers took over, and once the exhibition went down, the score got relegated to the vault at La Casa del Libretto. Then, about six months later they staged *La Bohème*, and that's when Giancarlo and Auldhilda fell in love, and—"

"And that's how a job is born," Nando cut in. "And, this Saturday, reborn."

"And Saturday, Auldhilda's singing?"

"Of course! She met Giancarlo because she had booked the role of—"

"Mimì," I said.

"Who else? Auldhilda's Norwegian. Hates the cold."

He had a sudden coughing fit and took a sip of his sparkling water. He'd already drunk half the glass. He recovered and said, "Appropriate for the song that she hates the cold, no?"

The Puccini score. *Che gelida manina, se la lasci riscaldar*. "What a frozen little hand, let me warm it for you." Or, what I liked to think of as the "Light My Candle" song from *Rent*.

"Wait," I said. "Isn't Mimì's whole story a tragedy? She falls for this guy, and she's got HIV and then dies, right? How's that supposed to be romantic?"

"Tuberculosis," Paulie said.

I tried not to see if Dad had picked that up. I wasn't up for a lecture on how *Rent* was overrated. Ginny always said he was so weirdly snobby about art because he'd had to learn it all on his own; he didn't want to admit that he also liked regular stuff, and that made him extra annoying about it.

"Right," I said. "TB. The guy sings '*Che gelida manina*' to her—"

"Rodolfo. He's a tenor."

"Rodolfo sings it to Auldhilda, or Auldhilda as Mimì, and they fall in love, but they're poor and he can't save her, and she dies."

Nando said, "Love that burns as bright as a candle can get blown out as easily as any other kind of love. It's a love story, Duke. You'll have to trust me on that one. At my age, you realize that everybody dies eventually anyway."

Helen smacked his arm. "It sounds like you're comparing our failed marriage to one of us dying. Nobody died with us, Nando. Sometimes people want different things. Our run was fine."

They looked at each other for an instant too long, and then Nando coughed once and said, "So of course, for Giovanni, what could be more romantic than to give his brother and his bride the Puccini score that inspired the same opera his brother commissioned a staging of, the staging of which ended up being the reason why Giancarlo and Auldhilda met in the first place. Giovanni believed, without that Puccini score, his brother might never have met Auldhilda, fallen in love. It was a gesture, Duke. Sometimes it's only about the gesture. That was enough for all of us to do the job."

"Plus," Dad said, "Giovanni's a hell of a host," and they all laughed.

There was part of me that thought their evident fondness for this job was kind of silly, but there was another part of me that got it. It's not like I was Robin Hood. I didn't break into vaults and crack safes out of the goodness of my heart. Yeah, sometimes I'd stuff a bunch of extra cash into donation boxes, and I did have a few other tendencies toward topping up the karma bank, and as a family we made a point not to hit places that didn't have it coming. We weren't shoving pistols into the faces of convenience store clerks or offering free samples of heroin, but you know, we were crooks. It was fun, but you had to be a complete psychopath not to know that we weren't exactly engaged in a noble pursuit. But this seemed harmless enough. I wanted to like it.

I said, "That's, I mean . . . okay. That's kind of sweet. Weird, though. Richa did tell me that Giovanni called it a crime of the heart."

Paulie reached out and patted my cheek, even though she knew I hated it. "That Richa's got her act together. By the way, Giovanni's reimbursing us for our flight over; you're square with me on the ticket."

Knowing Paulie, even though she'd agreed to do it as my aunt, she'd probably charged Giovanni vig for the money she'd fronted me.

God. Being broke again suuuuuucked.

"Does this mean I get to fly up front on the way back?"

"Act like a dick, you'll be right back in coach," Dad said. "Try saying thank you."

"Thank you." I said it in as snotty of a voice as I thought I could get away with. He narrowed his eyes, but let it go.

"And you're getting paid too," Paulie said.

Even though Richa had already told me that I was getting paid for the job, those were some sweet, sweet words, and I didn't mind hearing them again.

28

"ABOUT THAT," I SAID. Richa had alluded to how much Giovanni was paying me in a way that made me hopeful I might leave Italy with my financial straits significantly alleviated. Or at least make it so my credit cards were only slightly warm rather than absolutely smokin'.

Nando spoke before I could pursue my train of thought: "Your mother was the one who insisted we do the job, Duke."

"Come on," I said.

Helen nodded earnestly. "It's true. Given her relationship to your father, your mother believed in, oh, you could call it fate, I suppose. Plus, sure, it's not a complicated job, but it had a certain charm."

"I'd known Giovanni for years, and so had your mother, of course, so when Giovanni told us *why* he wanted us to do the job, well... Your mother said if she hadn't met your father, she might never have left... Where was that town she was from?" Nando said. "Would never have had you and"—he called up a well of tears from the depths so that they rimmed his eyes as he hesitated, long enough to make it seem like the hitch in his breath was natural and not him working me like I was a mark—"Ginny."

I couldn't believe I used to fall for this. Every single time, for a little while I'd think he and Helen were getting back together, and he'd treat me and Ginny like we were the most special people in the world, tell us stories about how wonderful our mom had been, and then he'd disappear without saying goodbye, without saying anything. And then, nothing, for a few months or a year or two, or since I'd been sixteen, and then acting as if he cared?

"What a load of crap," I said.

"Duke!" Helen cracked.

"Sorry," I said. I wasn't sorry. "I'm not talking about you, Nando." Of course I was. "I meant I don't believe it was Giovanni's idea to do the job. He asked you to do the job...or you talked him into it?"

"What?" Nando said. He looked befuddled and slack-jawed, an old man's face.

"There's no way Giovanni said, 'hey, Nando, how about you swap the original for a forgery so I can give my brother the original but never tell him.' That's *your* kind of grand romantic gesture. Except in your case, you'd definitely tell the person you stole it."

Paulie let out an honest-to-god guffaw, her broken arm giving an accompanying bounce.

Nando put his hand on his heart, a self-aware smile on his face.

"I remember *you*, Nando," I said. "And I remember all those stories about the extravagant, ridiculous things you did to impress Helen before you were married. And I was there for some of them, as well, like that time you hired the mariachi band, or that rock guy's shirt you stole."

"Mick Jagger," Helen said helpfully. "It wasn't ridiculous. It was incredibly sweet. I'm going to be buried in that shirt."

"And you'll be a gorgeous corpse, my dear," Nando said.

Nando. King of the grand gesture. The completely restored 1966 MG coupe in jet black he gave me for my sixteenth. In the mail, for Ginny, for no reason, a match-worn pair of sneakers pinched from Venus Williams's locker at Wimbledon, from 2008, when she won both the singles and the doubles title, the same year that Ginny was absolutely obsessed with tennis, which I hated. A watch for my dad that Nando won from Marlon Brando in a poker game. Dozens and dozens of grand gestures for Helen. He always had a trick up his sleeve for Helen. Was this another grand gesture? For Mom? For Helen? For me?

"Are you really going to try to tell me that Giovanni came up with the idea for the heist?" I asked.

Nando looked at me. "All I can tell you is the truth, young man. I didn't goad him into it. I did *not* con him."

"I'm not saying you worked a job on him, Nando. But I know you're the one who made it happen. You're good at getting your way. This was a job *you* wanted to do, not a job Giovanni wanted done. He might have *thought* it was idea, but no way."

Dad said, "Come on. Nando knows better than to plant a job on a friend like that. Maybe Nando led him a bit, but if Giovanni asked for it done, it was because he *wanted* it done."

I readied myself, tried to emulate Nando's body language and voice as much as I could, turning myself into "sincere" Nando. "What matters is that you know it's the original, my friend. What matters is that Giancarlo and Auldhilda are in love, and you can give them a piece of truth. And I can help you. *We* can help you."

Dad burst out laughing, surprised at himself, and Helen and Paulie both snickered.

Nando looked a little pained. "That's not exactly how I remember it."

"But you threw out a hook, and as soon as he took a nibble..." I jerked back an imaginary fishing rod, setting the hook.

"I wasn't conning him," Nando said, now fully aggrieved. "We truly are friends."

"Sure, but it's not like you weren't in it for the money too."

He stared at me blankly. "I'm telling you. We're friends."

"Yeah, but..." I looked around the table: Paulie looked like she was having stomach cramps, Dad glared at me, and Helen had the decency to look embarrassed.

"No way," I said. "For real?"

Dad softened in defeat, shrugging his shoulders and turning his hands over. "You've got a buddy who needs a hand, you don't ask to get paid, you just do it, right?"

"We're not talking about helping Martin move apartments when he got divorced! Giovanni's a billionaire. A six-pack and a pizza doesn't cut it as a thank-you from him. I mean, at least when we helped Martin move, he helped carry boxes," I said. Martin "the Czech Anvil" Moravek probably could have carried the entire truck by himself. "Money is money. You're seriously telling me Giovanni didn't pay you?"

Nando shook his head. He helped himself to some of the arugula and lobster salad. More lobster than arugula for him.

"And none of you are getting paid now? What about the golden rule, Dad?" I said belligerently. "It's one thing to do a favor for another pro, but to do one for an amateur is stupid. Ow!"—Dad had slapped me on the back of my head—"Don't touch me."

"Then don't be a smart-ass. What do you want me to tell you? I don't even think *you* should be getting paid for this job, but Paulie insisted."

I looked at Aunt Paulie, who nodded.

Dad added, "And your mom liked the idea behind the job. She thought it was romantic, and . . . what did you call it, Helen?"

"Charming."

"Charming. Your mom liked the hidden doorways and the whole romance angle."

I had no memory of there being hidden doorways as part of the job, but I could see how that would sound charming to my mom.

Dad said, "And your mom liked Giovanni. He could be a lot of fun. Nando gave me a call, and your mom said she thought it would be a hoot and that we should do it for the sake of it, and she wouldn't *dare* let us ask to get paid. We were going to be Giovanni's guests for a while, and this would be our housewarming present to him. That's what she called it. A housewarming present. It's what she wanted. There's an exception to every rule. It was a vacation with a little work thrown in. So I didn't get paid. So what? It was a good time for everybody. Why do you make such a big deal out of everything, Duke?"

One one thousand, two one thousand. Back to Nando. "Okay, fine. I believe you. It was Giovanni's idea."

29

I DIDN'T WANT TO ADMIT IT, but I was starting to warm to the job, particularly now that I knew that I was getting paid, even if I didn't know how much.

I always felt a bit odd about stealing things like the Puccini score. Cultural artifacts. Religious icons. Art that was transcendent. Things that had some additional value attached to them because of what they meant, rather than their value as only cold, hard cash. Expensive things that came with a story attached. For instance, a few months ago, when I'd done the Volkov Job, the billionaire had been, well, not exactly pleading, but at least trying to convince me to let him live. And he'd talked about a Degas painting that we had history over, and how it reminded him of his mother. Obviously, it hadn't stopped me from killing him.

Point being, the scrap of paper that Puccini had scrawled those words on, I liked the idea of putting the real one back. Maybe it didn't matter, but even if opera wasn't my passion, I had to admit that *La Bohème* was a beautiful piece of art. I didn't know what the heirs of the original owner intended to do with it, but there was at least a little justice there.

"Richa said Giovanni's grandparents were some of the founders of La Casa del Libretto. They donated the scrap when it was founded?"

"Yes," Helen said. "Did you know the building used to house a bank? Hence the vault."

A Frankensafe, inside a vault, which was inside another vault, all inside La Casa del Libretto. A libretto is the written text for an opera, the words that are sung to accompany the music. *Che gelida manina, se la lasci riscaldar.* We'd be returning the scrap of paper upon which Puccini had first dashed those immortal words to a safe inside a building literally named after the item itself. And we'd be doing it during a gala. I wondered, when they had done this the first time, if Mom —

I suddenly wondered if Nando was putting me on. Had it been a grand gesture for Mom the first time, and was it some sort of grand gesture for me, now? Sure, *I* was getting paid, but back when they'd done the job, Dad had been working for free. Donating his time and expertise to this selfless act of generosity, giving the two lovers, Giancarlo and Auldhilda, the gift they *really* deserved...

I didn't know what else to do other than laugh. "Is the job really that easy?"

Helen touched the tips of her fingers to the underside of Nando's chin. "Why don't you get Duke the bundle, and then you can have Knox show Duke how we worked it the first time? I know we'll have some updates in Venice, but the bundle is good enough for now. It might answer a lot of questions and save us some time if Duke knew the shape of the job. Plus, there's a photo of the Frankensafe in there," she said, turning to me. "It's very blurry and won't show you much other than that it's a single dial, but it would be good for you to at least start thinking about that part."

Dad tapped the table with his fingers. "You'll see the whole job as soon as you start looking. I'm telling you, once you open the bundle"—what he called the plans and pictures that made the spine of the research for any job where he was the blueprinter—"it's right there. A classic Cleveland Swing," he said with an absolutely, crushingly embarrassing grin. "I hope you all brought your dancing shoes."

A Cleveland Swing is an old con that relies on an almost slapstick sense of timing. You know those old comedies, where a door is opened as another is closed, the kind of farce where people keep missing each other by an instant? A Cleveland Swing con, done properly, is related enough to the Farmer's Daughter con that the mark usually walked away wiping sweat off their brow in relief, happy to get off with only a lighter wallet, believing they'd almost missed sheer catastrophe.

But for a heist, a Cleveland Swing meant a job where there were a bunch of different roles that needed to be played by separate people, but nothing complex about it other than the timing. For instance, if you were breaking into a secure server building, you might want to cut cell service, but you have to wait until a different person has gone through the exterior door, while another person is hijacking the video feed, and at a predetermined time, somebody works a big, noisy distraction. I have absolutely no idea why it's called a Cleveland Swing—the naming conventions of many grifts are lost in the sands of time—but the real point is that it requires you to work as a team. The degree of precision depends on the job; the Venice Double had a big margin of error.

I moved my water, espresso, and plate to the side—I'd had half a sandwich and several bites of the lobster salad and was feeling close to alive again—and Dad lifted his beer so that there was space for Nando to put the bundle down on the table. I scooted closer to Dad and snagged one of the photographs. It wasn't old enough to be completely washed-out, but it had faded with time. It was a Polaroid picture of a section of an external courtyard: brick in a herringbone pattern on the ground, a pedestal supporting a classical statue of a naked man with a centurion's helmet, the edge of a window covered by heavy iron scrollwork.

"All this from the original job?" I asked, even though the answer was obvious enough.

"We don't have to reinvent the wheel," Dad said. He spun the blueprint I was looking at ninety degrees.

"I know how to read plans," I said, "and I'm not arguing we should reinvent the wheel. You guys are acting like nothing has changed in the last thirty years."

Nando wagged his finger. "That's the beauty of this. It will be like old times."

Helen said, "According to Nando's info, the alarm system has been updated. We're pretty sure they've added cameras to the entrances and exits, but that doesn't impact us. Once we're in, the vaults are the same as they were when we did the job, and they won't be an issue at all. The problem, of course, is the supplemental safe"—she pointed to the blurry photo of the Frankensafe—"inside the two vaults. Even though we don't have make and model, you can see you'll be fine.

"But other than Frankensafe? You've got to understand, this place is as much a social club as it is a museum. They use the vaults for storing the more expensive pieces from the museum collection that aren't on display, but if they didn't already have these vaults, they probably would have put a slightly better lock on the storage room door and that would have been good enough."

"Then why did they buy the Frankensafe?"

"They didn't. It was given to them. One of the members left it to the museum in his will. He even left money to pay for it to be installed. This is *not* a hard target. Sure, there are some superficial things that have changed, but given the history of the building and the organization? There's no reason to change our play from thirty-three years ago."

"Thirty-two years," Paulie said, sitting back down at the table, evidently having decided she could wait for a drink.

Dad shook his head. "Thirty-one."

"No," Nando said, "a bit longer, I'm sure. I think Helen's right. It's been thirty-three years. Might even have been thirty-four or thirty-five."

For the next five minutes, Dad, Paulie, Nando, and Helen argued over how long ago it was exactly that they'd done the original Venice Double. I didn't bother pointing out that given that Mom was pregnant with Ginny at the time, the math was simple.

Sometimes it was easier to let the old folks go at it and settle things on their own.

30

WHILE THEY WERE BUSY ARGUING, I used one hand to eat another half sandwich, and the other to sort through the bundle.

La Casa del Libretto used to be a private residence, but to call it a house was absurd. It had been built by a doge in the fourteenth century. *Doge* literally translated to the word *duke*, which amused me for obvious reasons, but the doge of Venice was elected leader from among the city's rich and powerful. This particular doge had been in office less than a year, and, other than his short tenure, was completely unremarkable. His palazzo was grand, however, completed by his heirs and built to overwhelm with splendor.

La Casa del Libretto—the Libretto House—had twenty-five thousand square feet of indoor space spread over three floors, with turrets on each corner that went between ten and thirty feet higher, depending on which turret you were talking about. The building itself was a rectangle with a private courtyard on the interior. The courtyard had been enclosed with a roof between the two World Wars and turned into the organization's main banquet room. With their overflow rooms, they could do a seated event for nearly seven hundred. The building was essentially on a corner "lot" at the end of a row of mansions. A different palazzo was pressed hard against one side, but according to the plans I saw, there were three main entrances: two with direct access to the water, and one to a central square. The square would be bustling with passing tourists during the daylight hours and early evening, and the "main" water entrance was on a larger waterway that saw constant traffic, but the shorter side of the rectangle led to a smaller canal.

Sometime in the seventeenth century, part of it had been converted to a bank, and that was when the first "vault" had been installed underneath one of the turrets on the corner that was adjacent to the open square and the small canal. *Vault* in quotes because, by modern standards, it wasn't a vault, but rather simply a secured room on the ground floor. Then it was a private residence again for a while, and then something else—I couldn't tell from the plans—until about a hundred years ago, it became a bank again. The bank converted the secured room into what was considered a real vault at the time: stone walls, ceiling, and floor, and a heavy, armored metal door with a locking mechanism. And inside that vault, a few years before the second World War, the owner of the bank had installed a "modern" vault, with reinforced metal walls, and another door. A box within a box.

But the best part, now that I was looking at the plans, was that the guy who had owned the bank at the time, the son of the original owner, had been a bit of a mad genius. There wasn't biographical information, so I didn't know if he'd been thwarted in pursuing an architectural or design degree, or if he was simply a self-taught engineer and tinkerer. At the same time as he'd installed the second vault inside the first one, he added two different secret passageways: one an entrance to the vault antechamber, one an exit. It didn't say why he'd done it, but there was a note about him being part of the resistance, so maybe it was in reaction to the rise of the fascists.

I could absolutely understand why my mom would have romanticized a job like this. Sure, Giovanni sounded ridiculous to me, but for Mom? Between her love of opera and art, Puccini and *La Bohème* and this sketchleaf that was supposedly so instrumental, the lovelorn, charming Italian billionaire, his bird-in-the-water brother and the opera singer Auldhilda, the chance for Mom and Dad to spend time with their best friends, Helen and Nando, in Venice, with Paulie along for fun, and throw in not one, but *two* secret passageways?

Obviously Mom loved the Venice Double! And I had to admit, despite my tensions with Dad and how much I didn't like the way Nando was creeping up on Helen or the little jokes about Paulie and Giovanni, I was coming around to the idea of a trip down memory lane. Maybe this job was all a fairy tale, but heck, sometimes you need something to believe in.

If nothing else, the job would keep my mind off waiting for news about Ginny, and frankly, I needed a break from sitting in the Florida heat wait, wait, waiting for Janus to show up so I could kill him.

I probably would have fallen for any story Nando put out there even if I hadn't been rushed into this job; the easiest sucker to con is the one who *wants* to believe. I *knew* Nando and Dad and even Helen and Paulie were all trying to sell me some sort of story about Mom and how great things used to be, and I wanted to believe. So what if there were times that it felt like being forced to sit at the kids' table at Thanksgiving? At least it seemed like I'd have Richa sitting there with me. I was looking forward to getting to know her a little bit. I wondered if she—

"Duke?" Helen said again. I realized I'd missed the first time she'd said my name. "You're off in the clouds."

"Sorry," I said. "Visualizing the plan. I guess I get why Mom thought the whole thing was fun. It's a little goofy."

Paulie and Nando were still heatedly debating what year they'd done the job, but Dad caught my comment and looked sheepish. He said, "Not our typical job. But she loved the secret passageways in and out of the antechamber. She called it a 'Scooby Doo' job, and she thought the banker who installed the secret doors was cool. He fought in the resistance, and your mom said he was like a guerrilla artist. Something like that. You know how she was."

I did, but I didn't. I could always hear more stories about her.

But then Nando interrupted and asked for clarification on what year they'd been in Switzerland for the gold truck thing, and Dad and Helen and Paulie and Nando went back to their bantering while I continued to study the bundle.

The whole thing was ridiculous, but based on what I could see, I understood why the grown-ups were dripping with confidence. The job itself wasn't that hard. At its most elemental, it could be divided into four simple steps.

31

STEP ONE: SHOW UP AT THE GALA and split into two different teams. Dad, Paulie, and I blending into the background, taking it easy until the time came. We would have no interaction with Nando and Helen once we were at the gala. They would be at Giovanni's table, aggressively socializing and doing their best to put themselves at the center of attention in the banquet room.

Step two: At a predetermined point in the middle of the festivities, Dad, Paulie, and I would slip out. Dad and I would make our way to the vault, while Paulie dealt with the alarm.

Getting into position wouldn't be much of a problem. The nature of La Casa del Libretto—built as a doge's palace, transformed into a bank, turned into an opera society–cum-museum-cum–party venue—was such that, even with the central courtyard roofed over and turned into the banquet space, it was still a labyrinth of rooms. There were going to be at least five or six hundred guests—a similar number to Auldhilda and Giancarlo's wedding—which was more than enough people that you could get lost in the sea of the crowd. As long as we weren't wearing bandit masks and carrying bank robber gunnysacks with dollar signs painted on them, we could wander around without much worry. On the off chance we ran into a staff member on their rounds, we'd act confused and lost.

Paulie barely had to do anything more than walk upstairs. For some reason, the alarm system panel for the vault area was in a medium-sized storage room. The best part was that the only lock on the storage room door was on the inside, *and* it had a window that overlooked the banquet hall! Paulie simply had to walk upstairs, lock herself in the closet, pop the cover off the alarm panel, and attach an alligator clip between two screws. After that, she'd wait until Helen and Nando made their move—she could look through the window to the banquet hall—and then unclip the screws, close the panel, and casually walk back to our table. A well-trained poodle could do her job. Not that I was dumb enough to say that to Paulie's face.

For me and Dad, it was slightly more complicated, but even then, not difficult at all. There were only two ways into the vault anteroom. The first was through the old cashier's cage, left over from when the building used to be a bank. The second was at the base of a turret that you could access only through a tunnel that was below grade.

The cashier's cage was a nonstarter. In the first place, it was basically the lobby of the building. It was high traffic, since guests had to go through it to access the bathrooms, and it also opened right onto the square were there would be additional—likely armed out there—security in the form of Venetian police. But even if the lobby was quiet, the cashier's cage had been turned into the front desk for La Casa del Libretto: It was staffed 24-7, and there was no plausible reason for us to go behind the cage. Even though there wouldn't have been any armed security when they did the original job, and even though Nando and Giovanni had arranged to keep cops with guns outside this time, it was still a bad idea. Also, an interesting note that explained why Dad wouldn't brook any ideas of going in early: except for during major social functions—such as, for instance, Auldhilda's wedding, or the gala this coming Saturday night—the door between the cage and the vault anteroom was left open and we'd be visible not only from the cashier's cage, but the lobby itself. In other words, we *had* to do it Saturday night or another similar event.

The tunnel, on the other hand, was a hassle, but secluded. A hassle, because it was partially exposed to the elements. When they'd done the original job, it had been during Auldhilda's wedding, during the summer. This time, we'd have to go through it in the Venetian winter night in only our formal wear. Depending on how long we had to wait for the performance to end, we might get chilly.

The upside was that getting in was a breeze. We entered the tunnel at the other side of the building, but once we made sure a staff member wasn't in the middle of doing rounds near us, all I had to do was pick a single padlock keeping an iron gate closed. Past the gate, it was as simple as walking down some stairs to the tunnel, entering the tunnel on our cue and then waiting for our exit cue—the waiting was when we were going to be cold—and making our way back up some stairs, and then waiting once again, but this time in relative warmth, until it was time to yank on a rope that opened the first secret door, which led to the vault anteroom.

The banker who'd designed it was a brilliant, crazy bastard. He'd converted part of the turret to a tube. The counterweights for the doors—nearly a thousand kilograms of rocks for each counterweight—slid up and down as the doors opened and closed, kind of like an elevator chute. At the top of the turret there was...

I looked again at the blueprints and then flipped through a few of the photos, thinking about the top of the turret. The turrets were decorative—unlike castles built with defense in mind, there weren't outside walkways between the turrets for guards—and that meant there was no *easy* external access, but that wasn't the same as *no* access.

There was a Juliet balcony over the canal, and a matching one on the inside of the courtyard, and the turret across the building was taller. The courtyard in between had an enclosed roof, and it might not have worked in the height of the summer when we'd be silhouetted across the sky, but in the middle of winter, the dark night meant we could zip-line across undetected. The big issue would be figuring out how to attach the zip-line rope from one turret to the other.

"Hey, Dad," I said, "just curious, but instead of going in through the tunnel, did you ever consider using the turret as an alternative—"

"Not unless you somehow learned to fly," he said, not even bothering to hear the whole question.

"But—"

"You got wings?"

32

IT HAD SEEMED LIKE a harmless question. However, I did not have wings, so I shut up.

I didn't love the idea of shivering in the tunnel while we waited for the performance to end during step two of the job. Basically, because of the tunnel's age and construction, and because of the layout of the banquet hall and the stage, we had to enter the tunnel just as a performance started, wait in the tunnel during the performance, and then exit just as it ended. We'd be using the transition of the houselights as camouflage. If we didn't, entering and exiting the tunnel would cause light leakage that would make us—briefly—visible from outside the building.

Even though we were rigging it by having Giovanni's guys play the role of armed guards inside the building, *outside* there'd be real Venice cops. Quick or not, if we got the timing wrong on entering and exiting the tunnel, it would be as bright as a flashbulb out in the square for anybody who happened to be looking in the right direction. Obviously, a cop seeing us would be bad, but almost worse would be if it was a nosy tourist with a camera.

Too much risk. I was going to have to suck it up. Being cold in the tunnel for a few minutes was better than being in jail.

Once we were out of the tunnel, we ended up in the exact same place we'd have been if we'd used my zip-line alternative to come down through the turret: in front of the secret door that led to the vault antechamber. At that point, all we had to do was pull the rope and trigger the stone door's opening. As long as there was enough crowd noise to drown out the slight grind of the door's counterweight—which there would be, because with the light leak, we couldn't leave the tunnel until there was a break between performances anyway—there was nothing to worry about.

Whether it was turret or tunnel that got us to the first secret door and into the vault anteroom, we were going to have to take a different exit: The secret door leading into the anteroom would only stay open for a solid ten-count before it swung back closed.

But once we were in the anteroom it was time for step three: Open the first vault, open the second vault, and then close me up inside.

The problem, once again, was how wonky everything was because of the building's age and the banker's architectural alterations. The secret door and the first vault door both opened toward each other, and you could only have one open at a time. If we jammed the secret door open, we wouldn't be able to open the first vault door. And the second vault door opened inward, facing the Frankensafe, so once again, it was impossible to have both doors open at the same time.

Pretty much the only important thing Dad had to do was to close me up in the second vault so I had the space to open the Frankensafe . . . and then let me back out once I was done.

Then, we'd close up both vaults and wait in the vault anteroom for our next cue.

Step four: Nando and Helen.

If the problem with getting in and out of the tunnel was being seen, and the problem with opening the secret door into the vault anteroom was being heard, on our way out, we had to worry about both.

But once again, as Dad had meant when he called the heist a Cleveland Swing, it was just a simple matter of timing. All we had to do was wait for a break in performances.

When the banker had originally made his mad architectural changes, the secret door that led out of the anteroom had opened out to a storage area, but after La Casa del Libretto purchased the building, the storage area had been converted... into the stage.

Thankfully, the secret door opened in the wings, just offstage, rather than directly in front of the audience. In between performances, Helen would take her fall, Nando would turn it into a commotion, and while everybody was distracted and looking away from the stage, we'd trigger the secret door, the grinding noise covered by the crowd, and slip out unnoticed.

At that point, once we were offstage and headed back to our seats, Paulie would take the alligator clips off the alarm, and much to Nando's relief, Helen would have a miraculous recovery. All that was left was to enjoy dessert and the last few performances.

Getting the timing right required us to coordinate, but from a technical perspective, it was a simple job. The grown-ups were right about that.

There were a few extraordinarily small differences from the original job other than the Frankensafe. The old alarm system had an "off" button, but Paulie could handle a pair of alligator clips for the new one. And while I would have enjoyed seeing Helen throw a drink in Nando's face like she did the first time—accusing him of infidelity and getting in a scrap with whichever poor, innocent woman Helen claimed was making eyes at Nando—her pratfall and Nando's overreaction would have the same effect. All we needed was people to look in Helen and Nando's direction for the few seconds Dad and I required to scram. And in the unlikely event there was anybody still looking in our direction, with all the hubbub, it would take a while before they thought to ask questions. And by that point, the job was over anyway.

Swiping an apple at a farmers' market was scarier.

Then why did I feel so unsettled?

I took a last bite of my lunch, wiped my mouth and my fingers with my napkin. It seemed too simple. It couldn't be this easy.

Nando was right to think of it like a revival: If nothing else serious had changed, all we had to do was pull the costumes and backdrops out of storage and put on the same old performance, and other than me and the Frankensafe, once the curtain was up, all the grown-ups had to do was play their parts almost exactly as they had in the past.

Except, I found it hard to believe that *nothing* meaningful had changed in the last three decades other than the addition of a safe inside the second vault. Yes, Venice was a historical city, and I suspected that the board of La Casa del Libretto didn't truck in modern design, but that didn't mean everything stayed the same. Maybe I'd feel better once we were in Venice and Dad did his standard due diligence, rather than trusting some updated notes from Nando for an old plan. Even if the building hadn't changed much in thirty-something years, the world certainly had.

Except, there was a math problem.

Even if everything else *had* stayed the same, we didn't have enough bodies to pull the job off properly.

33

"HEY," I SAID. "WHEN DAD AND I go into the tunnel, who reattaches the padlock to the gate?"

"No," Helen said to Paulie, "I remember, because *that* was the same year we were in Saudi Arabia and decided *not* to go after that horrible man from British Petroleum."

"Helen, that's not right," Paulie replied. "BP was the year after that, and it wasn't Saudi Arabia, it was Qatar."

"This doesn't make any sense," I said, tapping the bundle.

"Of course it makes sense," Dad said. "We *literally* did the job already. It was a breeze."

Nando said, "No, Qatar was the year *before* the Venice Double, and—"

The four of them started talking over each other, continuing to argue about when exactly they'd done the job for Giovanni, when Qatar—or maybe it was Saudi Arabia—had been, and whether it had been an executive from BP or Chevron they'd been targeting.

I gave up and looked back at the plans again. I didn't understand it. If Paulie was on the alarm, Dad and I were dealing with the vaults, the Frankensafe, and the switch, and Helen and Nando were off causing a distraction, then who was going to close the gate and lock it back up after Dad and I entered the tunnel?

If it had been an old-school, iron-bars-you-could-pass-a-toddler-through kind of door, it wouldn't be a problem, but when the banker had done his construction project, he'd replaced the entrance to the tunnel with something more of a pain in the ass. It was decorative, and probably looked better than what had been there before, but the intricate scrollwork was so thick you couldn't reach through to lock it back up after yourself. It was a relatively quick job, and from the second we left our seats in the banquet hall until the second we returned wouldn't amount to more than thirty minutes, so I supposed I could just come back around and close it up after we were all done.

Except, at least back when they'd pulled the job originally, the staff did rounds every thirty minutes, and the door to the tunnel was on the list of things they checked. There's no way Dad would have left it unlocked then, and I didn't understand why he wasn't concerned about it now.

How did they pull it off with only Dad, Nando, Helen, and Paulie? That gate into the tunnel being left open seemed like a big "well, let's hope nobody notices!" kind of detail for Dad to have missed. He never forgot about that kind of stuff, and . . . I searched for it and found it: He'd marked "close" on his notes. He'd even underlined the word three times.

I didn't like it.

I didn't like the way the grown-ups kept their secrets and had their sly little grins as they told stories with layers that went over my head. And every time I asked a question to clarify, Dad or Nando gave some sort of song and dance about how everybody else saw it, so why couldn't I? And Paulie and Helen applauded their soft-shoe performance, and even Richa seemed to have a handle on what was happening. So how come I couldn't get it to add up?

Nando and Helen working the crowd was two, Paulie on the alarm made three, me plus Dad for the vaults and Frankensafe got us to five . . . plus one to close and lock the gate into the tunnel.

We had five, but we had to have six for the job to work.

All I needed was Ginny and a glass of milk to feel like I was a little kid asking questions about Santa Claus: How does he fit down a chimney, how do those reindeer fly, and how on earth do we pull off this job with a crew of five?

"The plan is hinky," I said.

Dad was looking at a piece of melon on his plate as if he was scared it might attack him. He gave an exasperated grunt and pushed it to the side. "Already? You're already telling me why my plan sucks? You've looked at the plans for like thirty seconds."

"I'm not saying your plan sucks. I'm saying it's hinky."

Nando wagged a finger. "You simply aren't seeing all the pieces, Duke. As Helen said, there are aspects of the plan that we have to update, but as a whole? You'll simply have to trust that it's a simple job."

"You're not hearing what I'm saying." Dad started to rise, but I added, "I'm *not* saying the plan is a bad plan. And I'm sure there's stuff I'm missing. It's, well, the numbers don't add up."

Nando frowned. "I think you're being paid fairly. Giovanni is being quite generous."

"That's not what I'm talking about, though I wouldn't mind—"

Dad pushed his plate forward in disgust and cut me off. "What, you're suddenly the expert on *this* job? You were here when we did this job already, before you were born? It's a sound plan. What's your problem?"

"I'm not trying to start an argument," I said. "I don't understand how we're going to pull this off with only the five of us, because by my count, to lock the gate back up after we head down to the tunnel, we need a sixth."

"Of course we need a sixth!" Nando tapped his fingers on the pile of papers. "Nobody would argue that. You don't need the detailed documents to see that. Anybody can see that we need six people!"

"Okay," I said. "Right. But like I said, there's only five of us."

Dad fidgeted in his seat and bent his head down, so he was staring at the table. Paulie suddenly had something urgent on her phone.

Helen looked at her ex-husband. He wouldn't meet *her* gaze either.

She said, "Well, nobody expects Nando to be the one to break the bad news, but Paulie? Knox? You ridiculous idiots. I know you were in a rush, and I know you didn't get a chance to tell him much, but you didn't at least tell him *that*? Did you think Duke wouldn't notice?"

I got that sinking feeling that I'd had so often when there was information Dad had held back. "What?"

"It's fine," Dad said. He still had his head down, and he mumbled like a petulant child.

"Knox." Helen's voice could have boiled water.

"Fine," he said again. He muttered a few inaudible words again.

"What?"

He muttered again, but this time I understood him: "We've got our sixth."

"For the love of god, Knox,"—Paulie snapped at him—"just tell Duke."

Dad let out a long breath, lifted his head up, and looked at me.

I looked at him.

Waiting. Waiting. Waiting.

Finally, he said, "Giovanni is our sixth."

I picked my jaw up off the floor, held up a hand, and said, "Are you stupid, or are you out of your fuc—"

34

"GRANTCHESTER DUCAINE!" HELEN SAID SHARPLY.

"No." I knew the tone of my voice was too hostile, but I couldn't stop myself. "I'm sorry, Helen, but..."

I turned to Dad. "So what, one rule for me and Ginny, a different rule for you?"

"It's not like that." Whatever hesitation or embarrassment he'd had at not telling me before had turned into an unassailable smugness. "Giovanni's good. We're not asking him to dial a Grand Talent XL. The most complicated thing he has to handle is closing a padlock, and if staff ask him what he's doing, he's on the board. He can talk his way out of it. Giovanni would have made a fine professional. Heck, he's better than some of the pros we've worked with."

"Except he's *not* a pro. He's an *amateur*." I said the word with all the malice I could muster. "Hasn't that always been one of your unbreakable rules? Forget working for free *for* an amateur. Now you're working for free *with* an amateur? You *never* work with an amateur, that's the rule! Or was all of it lies? All those rules of yours, so careful. Do it *your* way, because that's the only way to be safe, right? Our whole life, it's 'this is the way to do it, follow the rules no matter what,' unless, of course, *you* happen to feel like bending those rules because, what, you *like* Giovanni? And don't tell me *Mom* convinced you to allow him to tag along on the heist. This whole job was somehow *Mom's* big idea now?"

Nando reached out and patted my back. "Now, Duke, you weren't there. You're getting upset over nothing."

"I'm here now, aren't I? I've been here this whole time. Where were *you*?" The spite dripped from my words.

He pulled his hand back like he'd realized the dog he'd been petting was a wolf. The grown-ups looked at each other. Helen seemed to signal to Paulie, because she shook her head, and then Dad decided to take up the charge. He spoke firmly: "Now, look, you're being unreasonable. I know what I'm doing. All he has to do is close up behind us. There's nothing to it. I say Giovanni is fine."

"And I say, I'm not working with an amateur." I stood up. "I'm out."

Very quietly, Helen said, "Duke, sit down."

"But he—"

"Duke, it's not just your dad and Nando and Paulie. *I'm* saying Giovanni's good. You're just going to have to trust us. What more do you need?"

Dad glared at me, and I glared back. I wanted to pop him in the mouth.

But Helen. She was looking at me with such disappointment.

I said, "I'll talk with him, I'll give him a fair chance. Maybe he's as great as you all say. After all, Mom liked him, right?"

I gave a half smile, and when she didn't smile back, I turned it up to the full wattage and said, "I promise. I'll play nice."

Helen clapped her hands, suddenly glad. "Good, because it's time to go to Venice."

35

IF IT WAS AN INTENTIONAL MANEUVER on Helen's part to keep me away from Dad and Nando to give me extra time to cool down, it was done subtly, but the grown-ups were in one car, and Richa and I ended up in the other one, together again.

Richa seemed completely unaware of how pissed off I was at my dad over the Giovanni bombshell. She gave me a smile as I buckled in and said, "It will be approximately a twenty-minute drive to the station. The train itself is a little less than four hours. Giovanni will be meet us later."

"Why? I was hoping to get to chat with him," I said. "Chat" didn't cover it, but if he was, indeed, going to be part of our string, I wanted a chance to take the measure of the man before I trusted my life to him.

Okay, maybe it was a bit hyperbolic to say I was trusting my life to him.

But even though all Giovanni had to do was look both ways for staff members on rounds, close a door, and then shut a padlock, if he messed things up, there'd be a security response, and then things could get messy. Nando and Dad could claim the job was a cakewalk all they wanted, but there was no such thing as a truly safe job in our line of work.

Ginny was proof of that.

Though, if I was being honest, other than having to figure out the Frankensafe on the fly, and other than planning to use an amateur to help us out, redoing the Venice Double did seem like a sweet gig.

Depending on how much I was getting paid, of course. Sooner or later, I was going to get somebody to answer that question for me.

Richa said, "Giovanni is traveling separately. But you will have time to talk with him tonight. We are all having dinner together."

"All of us?"

"Not Auldhilda, of course. As I said, she knows of Nando as Giovanni's friend, and you as... Tell me about Panama City?"

Right. Our cover. The Panama job.

"It was the last time we were all together, though we'd used the dodge before. Helen and Nando played the part of a married couple for the setup. I'm kind of only realizing this in retrospect, but there was a lot of underlying tension with the two of them for that job. More than normal, because, you know, they'd been married, and I'm assuming they got divorced for a reason, so there was always a lot of tension."

"You don't know why they got divorced?"

"Why does anybody get divorced? It didn't work out. But I was seven when they got divorced. My mom had just died. I don't know. Dad told me that Nando was gone and maybe we'd never see him again."

"You were seven?"

"I mean, Dad probably didn't use those exact words. Like I said, I was seven. But we'd all done work together since the divorce, and it had been fine, or maybe I didn't notice, but for sure, there was more tension for the Panama City job. I was sixteen, I remember that. It was fun, even if Helen and Nando were being weirder than normal."

A fun job, but a full production kind of job, with Dad acting in the role of gofer slash driver slash bodyguard slash all-around glowering menace—Nando referred to Dad as his "valet"—and Paulie, taking a vacation from her management role, buttoned up in professional clothing acting as Helen's personal secretary. Ginny and I got to be Helen and Nando's niece and nephew, because Nando's much younger "kid sister," who was our ostensible mom, was a ne'er-do-well drug addict and out of the picture.

All Ginny and I had to do—other than open a safe belonging to the mobster we were hitting—was act like a pair of spoiled brats. Which was fun, because at least publicly, Ginny and I could order both Dad and Paulie around; as Nando and Helen's "employees," they had to hop to it. Though Ginny and I quickly discovered that if we pushed it too far in public, once we were in private again, Dad and Paulie had a limited sense of humor about the situation.

Richa found the story of how we'd pushed Nando's "valet" into a fountain to be amusing, however, which, years later, made it almost worth it. Almost, because Dad had made Ginny and me run wind sprints until we puked as a punishment, and Paulie... Well, Richa's laugh was a delight, and the job itself had been a rich vein to tap.

If we were going to play our Panama City roles again, there were some gaps that needed updating, I told Richa, because while I assumed I hadn't turned into the same kind of burnout as my "mom" had, I doubted I had magically turned into a well-rounded, thoughtful adult version of my Panama City self.

Richa assured me that we'd have time to get our stories straight, as we were unlikely to see Auldhilda until the night of the gala.

As we worked our way through traffic at the train station, Richa told me not to worry about my bag—Bosco, who was driving our car, and Fio, who had been driving the other car, would take care of everything. She also said that there was a coat for me here, at the station, so I wouldn't be freezing when I got to Venice, but that there would also be a weather-appropriate new wardrobe waiting for me at Giovanni's palazzo when we arrived.

I laughed, and then had to explain about the Volkov Job. I mean, not about the job—there was no reason she needed to know any of that—but rather about how on my last job, I'd also had a new seat of threads provided to me. I'd liked them enough that I kept them. I was hoping Richa had good taste.

"You do realize I did not personally shop for your clothing, Duke. Yes? I simply gave Giovanni's shopper the measurements you gave me. The choices were not mine. I do not care what you wear. And it wasn't only for you. For your dad as well."

She seemed to pull away from me as she said it, though it could simply have been her preparing to get out of the car. Ahead of us, Fio had already parked. The grown-ups were milling about, waiting for me and Richa.

"Well, thank you anyway," I said. "I packed for Florida, not Venice."

Richa hesitated, as if she had given a secret away that she intended to keep hidden, but she didn't say anything. I followed her in, watched Dad take a package from Giovanni's stylist—a slim man who looked bored and unimpressed with the world around him—took my own package, and then we all trooped onto the train.

As if in apology, though I wasn't entirely sure what she was apologizing for, Richa suggested I go try on the coat, see what I thought.

I took the box from the stylist into the bathroom with me. The box was neatly wrapped with twine. The blouson-style coat nestled inside was a wool and silk blend. I put it on and looked at myself in the mirror.

Well. The stylist had good taste. I was hopeful the clothes waiting for me in Venice would look half as good. I took the coat off, stared at the label, and then gave a snort. Good taste or an unlimited budget. I put it back on and looked in the mirror again. There was no chance the coat was worth the money. It had to be at least as much as my monthly rent. But even if I didn't have the cash to pay for it myself—I probably needed a good haircut more than I needed a designer coat—I did have to admit that it suited me. As

I was admiring myself, the train started to move, and I once again marveled at the pure civility of traveling by train. I'd always wanted to take the sleeper train from Chiang Mai to Bangkok, and I remember, as a kid, the whole family taking trains through Europe, Mom delighting at showing us what she loved about each city we visited.

I took the jacket off, draped it over my arm, and came back to our compartment. The grown-ups had colonized a four-person section and were already playing cards. Dad's box, which also, I assumed, had a coat in it, was unopened and stuffed into the rack above their seats. I was sure it was an equally nice and appropriate jacket.

Nando was riffling the cards. I watched him shuffle. If it was a hot table and he'd been trying, he could have wrung a sucker dry. Quick cuts and waterfalls, a deliberate stutter that looked like a mistake but allowed him to swing an ace from the middle of the deck to the top, his fingers making the kings and queens bow to his commands; even knowing what to look for, I could barely spot the tucks and pulls when I was younger. But I could spot them now, the slight tremor, the blotches of age, the thinness of the skin on the backs of his hands.

I watched him put the deck of cards down, cough, drink some water, and pick the cards up again, a fragility to his movements that was new to me.

The moon waits for no man, I thought. That's what he'd said to me earlier, when he was trying to talk over me, to stop me from bringing up my concerns about the job: The moon waits for no man, and there's nothing new under the sun. But even for Nando, the sun sets, the moon rises, and time marches forward with ruthless relentlessness and no compunction.

Everybody starts to slip at some point.

He might be able to deal a crooked deck to Helen, Paulie, and Dad, but he couldn't fool me.

I walked up the aisle and Nando spotted me. He leapt to his feet, slammed the cards on top of the table, hoisted his drink in the air, and trying hard, he pronounced in his regal, booming voice, "The prodigal son returns!"

Dad didn't even crack a smile.

36

I DIDN'T BOTHER POINTING OUT to Nando that when the prodigal son returned, he was greeted with open arms by his father, rather than a combination wince and scowl. But I was as good as my word to Helen. I didn't make a peep about Giovanni being our sixth.

We were in the VIP section or one step up from first class or whatever Giovanni's money and Richa's skill could arrange. The seating worked nicely, with Richa and I close enough to the grown-ups that we could lean in and ask questions if we wanted to, but far enough back that if we reclined away from the adults, we could have a private conversation. Because Richa had bought out the entire car, except when an *assistente di bordo* came with drinks or to otherwise see to our comfort, our group had enough space to talk if we used a small amount of delicacy.

For instance, the first time Giovanni's name came up, instead of getting into specifics, Dad said, "Honestly, he's good. He might not be a pro, but he's got the nerves, and it's super easy. Don't worry, he won't let us down."

Okay, so maybe I wasn't overtly complaining about Malanari being in on the job, but I was still feeling pissy. Even though Dad's head was turned, the words clearly aimed toward me, I didn't acknowledge the comment.

He tried again. As he took the next trick, he added, "We can trust him. He's probably the only person I've ever worked for who I'd take an IOU from."

We were crooks through and through: Nobody worked on the "pay ya later" system, and if somebody tried to stiff you on a job, there was only one way to settle it. Saying he'd take an IOU meant something from my dad.

I realized Helen was giving me the stink eye.

"I'm looking forward to meeting Giovanni," I said. "I'm sure everything will be fine."

I almost meant it.

We had wine and beer and cocktails and nuts and cheese and were essentially pampered the entire way. I didn't know if we were in some special VIP class or if Richa had simply arranged additional service for us, but it was a luxurious way to travel. Not quite as exclusive as Giovanni, who was evidently flying private jet, and not quite as quick, either, but in a lot of ways, much nicer, and certainly lower impact. But it did make me want to ask Nando if he was as good of a friend of Giovanni's as he thought, then why was he on the train with the other employees?

Instead, I asked Richa why Fio and Bosco were strapped.

"Strapped?"

"Slang. Sorry. I know they're working security for the event, but why are they carrying guns in the first place?"

Richa shifted uncomfortably. We were huddled together, earnest, focused on what was at hand. "How do you know they are carrying guns?"

"Because I'm looking for it," I said.

"There have been some . . . problems."

"Problems?"

"A break-in."

"And that was enough for them to start carrying pistols?"

"And some threats against Giovanni." She sounded uncertain. "They have only started carrying the guns recently, but they have been licensed to do so. You have been told that they will be working at the gala because of the necklace?"

"Because of the— Oh, Auldhilda's necklace! Yeah," I said. "But these threats, or whatever it is, they aren't going to be a problem with the job, are they?"

"It is a convenience. Do not worry about the reason why Fio and Bosco are licensed to carry pistols; it is not connected to this job," she said firmly. "Giovanni is a wealthy man, and with that, there comes people who wish to take his money."

"Speaking of money, I still don't know how much I'm getting paid for this."

It was like a light switch.

Maybe I wasn't making threats against Giovanni, but to Richa, at least in that moment, I *was* somebody who wished to take Giovanni's money. Which was true, but also ridiculous on her part. Why should it make a difference to Richa that this was a *job* for me? This was a job for *her*, so why should I be in it for charity? I didn't expect the nurses working for Ginny to work for free, even if they were rooting so hard for the surgery to work that one of them had convinced herself she'd seen a thing that wasn't there. But Richa thought me wanting to get paid was the *only* reason I was here?

It didn't matter to her that Nando was clearly over the hill, or that he was calling on a debt that I had no part of. It didn't matter that I was supposed to be settling an old score of my own in Florida, instead of romping around Italy, and it didn't matter that right up until that second, I thought the two of us were hitting it off nicely.

I changed the subject, and said, "He needs better security than those two guys."

"That is not part of your purview."

"Part of my purview? Is that a defense mechanism? Speaking like you learned English out of a textbook?"

She could have gone either way with her response. Thankfully, her mouth widened, almost approximating a smile: Maybe she didn't like me right at this second, but at least she was self-aware.

"Occupational hazard," she said. "Even though this is a personal matter, I often represent Giovanni in a professional capacity that requires a certain amount of formality." Then the smile reached her eyes, and she laughed. "But yes, actually, I learned English during business school. From a textbook."

She'd been born and raised in Florence—her paternal grandparents had moved there from Delhi in the 1970s. She laughed again when she said that they raised her father on the money they made selling curry to English tourists who'd gotten sick of spaghetti. Her mom moved in with her dad and his parents once they were married, and so Richa herself had been raised speaking Bengali, Italian, and all the necessary scraps of French, English, Chinese, German, Russian, Spanish, and Japanese that she could learn while helping in the restaurant as a curious teenager. Fluent now in Bengali, Italian, English, and Japanese. Conversational enough in eight other languages that she could get by without a translator unless she was negotiating a contract that required legalistic scrutiny. Though to be fair, she corrected, since her grandparents had died, she'd barely used her Bengali and was quite rusty.

"You negotiate contracts for Malanari?"

Her friendliness evaporated in an instant. I think she audibly sniffed.

"Yes, I am empowered to act as a financial agent for Giovanni." She crossed her legs, pulled her phone from her purse, and started thumbing at the screen.

I said, "Flick, flick. On, off. A light switch."

She kept at it with her phone for a few seconds, clearly trying to decide if she wanted to ignore me or not.

She put the phone down.

“You are a frustrating man. What do you mean, a light switch?”

“On or off. You forgot for a few seconds that you don’t approve of me, and it’s like the lights are turned on, and then I say something that makes you think I’m only in it for the money, and it’s lights-out again.”

“Aren’t you?”

“In it for the money?”

“Yes. Are you doing this for the money?”

“Of course,” I said. “Why would I do this for free?”

“Your father, Nando, Helen, Paulie,” Richa said, “they are all doing this because they’re Giovanni’s friend. You would like him if you gave him a chance. He’s a good man.”

“If that’s true, he wouldn’t have had the Puccini score stolen in the first place. Or he would have given it back to the heirs the Nazis took it away from in the first place instead of making this big, romantic gesture that nobody knows about. If he was a good man, I wouldn’t need to be here in the first place.”

No stone ever harder, no ice ever colder; Richa looked like she wouldn’t mind belting me. And then, almost as quickly, she recovered her composure. She started to speak, but then she pulled the words back, reconsidered, and said, “Giovanni Malanari *is* a good man, and if you feel otherwise, you would be well reminded that the others are here as his guests, but you are here in his employ. He is paying you handsomely, and you should treat him with all due respect.”

Every word could have been dipped in acid.

“Maybe they don’t teach you this in business school,” I said, “but respect can’t be bought. It can only be earned.”

Thankfully, Helen needed to go to the bathroom, and she summoned me to play for her in their card game. I picked up a hand that was rife with mediocre clubs and weak diamonds, and by the time my dad cackled and called me a loser, Richa was hard at work on her laptop.

But the trip was still, somehow, fun. As they continued to play hearts, Helen caught Nando palming the queen of spades and docked him a hundred points, and to his delight and Paulie's annoyance, Dad collected all the tricks to shoot the moon not once, but twice, and for most of the trip, we chatted and told stories—as much as we could in our mostly private public space—and by the time we were standing by the Grand Canal, it almost felt like we were on vacation. Even Richa had closed her laptop and deigned to join us for a glass of wine, and if she had looked ready to strangle me earlier, now she only seemed to want to poke me in the eye.

So much for chemistry.

37

RICHA HAD GIVEN US THE CHOICE of being met by a boat or walking to Malanari's palazzo. Paulie hemmed and hawed for a second, but we all decided that after four hours on a train, a ten-minute walk seemed pleasant. Didn't hurt that Tweedle-Fio and Tweedle-Bosco were taking care of the luggage.

With the early winter nights and the moon not yet risen, even though it was barely past seven o'clock according to the clocks in the train station, the darkness spilled across the water and the land, broken only by islands of light. A few restaurants still had holiday lights, a siren song for the tourists who'd come to Venice in the offseason, though I wasn't sure if there was such a thing as an offseason anymore.

There was a breeze that was as damp as the Adriatic Sea. I pulled my coat tight, my hands pressed deep into my pockets. I tapped Richa's elbow and thanked her again. She glanced at me, gave a nod of approval at the way the coat looked, and went back to her conversation with my dad.

We passed a small trattoria that was bursting at the seams and had a line nearly a dozen people long waiting outside. Richa made a comment about the risotto to my dad. Through the window, a pair of women who seemed to split the difference in age between me and Aunt Paulie watched us pass. Helen and Nando lagged behind, strolling leisurely, all the time in the world, hand in arm, the occasional peal of laughter catching up to us.

Richa moved confidently, neither rushing nor stalling, but guiding us forward, and I tried to keep our movements aligned in my head with the map of Venice that I'd studied. The bridges and alleys, the twisting water, the accumulation of buildings over the course of centuries, all meant that Venice could be a labyrinth for the uninitiated. But after we'd been walking for six or seven minutes, I called out to Richa. She and Dad stopped, waited for me.

"It's over there, isn't it? If we turn left here, can we walk past it on the way without attracting notice?"

Dad didn't seem to understand what I meant, but Richa looked at her watch. "I can do better than that. How about a drink?"

Two minutes later, we were inside a tidy little *bacaro* across the square from La Casa del Libretto. Nando, Helen, Dad, and Paulie had stools at the bar, and Richa and I were standing at a chest-high shelf by the windows. She'd ordered us all an *ombra de vin*, literally "a shadow of wine," and a few *cicchetti*: olives, sardines on fresh bread, pickled vegetables.

I watched the ebb and flow of pedestrians crossing the square. An almost equal mix of tourists and locals heading out for drinks and a small snack to start the evening, a few families with children, tired workers heading home.

None of them paid any special attention to the palazzo that we intended to break into.

It was Thursday night. In forty-eight hours, on Saturday night, the square would be crowded, tuxedos and ball gowns on the red carpet, Auldhilda wearing her fancy necklace, photograph hunters and opera fans, tourists drawn to the idea of a spectacle even if they didn't know what it was about.

I'd studied the bundle, but seeing La Casa del Libretto in person was different. You can understand scale in a picture or on a set of drawings, but you can't *feel* it. The palazzo loomed over the square, the turrets like points on a crown. Your eye was drawn to the building as if it was a boulder balancing on a precipice: The palazzo was the focal point you came back to.

Except, when I'm describing it, the building sounds like it is threatening or imposing, when it *felt* like anything but. Passing tourists made it easier for me to see the sheer scale, but despite the stone used to construct it, La Casa del Libretto had an almost unearthly lightness to it. Even competing against a nearly full moon on a cloudless winter sky, the paleness of the palazzo almost gleamed, a moon unto itself.

Maybe the atmosphere was infectious, because when Richa interrupted my musing, the tension between us from the train had been replaced with that pleasant, tingling, flirty buzz again, as if it was only the two of us, alone in the bar.

"That man," Richa said, pointing to a passing man, lanky, besuited, a face that could reasonably have belonged to an aardvark, "rented me my first apartment in Venice, after I'd graduated from university."

"I was thinking of the beauty of this place."

"He was a terrible landlord. All the windows leaked. Living here is not all so romantic."

"You're killing the poetry."

An enigmatic smile. "Have you read Brodsky?"

She waited, that same crook at the corner of her lip, settled in to see how I responded. A challenge.

Okay. That was interesting. Something had shifted again with her. That light switch. What had I done differently this time? What are the rules to this little game?

"You mean *Watermark*?"

"Yes!"

"Thank goodness," I said, "because that's the only thing I've read by Brodsky, and only because my tutor was, well, never mind. It doesn't matter."

"It wasn't a trap. Much to my employer's displeasure, I do not love art in the same way that he does. I read a few novels a year, I like movies, I listen to whatever music my phone recommends when I'm working out. But I get more than enough culture in my life accompanying Giovanni. He's not faking it when he says he loves opera: He's taken voice lessons for years. Of course, not to the same degree as Giancarlo did, or for that matter, Auldhilda, but it is the same with painting. And acting lessons. And writing poetry. He does not take singing lessons because he has any belief that he will perform at La Fenice. But simply because he enjoys it. I am not sure if I am saying this word right, but he is a... dilettante?"

"Yeah."

"He finds a new skill to be enthusiastic about, and then he masters it to the point where it becomes so that the difference between a hobby and a profession, it is not such a great distance after all. Maybe what people might call a skilled amateur enthusiast. For physical things as well. Skiing, rock climbing, and he has made a study of food and wine and many things that are considered signs of culture. He can be disciplined if he wishes to learn new skills, and if he is not the same as a professional, he is good enough to be taken seriously by people who do those things professionally. They understand that, with a different life, he could have been one of them. Do you understand what I mean?"

"Are you trying to pick a fight?"

"What?"

She was genuinely confused.

"You didn't know, right?"

"Know what? I didn't know that...?"

"Oh. Yeah. That makes sense."

"Duke. You're speaking in haikus."

Which, I realized was literally true, but what I said was, "Giovanni is going on the job with us."

"Of course." Richa bit her lip. "Oh. I see. *You* didn't know?"

"I *should* have known better," I said. "But you do realize you could have said Giovanni's a Renaissance man. Which, given the history here, is appropriate."

"My point is less that Giovanni is a Renaissance man," she said, with a wink so quick I could have missed it if I wasn't turned toward her, "and more that I have learned to enjoy the opera and museums and art galleries and all the higher arts because I have accompanied Giovanni so often. He is a lover of the arts, and a true romantic. But no, left to my own devices, I probably would not have read a long essay by a Russian poet on why he loved coming to Venice on vacation. There is nothing wrong with spending some of your nights watching *Survivor* instead of attending the opera."

"I know what you mean about the opera. But still, Venice, Brodsky. It's beautiful."

A crinkle around her eyes, and then her face in profile as she turned to stare through the glass.

"Which? The city, or the Brodsky essay?"

But I was too distracted to answer. When she'd looked out the window, I'd lingered on her face for the smallest snatch of time, and then followed her gaze to the whirls and pools of pedestrians in the square in front of us, the pattern of movement a predictable sort of chaos. And in that chaos, some imperceptible shift from what I'd seen before caused the skeletal hand of fate to reach out and pluck the strings on my paranoia and settle down into the idea that there was something amiss.

There.

Diagonally across, three trattorias in a row, under the canopy of the one to my far right, a bearded man with slicked-back hair, opening the door for a short-haired woman wearing a motorcycle jacket. They'd been split before. Beard by the fountain, on his phone.

Motorcycle jacket with a cocktail on the far left. Oriented so they could see the palazzo.

And even from a distance, I could tell by the way they moved.

They were pros.

Another team was working.

38

"WHY'S HE DOING THIS?"

Richa frowned. "I'm sorry. I don't understand."

"You understand. We'll talk around it since we're in a public place. But you understand exactly what I mean when I ask, why is he doing this?"

Nando plonked down two more shadows of wine in front of us, made a bawdy joke in Portuguese, explained it in Italian when he realized neither of us spoke Portuguese well enough to follow him, and then switched to English to tell us a story about a heist he'd pulled when he'd read the currency conversion rates wrong, and instead of clearing nearly ten million, had come out in the hole more than forty grand.

Dad and Helen and Paulie were in their own little bubble while Nando talked at me and Richa. There were strings of dim lights layered across the ceiling, a brighter light behind the bar, the overall effect like candlelight; you could read a paper menu, but you wouldn't want to read a paperback.

When Nando was rewarded with Richa's giggles, we clinked glasses, and he went back to join the rest of the adults at the bar.

"He is impossible not to adore," Richa said.

I looked out over the square. Not everything was lit with as much delicacy as our *bacaro*; the trattoria I'd seen the couple enter was lit up so that the inside was a stage. I could see Beard and Motorcycle Jacket sitting at the table in the front window, turned enough away from each other that it was clear, even though they were together, they weren't there to *be* together. Wary, watching, but somehow the way they occupied space showed that they were not wary of each other. Not a date. But partners. They trusted each other.

Richa, surprising me, switched to Japanese. "You are conversational?" she said. I nodded, and she said, "Nando gave me the idea, the way he was jumping around from language to language."

It was a little bit like trying to loosen a rusty bolt. It took a lot of effort to get it moving, but once I spoke my first word in Japanese, it came back. "If you can stand my accent, then yeah. I'm good with languages, but not like you and Nando."

"Yes, I understand what you mean when you ask why Giovanni is doing this."

"Okay, so, why?"

"Why?"

"Yeah."

"No," Richa said, "I'm asking you, Duke, *why*? Why do you need to know now? You are going to be having dinner with him in, oh, perhaps half an hour. We will be staying with him in his palazzo. He has already agreed to talk with you and answer all your questions."

"I don't want to wait."

"Which is what I am concerned with. Something has changed in the last minute for you. You are acting as if you are haunted."

"Spooked," I said in English.

In Japanese again: "What is it? Is it the building? Security? Another thing? Whatever it is, the . . . elders don't see it, do they?"

The way she was sitting, the trattorias would have been on the edge of her field of vision. A blur, at best, the shape of a thing rather than the thing itself.

"Okay, so don't make any sudden turns or anything, but—"

"Don't insult me."

She took a sip of her wine. She switched to Italian and held out her glass. *"Saluti."*

"Cheers."

We clinked wineglasses, finished them, and then Richa collected them, took them to the bar, and came back and sat down, going all the way around the bases from English to Japanese to Italian and back to English.

She said, "The man with the beard and the woman wearing the black leather jacket with the zippers."

A statement. Not a question.

"It's a motorcycle jacket."

"Ah! Yes. I couldn't remember what it was called."

The couple in the window wasn't doing anything noteworthy. They were sitting there. There was no way that Richa should have been able to spot them that easily. Not without me giving her more of a hint than simply it was out of the field of her vision.

Richa seemed worth getting to know better.

"How'd you know?"

"You can tell they're working. Everybody else is having dinner. This couple," she said, "there's food in front of them, but they are *working*."

"Sure, but how? How can *you* tell they're working?"

"How am I supposed to know?" she asked. She put her hand on the shelf where we'd been resting our drinks. "I looked, and I could tell. I think it is like... Giancarlo's wife, Auldhilda, she has, oh, I'm not sure what it is called in English. When you can hear music, the notes, exactly, so you know if it is in tune or not?"

"Perfect pitch?"

"Yes! Perfect pitch. Auldhilda has perfect pitch, and she tried to explain to me how to have perfect pitch. But of course, you cannot explain how to have talent that simply comes naturally to you."

I chortled. "I'm supposed to believe that you have, what, perfect pitch, but for spotting... people like me? Beginner's luck and all that?"

She stared at me for several long seconds. It could have been minutes or hours.

And then, in Italian, she said, "I know how to spot the bad boys."

She stood up, and as she did, the reflection of the hanging lights twinkled in her eyes. "I'll pay the check," she said in English now with a cheeky grin. "Giovanni is waiting to meet you. And don't worry. I won't stare at that couple on my way out."

39

IT WAS A GOOD THING it wasn't much farther to get to Malanari's place, because I felt like I had whiplash. One minute Richa was a machine speaking in a code I couldn't understand, turned overly formal and distant, and the next minute it was like we had our own secret, shared language. Or, rather, languages, though I was more comfortable in English or even Italian than I was speaking Japanese.

But with Dad and Paulie and Nando and Helen, she was simply charming and efficient, clearly adept at making small talk in any kind of situation. She was now making the four of them laugh by telling a story about her missing an important meeting at her first job. She'd tripped and literally fallen into a toilet in the process, losing a shoe and an earring and tearing her skirt. When she'd told the story of falling into the toilet to her boss, her boss laughed so hard that the boss—again, literally—peed herself. And somehow, that led to Richa getting promoted instead of fired.

It was a story that felt a little too tailored, like a tale Nando would have told as part of a con. The story Richa told about herself lining up too perfectly with who she presented herself as.

"Did you really get promoted?" I said.

"Turn left here. What do you mean, did I *really* get promoted?"

Nando stopped and held up his hand. "No! Do not answer that. He's looking for the con."

"That's not fair," I said half-heartedly.

"He wants to know why you tell *this* as a story," Nando continued. "What's the long con? Think of the woman who tells the story in line at the dealership about how she saved her own life by double-checking the brake line, but also, she happens to be a big-shot investor and is late for an important meeting that is for big, big money, so she can't talk more now. But later that day, it so happens that you get a hot tip on a big deal of your own. And then, coincidently, that night, you walk into a bar, and what do you know, the woman from the dealership is there. And you remember that she's a big-shot stocks and bonds kind of person, so you tell her about this deal that's come your way. And she says, oh, that is an awful scam that is going around... but, I so happen to have this *other* thing, which *is* a guaranteed winner. He wants to know what you are saying now that will have been a lie later. What is the con?"

"Nando," I said. "Come on. I don't think it's a con."

"No," Richa said. "I think I'd like to hear more, Nando."

Nando furrowed his brow and turned on his professor voice. "Even if the job pays well, sometimes you say no if you must work with somebody you cannot trust. Some you can work with, some you cannot, but working with a person is different than being with a person when you are not working." He dropped the voice. "As you can imagine, Richa, it is difficult to trust other thieves. We all tend to have one thing in common, which is that we aren't dissuaded from doing things simply because we shouldn't do them. Whether that is good or bad I do not wish to debate. But what he's asking is are you steering him with this story?"

"Steering him?"

"Not to be the voice of reason here or anything," I said, "but maybe we walk another fifty meters or so and have the rest of this conversation inside. You know, in private? Because that's it, right?"

I motioned to the palazzo. It was Renaissance era, restrained but pleasing, easy to slide past without noticing given the symmetry, and so neatly matching in size and coloring to the buildings surrounding it that at first, I hadn't even noticed it. But when I studied it again, I realized it was a trick of proportions. Hiding in plain sight.

That one was Malanari's. I would have bet my paycheck on it. I mean, not at like one-to-one odds, but at, say, seven to one, yeah, I'd lay that down.

I gave myself a mental fist pump when Richa confirmed that I was correct; if I'd made the bet, I would, indeed, have been paid... seven times whatever my paycheck was supposed to be. Mostly I hadn't been placing bets. Paulie had blackballed me in her territory. But maybe when I got back, I'd go to Vegas. It wasn't a bad drive. If Malanari paid me enough, I'd have the cash to make sure I got comped on the hotel.

A neatly dressed man in his early thirties opened the door to our knock. He and Richa kissed cheeks, and he introduced himself as Alvise. Richa told us that Alvise was considered as secure as her or Fio or Bosco. The same for all the staff in the building. If we needed anything at all, from a coffee to a tuxedo, Alvise or any other member of the staff would be happy to arrange it.

I wondered if anybody else noticed that Alvise was also carrying. Same as Bosco and Fio. A small gun under well-tailored clothing. But the difference between him and Abbott and Costello was that Alvise moved with that coiled calm that made me think he might be able to handle himself. I kept an eye on him as he gave us the grand tour:

Let me show you to your rooms, once you're settled, drinks in the library with small snacks, dinner to follow, here's a copy of the menu, if you'd like anything special in your rooms or have any dietary restrictions we're unaware of, please let me or any member of the staff know, there are only six staff and you've already met three of them—and here he mentioned Fio, Bosco, and the personal chef from Rome—and you have met me, and I will introduce you to Nicole and Filomena. Because of increased security, we are less staffed than normal, so some requests might take longer than normal.

"Yeah, Nando," Paulie said. "Don't order quail eggs again."

"It was emu eggs, as you well know, and in the context of the job—"

"In the *context of the job*?" Dad said, laughing as the words came out. "You were supposed to be a Scandinavian general, not the king of Siam."

Helen came to Nando's rescue, claiming that given the character he was playing, extravagance was not out of character, but I disappeared into my room to clean up, so I never heard whether Nando's decision to order fried emu eggs for breakfast was what soured the job or if it was one of the other thousand ways a sweet setup can come undone.

40

MY ROOM WAS AS ABSURD in its splendor as I expected from a bazillionaire's Venetian palazzo. The soaring ceilings featured intricate cornice moldings and a glittering chandelier, and the arched windows were draped with layers of fabric that hung to the floor, letting me choose between the sheer gauze of daytime privacy all the way through a complete blackout that would suffice if for some reason I had to comply with a wartime air raid. There was a heavily brocaded chaise longue draped with a cashmere throw, as well as an antique writing desk and matching chair. The bed itself was made with crisp, white linens, topped by an ocean of blankets. The mosaic tiled floor extended into the bathroom, crawling ropes of ivy and flowers.

I chucked my jacket on the chaise and went to the bathroom. I took a shower, dried off, hung up my towel, and then looked for my suitcase. One of the staff had already unpacked it for me in the immense wardrobe; closets weren't a thing in the same way as they are now when the palazzo had been built. Thankfully, I wasn't stuck with the clothes I'd brought to Florida. As Richa promised, Giovanni's stylist had come through. The wardrobe had a mélange of options for me, head to tail. I put on a pair of charcoal pants, a casual black button-down, and a full-front, cashmere, zippered cream sweater with blue bands around the cuffs, and a pair of Tom Ford sneakers. I gave myself a quick once-over in the mirror. Not that I cared that much given this wasn't clothing I picked out for myself, but I thought I looked good. I was sure if Meg was here, she would have agreed.

Speaking of which, I shot Meg a text checking in. She responded asking how Florida was. I told her Italy. We bounced back and forth a few times before she said the couple she was giving a surf lesson to had arrived, and she hoped I was having fun, glad I was in Italy, hopefully without my dad because it seemed like I needed some space from him, and by the way she was going on a long weekend with her new partner, Theroux, at the end of March, and if I was home when they were gone, could I walk their dog? Heart emoji.

Their dog.

Yes, I texted. I could walk their dog if I was home. Not sure if I would be, though.

I hit send.

I looked at my phone.

I was happy for Meg, right? I wanted to stay friends with her.

I thought about Janus for a minute. I knew where he was going to be. I had a window of a few more months before the information I had on him would go stale, but even so, I had enough to go on past that, so if I needed to, I could start over and still dig him up. Or I could take care of it quickly, as soon as this gig was up. Find him, kill him, close the book. I'd be done before the end of March.

I texted Meg again: *Yeah, checked my calendar. Can do. I'll make sure I'm home.*

Just to make it clear that I was cool about it, I started to type: *excited to walk...*

Was I supposed to text walk *the* dog or walk *your* dog? And what did *your* mean, anyway? What did *our* mean? *Our* dog? It had barely been any time since she'd given me the soft goodbye, and now, suddenly, *she* had a dog, or she and Theroux had a dog together?

I texted: *excited to walk dog.*

By that point, Meg must have taken her class into the water, because she didn't respond, so I called Ginny's care facility. I talked with Carlita, who had been Ginny's assigned care leader since she'd been there. We weren't exactly friends, and I would never have described Carlita as "serious," but she was good at her job, thorough, attentive, and I never worried about Ginny's care falling through the gaps with Carlita.

She said that even though Nurse Crusty pooh-poohed Daisy's excitement—not that Carlita called Nurse Crusty by her nickname, but the tone was there—she'd decided, as Ginny's care leader, to reach out to the doctor who'd done the operation. Carlita said the doctor wasn't overly excited—it was too early—but had ordered a battery of tests, and as such, Ginny would be taking a little "field trip" to the hospital today. If another caregiver had used the phrase "field trip" in a singsong childish voice, I might have reached through the phone and strangled them, but coming from Carlita, "field trip" as a euphemism for Ginny being transported to the hospital for testing was almost charming. Between her and the doctor spouting off nonsense about angels, I'd gotten good at ignoring the way people talked. The only thing I cared about was if they could help my sister.

So, the news from home: no good news, no bad news.

I gave myself one last, quick look in the mirror. Well, at least here, the news was that I didn't look half bad, and my confidence was all good.

41

I WAS THE FIRST ONE DOWNSTAIRS, but not by much. I could see the grand staircase from where I sat in what Alvise called the "parlor." I barely had time to ask him for a gin and tonic before Helen swept down, wearing a gray knit sweater, her hair neatly twirled up off her neck. A heartbeat later, Nando, and then Paulie, came down the steps. Alvise returned with my drink and ushered us all to a seat in front of the fire, and then dutifully took orders for cocktails.

He returned with a tray and accompanied by two women, who he introduced as Nicole and Filomena. Alvise said they were part of the "household," for security purposes; in other words, we could speak freely around them.

Nicole was about my age, though I would have believed five years younger or ten years older than me, and *exactly* the type of woman Ginny used to swoon for: Nicole looked like she'd been snipped from a boutique "active lifestyle" catalog and she had a double masters in applied something or other and something else, but I had stopped paying attention, because Filomena had almost made me do a spit take.

I had eyes on Nicole while she introduced herself, to be polite and for no other reason, but on my periphery, I'd caught Filomena flinch. And then I realized it wasn't so much of a flinch as that Filomena had come to attention. Not in a formal sense—she didn't straighten up or salute—but rather, suddenly, her *entire* focus was on one thing.

Which was over my shoulder.

So of course I checked it, because if there's one thing you learn early in a business where people try to kill you on an alarmingly regular basis, it's that if somebody is looking over your shoulder instead of at you, there's something interesting going on back there. I thought of the pros I'd spotted out in the Venice night, how they'd kept themselves at an angle, knowing that not everything came at you head-on. Because that was what a good partner did. They looked for the things you couldn't see, the things over your shoulder.

Somehow, I'd already processed that Filomena's attention wasn't from fear but rather a pleasure response, and I think I was ready to do my spit take at the same time as I rolled my eyes, because when I turned, I saw... Dad.

Dad.

Dad, padding down the steps, and Filomena drooling. He was wearing a pair of jeans and a jacquard shirt, and he was barefoot. His hair was still visibly damp. Filomena looked like she was going to offer to dry it for him; she had bedroom eyes so bad she was going to need to see an optometrist.

Okay, terrible joke, but it drove me crazy that most people thought my dad was attractive. No, not attractive. Hot. Because as one of my ex-girlfriends once said to me, "Lots of guys are good-looking in a picture, but your dad, he's *real-life* hot, you know? Hot is better than good-looking. He's got presence. Like, yeah, sure, he's an old guy," she said, "but when he walks in? Like, what do Denzel, Redford, and your dad all have in common?"

I didn't know the answer to what they had in common, and neither did she, but we broke up the next morning.

It was unbelievably annoying to have women respond to him like that. He was such a prick so much of the time, but with his mouth shut—and wearing clothes that clearly had also been picked by Giovanni's stylist—Filomena had reacted like... Well, I was sure

Filomena would change her mind about sleeping with him the first time he explained to her why she was an idiot, but if I was being totally honest, I hoped I aged even half as well as Dad was aging. Given his generation's long-held beliefs about healthy living—or maybe it was Nando's generation that thought an all-bacon diet was good for you?—aging well was inimitably possible for me. In fact, I was pretty sure my decision to use sunscreen alone would be enough for me to end up looking at *least* half as good as Dad at his age. But even if not, I was also already ten times better at what we did than he'd ever been, even in his prime—and he was past his prime as far as I was concerned—so I could live with it, and good for him that a woman was taking pity on an old man like him.

Dad slipped past me with an easy smile at Filomena, shaking her hand and then Nicole's, making some sort of a dumb joke about Venice's canals, which both women laughed at to be polite, Filomena tittering longer than was strictly necessary. Then Alvise, Filomena, and Nicole turned themselves into ghosts—Giovanni's staff had the knack of invisibility that comes only with complete attentiveness—and yet we all had drinks. I sipped my gin and tonic and watched Dad talking and laughing. Getting Paulie to tell the story about the time he bought the wrong kind of paint, and the two of them were cackling, Dad like he didn't have a care in the world.

It scared me.

Because it meant he'd missed it. He should have seen and marked the couple in the trattoria back when we were at the *bacaro*. Nando and Paulie and Helen too. The four of them were having drinks with each other like there was nothing to worry about. Just taking a week abroad together. This wasn't a job to them. It was a vacation. They hadn't noticed the other team at all. What else had they missed?

The grown-ups truly thought this was a vacation. They were going to get us killed if I wasn't careful.

But I was going to table that thought for now, because Richa had changed into an A-line midi dress, lace with embroidered daffodils, sleeveless, but with a silk shawl covering her shoulders and arms. Helen was in the middle of telling the story about when she and Nando celebrated their third wedding anniversary while they were hiding in an abandoned shopping center, waiting for an enraged Estonian mobster to stop hunting them, all because, of course, of some ill-timed joke or flirtation of Nando's. None of them paid any attention to the way Richa smiled at me, and while the adults relived old times, Richa and I entered our own conversation.

We sat on the floor, close to the fire. It was a small fire, freshly laid, and yet it crackled, the wood seasoned and ready to burn. Somebody took away my empty gin and tonic and gave me and Richa each a glass of prosecco, and then Richa asked me a question about Ginny, and I told her it was a waiting game, and she asked me if that was difficult and I told her about the conversation with George about Nurse Crusty and then I asked her if she had minded working in her grandparents' restaurant as a kid, and she said that she'd always understood it was the price of admission of being part of the family, nobody got to choose the circumstances to which they were born.

We were finishing our prosecco when Giovanni sauntered into the parlor.

42

HE WRAPPED NANDO IN A BEAR HUG, kissed Helen on the cheek, grabbed Dad by the shoulders and kissed him on both cheeks, and then he stopped in front of Paulie.

They stared at each other for what felt like an extraordinarily uncomfortably long time. It was probably no more than a few seconds. But it was weird. Then they hugged and said it was good to see each other again, and it wasn't weird at all anymore.

Just kidding. It was super weird. I wished Uncle Charles was there.

Richa and I had stood up by that point, and I noticed Giovanni and Richa were about the same height as they exchanged kisses on the cheek. Finally, he held his hand out to me.

I was all set to make a joke about him being the sixth wheel, but as we shook hands, he said, "Your mother was one of the smartest women I've ever met in my life, and I'm surrounded by incredibly smart women."

Three hours later, the seven of us—Giovanni, Dad, Nando, Paulie, Helen, Richa, and I—had finished off most of a case of wine. I was still catching my breath from dinner. We'd been assaulted by a cavalcade of dishes that seemed designed to prove to Giovanni that he was getting his money's worth out of his private chef; if anything, he was underpaying the man.

We'd abandoned the dining room and gone back to the parlor, drinking limoncello as a digestif. Nando and Helen huddled on the loveseat near the fire. She'd taken a cashmere blanket and covered her legs, and Nando was whispering near her ear. By the smirk on his face, he was telling a joke. Helen, by the lean on her body, was showing that she'd forgotten, at least for tonight, the old wounds of their marriage. And Dad, Paulie, and Richa were at the poker table, Dad and Paulie trying to teach Richa how to spot when somebody is stacking a deck of cards. Paulie had that shrewd look on her face, where she was clearly thinking five moves ahead, but Dad seemed delighted in the chance to teach—and show off—while Richa was earnest in her desire to learn. She watched his fingers move with the diligence of a committed apprentice.

Giovanni and I sat facing each other in a pair of deep, wingback reading chairs. He had his feet up on an ottoman, casually crossed, the pebble soles of his driving shoes at a polite angle to me.

He was naturally charming, his attention, when it was on you, like the sun shining on an early summer's day. But there was a part of me that couldn't help but be aware that it was an artificial sun, the wattage juiced by a fortune; he and his brother had inherited an empire, and while Giovanni had trebled it when he took over, and trebled it again, and then four more times since, it was hard to argue that it was anything other than the simple good luck of being born into money that was already well invested, at a period in time when economic growth meant that it was almost impossible for him to fail. In other words, he'd done almost nothing to *deserve* the cosseted life that allowed him to spend all his time devoting himself into becoming, as Richa had put it, "a skilled amateur enthusiast" at so many pleasures. He had handed off the running of his empire to a legion of experts and had, essentially, chosen as the profession of his life, to become good at things. To become professionally charming and interesting.

And he truly was. He had good taste. Of course we were surrounded by help, by a chef who was trying to delight us, by a stylist who could snap his fingers and turn Dad and I into properly presentable dinner dates, by a field general like Richa, who could align the moon and the stars for him, by Fio and Bosco and Alvise and Nicole and Filomena, the tip of the iceberg of all the ways in which he bought himself a life that bore little resemblance to what most people experienced.

I wondered if I should say anything to him about the other team working the job, the couple I'd seen in the square, but then I decided to leave it to Richa. That was her job.

And I'd tell Dad about it when the time was right. Hopefully when he wasn't primed to kill the messenger.

Giovanni and I each finished our limoncello. Then he had Alvise bring in a bottle of Yamazaki 25, which was a ten-thousand-dollar bottle of single malt whiskey. Even though I thought whiskey was expensive lighter fluid, I figured I wasn't paying for it, so why not? And then I took a sip and remembered why not: Whiskey is nasty. I hoped this wasn't going to be one of those "you can't waste whiskey like that!" kinds of situations.

As Giovanni took a drink from his glass, I wondered if he could even conceive of a life where anything was out of his grasp. He couldn't cheat death, of course, but he could buy the best doctors in the world, a personal trainer, a personal chef. He couldn't buy love—I couldn't remember if Nando said Giovanni had divorced his sixth wife or his seventh wife—but he could pay Richa and Alvise and Fio and Bosco and Nicole and Filomena enough that they'd keep their mouths shut and make even our most outlandish requests come true. Want an emu omelet on this job, Nando? Sure, why not.

I'd figured out a long time ago that rich people were as messed up as poor people. Usually worse, because their worlds were warped by their privilege, but while rich people could be charming and funny and smart, just as many of them were boring and crass and stupid, the amount of money in their bank accounts like a lead weight around their ankles, invariably pulling them under the dark surface of an ocean of money. The good ones had to fight like hell to keep their heads above water.

And yet, Giovanni could have been gliding to shore on top of a surfboard.

When he looked at you, he didn't do that thing where his eyes flickered over your shoulder, his attention focused less on the conversation he was having and more on his place in the room, looking for an opportunity to jump in to a more interesting conversation. He was fully and entirely present. He took the same kind of concentration into a conversation that he might have into diffusing a bomb. It made everything I said feel somehow important. He wasn't pretending to pay attention. He was *actually* paying attention.

Plus, he was telling me a story about my mom.

"So, the tailor says to me, '*stai chiedendo un miracolo*,' " Giovanni said, "and I say right back to him, 'no, it would have been asking for a miracle as a child for my mother to let Giancarlo wear light blue for his communion!' And, of course, the tailor laughs at this, but then I say, 'adjusting this dress for your mother tonight? I know that it is late, and I know that you must work quickly, but does this look like a woman for whom you have to work miracles?' "

The punchline cut across the room, and both Nando and Dad made a few good-natured comments about Giovanni's aristocratic tendencies and Helen said she thought she had a photo of Mom in that dress, not from the party Giovanni took them all to, but from when Mom wore it again, later at one of Helen's pieds-à-terre, either London or Bangkok, she couldn't remember, but she'd make a point of looking, and Richa said to me that she'd like to see a picture of my mom, and then Giovanni and I returned to our little huddle and, finally, got to the matter at hand.

I told him that I didn't understand why he'd wanted to steal it in the first place, let alone why he wanted to put the score back now. There had to be more to it.

"Of course," Giovanni said, "but you must understand, my brother was a lemon."

43

NOT A LITERAL LEMON, GIOVANNI SAID, but he had forgotten the word *sour. Lemon* was the best he could do. Because as a child, Giancarlo was always unhappy. He was neither mean nor cruel, not spoiled as you would expect given the wealth both boys were born into, and not even particularly entitled. Just sour. There was little that seemed to please him.

"He was not difficult. But he did not seem to enjoy things, and my parents, of course, refused to believe anything could be wrong with him. That is not true, because they must have believed it, must have known, but they would not take him to a doctor, as if to find out there *was* a thing wrong with him would be the same as saying they had failed as parents. They were, how would you say, behaving as if things do not ever change?"

"Old-fashioned," I said.

"Old-fashioned. Yes. They used to say that he was a 'little old man,' that Giancarlo should have been born in a different time, when children were meant to be adults because he was so serious. I wonder, had they taken him to a doctor early, if that would have been good for him. There is a word for it in Italian, but it is a medical term, and I do not know what it is in English. It is not...you know the word, *Asperger's*? That word I know, but Giancarlo does not have Asperger's, even if it is similar in some ways. But you are not interested in what a doctor has to say, are you?"

I was, in fact, extremely interested in what one specific doctor had to say...about Ginny. I kept patting my pocket, in case my phone had abandoned me of its own accord, but I took a sip of my drink and looked around the room.

Helen was sitting with her back to the arm of the loveseat, her legs across Nando's lap. He was rubbing one of her feet with his left hand, gulping a couple hundred dollars' worth of Japanese whiskey from the glass in his right hand. Helen said something I couldn't quite catch, and Nando Cheshire Catted her.

Paulie had her normal resting shark face on as she watched Richa, now shuffling under the close supervision of Dad. Richa was terrible at it: She couldn't even have fooled Mr. and Mrs. Donachanda, who were my grandparents' neighbors. Lovely people, but also perhaps the least suspicious people I've ever met, and Mom would have *killed* me and Ginny if we'd conned the Donachandas. It would never have occurred to them that anybody would cheat at cards, let alone somebody as delightful as Richa, but still, her clumsy shuffle could have been seen from Norway.

She had her ear tucked toward her shoulder, the tip of her tongue poking out the corner of her mouth, watching her own hands, which was always an amateur's giveaway. She ping-ponged five cards each to her and Paulie. She reached for her hand, but Dad stopped her, and then Paulie laughed, because Richa was still so raw that she couldn't tell if she'd fixed the deck properly until she'd checked the cards.

Even from where I was watching, I'd been able to see the deal. I knew what Paulie had in her hand: seven, nine, and ten of diamonds, the six and eight of clubs. A straight: six, seven, eight, nine, ten.

And I didn't need to look at the cards to know what Richa was holding either: a flush.

Five hearts beat a straight.

Now, Dad turned her cards over, and Richa threw her arms around him in triumphant delight, and Paulie was shaking her head, but she was laughing, too, and I thought maybe I'd go over and see if I could join them, when I realized Giovanni had said my mom's name.

"What do you mean, she didn't like doctors either?" I asked.

He swirled his glass of whiskey, sniffed it with evident pleasure—I had no idea why, because as far as I could tell, whiskey smelled like pain and despair, not that it stopped me from sipping it occasionally—and then sighed.

"Have you ever had"—he named a whiskey with a vintage that put the price of a bottle at about a quarter million—"because it's not very good. This," he said, swallowing some of the Yamazaki 25, "however, is quite serviceable. But it was a different time, and my parents did not take Giancarlo to a doctor, and so he was . . . I'm sorry. I have forgotten."

"Sour."

"Yes, sour. I will remember that word. *Sour*," Giovanni said. "I could make him smile, I was always his favorite, but he seemed as if he would be unhappy his whole life, until he turned twelve, and discovered the one thing that . . . What is it when a flower opens?"

"Blooms?"

"Sorry. I have had too much to drink."

Helen poked her head up and said, "What do you expect, Nando's here. You have to drink more when Nando's around just to keep up with him!"

Which got a knowing laugh and a raise of the glass from Nando.

Giovanni said to me, "Yes. Thank you, bloom. I lose words when I've had too much to drink. Bloom. The one thing that made him bloom. Opera."

Of course opera, I thought. My experience with truly wealthy people is that they are all a little bonkers. I think the sheer scope of their hoarded fortunes makes them as disconnected from the real world as a dragon. Some of them become dragons themselves, but there are always the harmless eccentrics who build their life around some obsession: sailing, skiing, playing bridge, watercolor painting. With Giancarlo, it was opera.

"For Giancarlo," Giovanni said, "once he discovered opera, it became simple for him to be happy. I do not mean that Giancarlo was simple. He was not stupid. But..." Giovanni shrugged. "Not sports, not food. It was only opera. He would try other pursuits, because I asked. He was a picky eater, and yet, he always tried. I got him to taste fried crickets once. Another time, a lamb stew in Mongolia after a long helicopter ride. And of course, he was a dutiful son, so he can ski and swim and be a useful companion on vacation. He is a quick learner, but if it was his choice. Opera. Always opera."

For some reason the others had turned their attention fully to us again, listening to Giovanni talk about his brother.

"Giancarlo loved the opera in the way that I love, well, other more earthly pleasures," Giovanni said, pulling back from taking himself too seriously. He was rewarded by a slight snicker from Nando. "But Giancarlo was kind. Not always. But mostly." A shrug. "I loved my brother, more than I have ever loved any person in this world. Perhaps I am not the best to ask. But he was somebody that other people loved as well, and I think that is also because of opera."

"Trust me," I said, "not everybody feels that strongly about opera."

"I will not try to convince you otherwise," Giovanni said. "You cannot convince somebody else to share an obsession if they do not want to. I learned to like opera for my brother's sake. To love it, even, though I could never love it as much as he did."

I noticed that he had the tact not to brag about the singing lessons Richa had mentioned to me. Or maybe he assumed that everybody knew that he loved opera enough that he could sing it?

Giovanni continued, "Yes, I would say that I learned to love opera. But for Giancarlo, opera transformed him from the first time he heard it. As I said, he became an open flower. Opera was all he wished to spend his time on, but he could pretend otherwise if he was required to be polite. Which is why I was so suspicious when he fell in love with Auldhilda."

"Whoa," I said. "His wife? You thought Auldhilda was a grifter?"

Giovanni looked helplessly at Nando, not understanding the word.

"*Una truffatrice*," Nando said. A scammer.

Giovanni winced. "I saw my brother as a flower, and I thought she had come to pluck him."

44

HYPER-RICH PEOPLE ARE HYPERSENSITIVE to the idea that somebody's after their money. Usually because it's true. Once you get enough zeros, nobody can see anything else when they look at you. I mean, mostly when I look at people who have more than they could use in a thousand lifetimes, I wonder why they don't choose to share. And yet, they are rarely inclined to do so in any meaningful way. Instead, their claws close ever tighter around their treasure, though it can be of no use to them past a certain point and would be of much more use for those who had less. Which is why I have such little compunction taking from them; if the government taxed wealthy people properly, maybe I'd feel a twinge of guilt about stealing from them. When you take twenty million in rare coins from some billionaire's seventh vacation home? It barely even stings.

But the point is that Giovanni would have spent his entire life assuming that every person he met who wasn't equally as rich as him, a small group of people, was after his money. And with a brother like Giancarlo, a dreamer, not quite Asperger's but somewhere in that territory, missing an essential layer of armor that Giovanni had, extra skepticism of a woman who was sliding into Giancarlo's life seemed warranted.

Giovanni was his brother's keeper. And to him, Auldhilda seemed like she *must* be running a con, because nobody could be as perfect of a match for his brother as Auldhilda. It was like she was created in a lab to be Giancarlo's partner. If their parents hadn't been incapable of such scheming, Giovanni would have suspected his mother of hiring an actress so that her oldest son would finally get married and start providing her with grandchildren.

Nando winked. "Even Giovanni's mother knew that it would take a saintly intervention to get *him* to stay married long enough to have kids. Marriage isn't for all men."

"No kidding," Helen said. Nando glanced at her. Like me, he seemed unclear if Helen was making a harmless joke to be taken lightly. He decided to turn it into something to chuckle about, but I hoped it meant that Helen could see through his empty promise that this time would be somehow different.

"You had her checked out, didn't you?" I asked Giovanni. "Auldhilda? You did a security check, and she came up clean, and . . ." I looked at Richa. I remembered the conversation about Fio and Bosco being strapped, about there being a break-in, some threats, a change in security.

"Hey," I said to Giovanni. "Let me ask you a question. Where was this break-in you had?"

Dad perked up. "What break-in?"

"It's why his guys are heavy," I said.

Dad said, "What guys?"

"Fio and Bosco. And Alvise. Just the men," I said, giving Dad a skeptical look. Maybe he was taking this "it's just a family reunion" thing too far, because that was the sort of thing he would have normally noticed.

I said to Giovanni, "Richa said there was a break-in. Some threats too. I don't know. But it's why they've got guns."

"It was nothing," Giovanni said.

I said, "It was *something*. These guys aren't used to carrying pistols."

"What happened?" Dad asked.

Nando chipped in, "Some tourists. You know how the English can get on holiday. Nothing to worry about, Knox. But because the licenses had already been processed, it made it easier for us to meet the obligations of the insurers of Auldhilda's necklace and provide the only armed security."

"Makes sense," Dad said. "I like it."

"But yes," Giovanni said, "I hired a detective agency to investigate Auldhilda. My family has a long-standing relationship with a private security firm. And they did a thorough job. Exceedingly thorough. Then, Jacobini hired— Apologies. Jacobini was my Richa at the time. I must admit, I didn't think I'd ever be able to replace him."

Richa nodded, acknowledging her place in the pecking order in a way that was neither deferential nor proud, and Giovanni continued. "And then Jacobini hired a different firm, a second firm, to investigate her as well. He was compulsive about making sure there were no mistakes, nothing overlooked."

"Neither of the security firms found anything on her, right?"

Giovanni shook his head. "Nothing. A few parking tickets. Actually, many, many parking tickets, which remains a problem, because she likes to drive herself. That woman seems incapable of understanding where you can park and... It doesn't matter. Parking tickets, but otherwise, no. She was not"—he searched for the word for a second—"a grifter."

Nando said, "It was love. Pure love. Nothing else."

I thought I saw Giovanni's eyes flicker in Paulie's direction, but I wouldn't have put money on it.

Helen stood up and said, "It's midnight. I think I'll go to bed before I turn into a pumpkin. Nando? Walk me up?"

He stood up, brushed the front of his shirt as if he was worried about wrinkles, finished the brown liquid in his glass, and hastened after her as quickly as a man his age could move.

And before I had time to interrogate *that* interaction, Dad and Paulie announced that they were wiped out as well after all the travel they'd done between getting to Italy and from Rome to Venice, and then Richa got a funny look on her face and said that she needed to go to bed as well.

Which left me and Giovanni by ourselves.

He swirled his whiskey, finished it, and looked at the fire. I absentmindedly took a sip of my drink, once again reminding myself that whiskey is disgusting, and then took another sip in case I was wrong.

Giovanni got up, took a wrist-thick piece of kindling from the basket, and then crouched by the fire. He used the kindling like a poker, moving the burning logs around for a bit, not with any apparent purpose in mind, but as an excuse to watch the flames curl and lick at the piece of wood in his hand. Finally he dropped the kindling on top of the burning pile, stood back up effortlessly—he was in between my dad and Helen, maybe sixty or sixty-five, but he would have been in excellent shape for a forty-year-old—and came back to his chair. He started to sit down, changed his mind, and grabbed the bottle of whiskey. He splashed a dollop more into his glass and looked at me, but I wasn't interested. I'd had enough.

I hadn't realized how dim the room had become. The lamp on the sideboard haloed a soft circle of light that reached halfway to the fireplace, and the twisting flames from the fireplace was unsuccessful in chasing the shadows away. We sat, the two of us, Giovanni still occasionally taking small pulls from his glass of whiskey. I'd pushed my glass away, done for the night. The fire crackled and popped, Morse code sending a message into the silence.

"Let's take some air," Giovanni said.

I looked at the time on my phone. It was half past midnight.

"Please," Giovanni said. "It's important."

I wanted to say no, to tell him that I was exhausted, drained from sitting on my butt for a week in Florida, waiting by the watering hole so I could pounce on Janus, and I was tired from flying first one way and then the other. In economy. And I was tired from spending the last two years picking up the pieces of my life after I was the one to shatter it.

But he sounded so plaintive, and I realized that even here, in this absurd monument to Giovanni's wealth, he was alone. As much as Nando might claim they were friends, other than his parents and his brother, Giovanni had spent his entire life surrounded by people who were on his payroll in one way or another.

It was a lonely way to live.

45

LONELY ISN'T THE SAME AS BEING ALONE, however; as we left the palazzo, I saw Alvise slip discreetly out the door behind us. Not that I was particularly worried about our safety—well, at least my safety—but with the other team I'd seen working the square earlier, and given that there was apparently some threat that had led Giovanni's employees to iron up, having a minder trail along seemed like a decent idea. I'd have to check with Richa on that. She hadn't said anything about a possible connection to the Venice Double, and the way Nando had described it as "some tourist" thing didn't feel like what I'd seen with Motorcycle Jacket and Beard. They were clearly professionals of some sort.

It wasn't quite late enough to feel furtive as Giovanni and I strolled through the mostly empty streets and squares. Two or three in the morning in most cities, and the only people out are drunks and lovers, scoundrels out for mischief, flesh peddlers and drug dealers offering their wares from the edge of the shadows, but we were still before the hour when the magic of Venice turned menacing and sour.

I was glad for the coat Richa—or rather, Giovanni's stylist—had procured for me, but even zipped tight, I could feel the chill from the breeze. The wind carried the smell of salt and a hint of darkness, decay, the canals in Venice never completely washed clean of all their sins. I had my hands shoved deep into my pockets, shoulders hunched against the cold.

And yet, I could have been walking in a spun-sugar castle. Most of the windows we passed were dark, but whatever Venice once was, it has become a city full of and for tourists: The streetlights mocked the shadows where we walked. Alvise kept a reasonable distance, drifting behind us close enough that he could move in, far enough away that it was possible to pretend he wasn't there. I wondered if Giovanni was so used to having help hovering near him, ready to address his needs at an instant's notice, that he truly didn't notice Alvise.

Either way, Giovanni himself seemed to float above the paving stones, moving with a slow calmness that I was hesitant to interrupt. Whereas before, at dinner, and when we first started talking in the parlor, he had an almost impish quality that made me understand why he and Nando got along, now, in the night, despite the electric lights that guided us away from the darker alleys, he seemed lost, almost alone even though I walked by his side.

As we entered the square by La Casa del Libretto, I noticed a guy sitting on a bench. For a second, I thought it was Beard, the professional from earlier, but as we got closer to him, I realized I was mistaken. He had a beard as well, and could have passed for the professional's brother, but he was younger, a kid, maybe early twenties. He was bundled up against the cold and smoking pot. He looked exactly like the stoner he was.

Giovanni gave me a sly smile, stopped, patted down his pockets, produced a thin sheaf of bills, and offered the kid a hundred-euro bill for the half-smoked joint and his lighter.

The kid stared at us both for a few seconds, deep in a fog, and then took the deal and took off. Giovanni went to light the joint, but I stopped him.

I said, "It's one thing for us to be here, but it's another thing for us to be here and smoking cannabis."

Giovanni chuckled and said, "Let's walk then."

We walked, and he lit the joint. We crossed one bridge, and then another. I took a couple of hits. It had been a while, and even though

I had to stop at one point to cough up a lung over one of the canals, I was feeling nice and loopy by the time we finished off the joint, just as we got back to the open square in front of La Casa del Libretto.

We sat on a metal bench next to an empty wall fountain. The building we were supposed to hit Saturday night was dim, with a single light above the front steps, the windows showing only darkness inside.

Alvise settled in at a distance, with his back against a wall, kitty-corner from us. He had a stillness that reinforced my opinion of him as somebody who could probably hold his own; his presence was more solid than either Fio's or Bosco's.

"We were so careful," Giovanni said, interrupting my contemplation. "It did not occur to me that we could be caught."

"You can always get caught."

He shook his head. "I do not mean caught stealing the score. I mean after, when we were done. When I commissioned the first copy of the score, I truly wasn't thinking of it as a forgery. It was just a gift, and I wanted it to be a perfect replica simply because I couldn't give my brother the real thing. And then, because of Nando, and your father and Helen and Paulie, I realized I *could* give my brother the real thing." A grin. "I just couldn't tell him or Auldhilda it was the real score.

"There was no difference, not to the eye," he continued. "Not between the forgery from thirty years ago that is in the vault and that everyone believes to be real, and not between the original score that you took from Auldhilda's safe, or the new forgery of the score that you left in its place. But it is not enough to be able to fool the human eye anymore. Nando has told me there is new technology, and under a, how do you say it? *Un microscopio?*"

"It's pretty much the same. A microscope."

"Yes, a microscope. Under a microscope, now, somebody who is trained in the field would be able to tell that the score that is inside there," he said, motioning at the building, "is *not* real. It would cause many, many problems."

I suspected he didn't mean a microscope. He was probably talking about Raman spectroscopy. It wasn't a new technique—it's been around since the mid-1900s—but it only started being used on cultural heritage objects in the early 1990s. It was the sort of thing that tripped up even the best forgers; under analysis, you could find pigments in ink and paint that weren't available at the time a piece of work was created. That was one of the ways Wolfgang Beltracchi, perhaps one of the most prolific forgers of all time, got busted: He used paint contaminated with titanium dioxide white on a piece that was supposed to have been painted around 1910, even though it wasn't available until the 1950s or so.

"When you say 'problems,' you mean because of Auldhilda potentially finding out?"

"My brother's whole life, there were only ever two things that made him happy: opera and Auldhilda. They were so in love. They deserved the real score. I was young and thought it would be harmless, but now, with Giancarlo . . ." His voice cracked. He paused for a moment, and then he said, "I wouldn't have wanted Giancarlo to be disappointed in me. If Auldhilda found out . . . I don't think I would ever be able to forgive myself. Do you know what that feels like, Duke, to do something that you cannot forgive yourself for?"

46

DID I KNOW WHAT IT FELT LIKE to do something I couldn't forgive myself for?

Sense memory: Ginny with tubes and wires, in a hospital bed in Paris, me holding her hand as if I was waiting for her to wake at any instant, the fresh ache of the bullet that had gone through me, the unbearable itchiness of my wound knitting itself back together. If she ever did wake up, would she forgive me? Because no, I would never forgive myself.

"But," Giovanni continued, oblivious to the conversation I was having with myself, "even if you can't forgive yourself, that doesn't mean that you cannot do your best to make things right. It *was* selfish, in its own way," he said, "stealing the Puccini score for my brother, even if it was truly a romantic gesture."

He stood up and put his hand on my shoulder to stop me from standing up with him. "I think I will walk a bit more on my own," he said.

"You sure that's safe?" I asked.

"Alvise will see to me," he said.

Which answered my question of if he'd even noticed our shadow.

Giovanni strolled off into the night, sticking to the brightly lit boulevard, Alvise in his wake.

I waited a few minutes, staring at La Casa del Libretto, and then I made my way back to the palazzo, using the shadowy alleys and dainty bridges.

The palazzo was locked.

I almost rung the bell before remembering who I was and that I still had my pen with the hidden lockpicks in my pocket.

Upstairs, I looked at the doors in the hallway. It didn't matter that I didn't know which room belonged to Richa, none of the doors were cracked open in invitation.

Ten minutes later, I was alone and asleep.

47

I WOKE UP AT A QUARTER TO NINE. Through the window, I could see winter rain coming down in a fine mist. I needed to go for a run, but it looked miserable out. I went downstairs, trying to work myself up for heading outside, but decided that a coffee was in order first.

I found Nicole in the kitchen. Unlike Auldhilda's mansion in Rome, Giovanni's Venetian palazzo *only* had two kitchens—the one Nicole was standing in, as well as a professional kitchen in the back for the personal chef. Nicole made me an espresso. She told me that everybody else was still sleeping, however, she would be happy to have Giovanni's chef make me breakfast. I said I wanted to get some exercise before I ate, but was hesitant because of the surly weather. She suggested that instead of going outside on a day like this, I avail myself of the exercise room. It would likely suffice my needs.

It would suffice.

The exercise room was perhaps twenty feet wide and twenty feet long, a square with mirrors on three of the windowless walls. It had the faint smell of vanilla and cinnamon. All the equipment was matched and spoke of money; if the gear hadn't been branded with a name I recognized, I would have assumed everything was bespoke. The weights and kettlebells were made of gleaming stainless steel and had walnut handles, the treadmill was curved, with brass accents and leather grips, and the rowing machine could have been an art installation. I was pleasantly surprised that there was a heavy bag but had no idea why somebody would want one in premium leather, let alone with matching boxing gloves. None of it looked like it had ever been used. Which, given how good of shape Giovanni was in, made me suspect that instead of his palazzo having a guest kitchen, it had a guest gym. Why not? It was only money. For the heck of it, I looked up prices on my phone.

A couple hundred grand worth of equipment.

Well, I was going to try to get my money's worth.

I started out on the treadmill, pounding through six miles at a six-minute pace. I was probably in the best shape of my life. Working out was a good way to avoid thinking about all the things I'd screwed up in my life; I'd been in good shape before Ginny's accident, but since then, between me pushing myself, and Meg pushing me even harder, I was a raw bundle of lean muscle. Not gym muscle, the useless accretion of bulges that looked good in front of a mirror, but functional strength and speed.

I finished running, took a few minutes to catch my breath, and then started working the heavy bag, using a timer on my phone to alternate between bursts of intense effort and longer, sustained sessions. Then, plyometrics, stretching, and body-weight exercises, following the program Meg had made for me.

When I was done, I was soaked in sweat, and even though I was wiped out, it was the good kind of tired. I stopped by the professional kitchen—I didn't quite manage to startle the chef, but he didn't seem particularly enthusiastic about having me in his space—and asked him to whip me up an omelet for a late breakfast. Nicole had been talking with the chef, and she gently encouraged me to wait upstairs, in the parlor.

The parlor was pristine when I got there: glasses and bottles gone, the fireplace emptied and swept of ashes, new logs neatly laid and readied so that all Giovanni had to do was cast a spark, no hint of the night before. I wasn't naive enough to think that it had been cleaned by enchanted mice; Dad had given me a few tough lessons when I was a kid about taking service workers for granted, and while it seemed like Giovanni's staff was on a different level—the watch I'd lifted from Richa's wrist when I met her, the "uniform" of designer professional clothing that Nicole, Filomena, Bosco, Fio, and Alvise wore, their watches, the jewelry, it all spoke to a level of compensation that made me think they were paid more than fairly—even after all of the time I'd spent at resorts and high-end hotels, it still made me uncomfortable to be waited on hand and foot.

Not that it stopped me from getting excited when Nicole brought my breakfast into the parlor: an omelet stuffed with salmon and herbs and topped with a small ball of burrata, a bowl of yogurt with a side of fresh fruit and muesli, another espresso, and a glass of fresh-squeezed orange juice. She informed me that Giovanni had instructed the staff to serve lunch at one o'clock in the dining room, and that in the meantime, I was free to do as I pleased.

She was professional enough that it sounded like a generous invitation, but it was clearly a command on behalf of Giovanni: Be in the dining room at one o'clock to meet with the boss. I might be doing the job *with* Giovanni, but when it came down to it, I was working *for* him.

But the omelet was sublime. Whatever Giovanni was paying his chef, he should double it; I could do worse than lunch in an obscenely rich man's Venetian palazzo.

48

WHILE I ATE, I READ THE NEWS on my phone, and then went upstairs. I thought about going out and doing some recon, getting the lay of the land in daylight, but when I looked out the window again, it hadn't gotten any nicer. Instead, I peeled off my sweaty clothes, threw them onto the bathroom floor, and then lay naked on top of the covers of my bed. As soon as I lay down, my eyes started to droop a bit. It was only eleven o'clock in the morning, but even with having slept on the plane, my body was struggling with the time zones. I set my phone to sound at half past noon, took what felt like a single, long blink, and then was awakened by the rude bleat of my alarm.

I took a leisurely shower, stretching out under the hot water, letting the steam fill the bathroom so that I had to wipe a circle on the mirror with my towel. By the time I was dressed and made my way down for lunch, it was a couple of minutes after one o'clock.

Dad, Nando, and Helen were in the dining room.

Helen looked like she'd started the day by seeing a stylist, which was to say, she looked about as she normally did. Nando was dressed as if he expected us to lunch out, at a restaurant where understated elegance was not only encouraged but required. Dad, on the other hand, looked like he'd fallen off a horse and been dragged a few hundred feet through a patch of thistles.

Nando was finishing a story about a guy named Joel the Vegan, a specialist in dice games. Joel had been working a mark for hours, eating away at the guy's bank until he'd worn the guy's wallet almost to the bone, Nando said, when suddenly, according to Joel, he realizes he'd forgotten to swap in the hot dice.

"And he looks at me," Nando said, giving me a wink as he affected Joel's flat American accent, "and he goes: The weirdest thing was that once I realized I was using straight dice instead of my normal loaded dice, I suddenly felt bad, like I was cheating. I hadn't conned the guy; I'd gotten lucky! No fair!"

Dad snickered, and then immediately grimaced and pinched the bridge of his nose.

"Duke, dear, I trust you're well rested, and not as hungover as your fool of a father," Helen said spritely as I leaned down to kiss her cheek.

Paulie came in as I was sitting down, looking slightly wobbly herself, followed almost immediately by Giovanni and Richa, neither of whom seemed the worse for wear from the night before.

I hadn't worked out the staff schedule yet, nor what Richa's odd role was, because she was between Giovanni's chief of staff and his surrogate daughter. Whatever it was, it didn't seem to bother anybody else, and Filomena and Alvise served lunch: grilled salmon with sautéed seasonal vegetables, a small salad, warm bread, and a bottle of chilled Soave. Richa and I stuck to water, and Dad, who looked distinctly green around the gills, also stopped Alvise from giving him wine. I suspected he might still be tipsy from his night of trying to keep up with Nando. Or, if not tipsy, then deeply remorseful of his actions. Which didn't stop him from leering at Filomena as she moved around the room; unfortunately, she leered right back. Yuck. But Giovanni, Nando, Helen, and Paulie all accepted a glass of wine, and Alvise opened an additional bottle and put it on the table for the informal meal.

It was light and pleasant, and other than occasionally wondering who was going to barf first, Dad from being hungover or me from watching him and Filomena shamelessly flirt with each other, I enjoyed myself. Giovanni and Paulie talked with each other harmlessly enough—though Paulie did make an innuendo about pasta that made me uncomfortable—and Nando kept up a stream of charming chatter, doing his best to keep Richa entertained even if his *real* audience was Helen.

After a lingering lunch, we split up: Dad and Paulie went to do a walk-through of exit routes, and Giovanni took Nando and Helen to his "club," so that they could put on their act as a married couple and make sure that by the time the gala rolled around tomorrow night, they felt like familiar faces again.

Richa and I went back to the square to get a look at La Casa del Libretto in the daylight.

49

OR WHAT PASSED FOR DAYLIGHT. The morning rain had dissipated, but it was cloudy and gray, a stiff chill hitting us as soon as we were outside. Last night, when I'd been to the square twice, once at the *bacaro* with Richa and the crew, and then again, after midnight, with Giovanni, it had been cold. I'd chalked that up to the shock of coming to Italy from Florida by way of Los Angeles.

We walked briskly. At one point, Richa took my arm as we crossed an uneven section of paving stones. She was wearing more casual clothes than she had been at dinner last night, and as much as I missed the charm of Richa in her embroidered A-line, she looked as good in a pair of jeans and a sweater. She had a belted, beige wool overcoat, and despite taking my arm for balance, her ankle-length leather boots were eminently practical, with a mid-height heel and lug soles. As a pair, we could have been returning home from a late lunch at a swanky hotel . . . or going to the hotel for an afternoon respite.

Instead of a hotel, I took us into the same trattoria in the same square as La Casa del Libretto, where I'd spotted the other team the night before. As a lark, I even took the same table.

La Casa del Libretto seemed different during the daytime. Even with the overcast flatness of winter, the building felt more rooted somehow. As if in the darkness, the doge's old palace was a painted backdrop in an old Hollywood epic rather than an edifice that had been standing there, in one form or another, for hundreds of years, existing well before Venice even became part of the kingdom of Italy. I took off my coat and, where the team from last night had sat at an angle from each other, their attention outward, I turned my focus—and my chair—fully toward Richa.

"You could see the building better if you turned your chair," she said.

"You can see it fine for me."

She held my gaze. The trattoria was nearly empty, but it could have been just the two of us in there, the overheated space a relief after our walk.

"I have a gift for you," she said. She reached inside her bag and pulled out a wrapped box about the size of a Rubik's cube.

"What is it?"

"A replacement."

I took off the paper and opened the box. It was a watch. I recognized the brand. Visconti. Satin finish, blue face with a multilevel dial and three time zones. A replacement for the one that had gotten fried when I opened the Nimsik. I loved it. I strapped it on, no longer feeling quite so naked without a watch. It looked good on my wrist. Somebody had already set the time on it.

"Giovanni's stylist has good taste," I said.

"I picked it out myself," she said. "That model of watch is the Opera. I thought it was appropriate."

A little heat came to my cheeks; earlier I'd thanked her for picking out my clothing, and she'd said it was the stylist. This time, I'd thanked the stylist, but it was Richa who'd picked out the Visconti. I didn't normally like it when women played games with me, but Richa had a way of keeping me off balance that made me feel like I was stumbling and might fall in her direction.

"Thank you," I said simply, letting the crinkle around my eyes speak for itself.

She somehow managed to combine a coy demureness into looking at me directly, and something seemed to be tickling her lips.

Before she said whatever was on her mind, however, the waiter came. Richa ordered us macchiatos, and as soon as the waiter turned away, Richa said, "There are cameras pointed at the entrance. Two of them. One on each side. If you are facing La Casa del Libretto, to the right, the camera is perhaps as high as you could jump with your hand up, and on the left side the camera is attached to the building below the second windows."

"Richa," I said. "I need a gun."

50

SHE'D BEEN LOOKING AT AN ANGLE over my shoulder as she described the camera placements, but her attention snapped fully to me now.

"No," she said. "You will not need a weapon. That is not what we have agreed on. There is no reason for a weapon."

"Because your guys are working security."

"As I said, you do not need a gun."

"Maybe Alvise can handle himself, but Fio and Bosco aren't going to be much good with their pistols."

"You will not need a gun for Saturday night."

There wasn't much of an offseason in European tourism anymore, but February in Venice was close. The restaurant was almost deserted; three middle-aged men had left as we arrived, and the only other two occupied tables in the oversized room were single travelers, both wearing headphones and both oblivious.

"I don't really understand how you pulled off replacing the security with Giovanni's guys at the last minute like this, but even though that's helpful, I still need a gun, Richa."

She crossed her arms. "What did Nando say?" She waited, a little pouty.

"About what?"

"This is because of the man and the woman who sat here last night, yes? This is your idea of a little joke? To bring us here, to sit us in the same seats, to tell me you need a gun after I give you a watch? When Giovanni agreed to do this job—when I agreed—it was because Nando said there would be no need for any of you to carry weapons, and that no one would get hurt. Isn't the point that it is easy?"

"Richa. This is serious. Nando and everybody else can treat this like a vacation all they want, but those two were professionals. They were working together as a team, and they were doing reconnaissance on the museum."

"It is more of a place for socializing and a shared enjoyment of opera, rather than a proper museum," Richa said.

"That wasn't my point, but fine. They were doing reconnaissance on the Libretto House, okay? And we don't know if it's only those two, or if there are more of them, or what they're watching for. I think we can assume it's not out of the goodness of their hearts. Unless you know something I don't, I need a gun."

"You did not answer. What did Nando say when you told him there were others watching the building, others . . . like you?"

Like me. I wasn't sure how I felt about the way she said that.

"I didn't tell Nando," I said.

"Why not?"

I gave a half-hearted shrug. "What's the point? Dad's the one I should tell, anyway, since he's the blueprinter, but they'll all tell me I'm imagining things, like it's a monster under the bed. Every time I tried asking a question about the job, I basically got told to shut up and leave it to the grown-ups."

"Ah," Richa said. "Like my parents."

"I figured it was better to get more information first, so they don't just dismiss my concerns."

Richa uncrossed her arms. "I didn't tell Giovanni either. My job isn't to tell him what's wrong. It's to fix it."

"That's why you get paid the big bucks," I joked.

"Actually, yes." She was comfortable with the idea that she deserved it, comfortable with herself in general. "But I will not help you get a gun," she said.

We sat and drank our coffee in silence for a few moments. A pair of Japanese men walked briskly past our window. A young man and two young women herded a group of nearly a dozen kindergarten-aged kids. The clouds parted long enough to paint the square in sunlight before returning to the muted winter afternoon.

"Why are you doing this?" I asked. We were talking quietly, soft pop playing in the background, the emptiness of the restaurant and our waiter's apparent disinterest in hovering, combined with an overstuffed decor, all combining to create a space that felt private despite us being in public.

"Having coffee with you?"

"No," I said. "Helping your boss arrange to steal a... well, I guess we're not stealing it. I know you're well paid, but this can't be part of your job description. So, why?"

"Because Giovanni does not wish Auldhilda to—"

"Not that," I said, cutting her off. "I mean, why are *you* doing this? Everybody seems to think it's safe and easy, nobody's going to get hurt, nobody's going to go to jail. But it *could* happen. Things go wrong all the time. For instance..." I made a helpless gesture that was intended to take in the trattoria, our table, to capture the uncertainty I felt about knowing at least two other people had an eye on La Casa del Libretto. "Giovanni seems to think this is a game. It's not a game."

"I am aware," she said.

"Don't give me any crap about how you're doing this because you work for Giovanni. That's circular. And that goes for the rest of them too."

"Who?"

"The Hardy Boys, plus Alvise, Nicole, Filomena, all of you."

"What is a Hardy Boys?"

Her English was so good that I forgot that it wasn't her first language, though even if it had been, I was prone to obscure references. "It was this old detective series for kids. The Hardy Boys were these two brothers, and they'd... You know what, look, it doesn't matter. I meant Fio and Bosco. But all of you are on board with this? Giovanni says we're going to run a heist at some charity gala and that's another day's work for you?"

She took the last sip of her macchiato and then motioned to the waiter for the check. He snapped to it almost immediately, and I waited while he came over with the tray and the credit card reader and Richa paid for the drinks. When he left, she stood up.

I said, "Where are we going?"

She said, "To show you."

I stood up. "Show me what?"

"You are worried about the couple that was here, but I am worried that we have a different problem."

"What?"

"Water."

51

WATER. THE PROBLEM WAS WATER. In Venice, the problem was always water.

I followed Richa as she left the restaurant. The long edge of La Casa del Libretto fronted the square on one side and a larger waterway on the back. Or, vice versa depending on whether you thought of Venice's water entrances as the front of a house and the land as the back door. But while one of the shorter sides of the rectangular building was directly contained by the building next door, the other side ran along a smaller canal.

She walked out of the square and around to an arched wooden bridge that crossed the lesser canal. On the other side, there was a narrow walkway, and we walked along it until we were across from La Casa del Libretto.

Venice is a miracle. A floating city that has existed, in one form or another, for a millennium and a half. A city constantly at war with water, a city constantly reinvented. The Venice that I love—that we think of when we think of Venice—carries with it a sense of ancientness that is almost impossible to find in America, where an "old" building might have existed for a century.

Venice rose from the lagoon well over fifteen hundred years ago. The city was officially founded at noon, on a Friday in March in the year 421, though that is as much myth and legend as historically grounded fact. The original settlers were likely seeking refuge from invaders—the Huns and Visigoths—and used the marshes as natural defenses. The same ground that protected them also made it necessary to drive wooden pilings through the silt and the mud into the underlying clay so that Venetians could build permanent structures on top. The anaerobic atmosphere petrified the pilings, the lack of oxygen and bacteria preserving the wooden stakes and turning them almost into stone; supposedly, both the Rialto Bridge and St. Mark's still rest on the original foundations.

Over the course of the city's history, residents have raised the streets and buildings to cope with flooding seawater, cleared the canals, and built gates and sluices in the eternal unwinnable battle against the ocean; the water is supposedly six feet higher than it was in the fifth century when the city was founded. The government has brought modern methods to bear on the quixotic quest to hold back the water; in the 1980s, the city started building an enormous, ambitious engineering project, the MOSE project, a series of gates that can be raised according to the tides to help stop the lagoon from flooding with seawater. But water is a pernicious, indefatigable enemy, and changing weather patterns present an existential threat to the city.

The exterior of La Casa del Libretto was impeccably maintained, a sign, I assumed, of the wealth of its benefactors. As Richa had said, it was not quite a museum, but nor was it entirely an event space, but despite giving a third of the building over to community groups, whatever you thought of it, La Casa del Libretto was very much a private facility. A well-financed one. A trio of boldly colorful flags hung from the third story out over the water, dancing in the breeze.

I kept staring at the building. On this side, on the canal, on the night of the event, there'd be lights spilling out the windows, exterior lamps reflecting off the water, and yet, inside the four turrets that cornered the building, there would still be deep pools of shadows, buildings and bridges and boats shifting the darkness to keep us hidden as necessary.

“I don’t get it,” I said. “Everybody keeps saying it’s the exact same job, except, I guess, in reverse. Water’s always been a problem in Venice. Why’s it a bigger problem now?”

Richa reached out and took my hand, but it was only so she could push back my sleeve and look at my watch. She dropped my wrist, pointed, and said, “It is an hour past low tide, but you can see the change in color, there, below the surface.”

A line of demarcation. Low tide.

Venice has what is called a semidiurnal tide cycle, which simply means that most days there are two low tides and two high tides. Because the full tide cycle took about twelve and a half hours, sometimes a low tide or high tide would occur after midnight, but in essence, every six hours or so, the water went all the way up, and then six hours later, it went all the way down.

I looked at my watch myself and did the math. Low tide today had hit around ten after three this afternoon, which meant high tide tonight a little before nine o’clock. Factor in the change between today and tomorrow, and . . . “Okay, so it will be basically high tide at ten o’clock during the gala. And?”

“And,” Richa said, “*la luna piena*.”

52

THE FULL MOON. TOMORROW NIGHT was going to be February's full moon. I wasn't sure if Italians had names for the full moons like we did in the States, but at home, it would have been the Snow Moon, a colloquialism that I always found amusing since the closest thing I'd ever seen to a blizzard in Los Angeles was a couple of party girls accidently dropping an open bag of cocaine.

But a full moon also meant higher tides. Syzygy is when the moon, Earth, and sun are in alignment, and it happens at both the new moon and the full moon and is part of the phenomena that contributes to some tides cresting higher than others.

"I mean, the tides will be higher than normal, but not *that* much higher, right?"

She shook her head. "Normal compared to what? Yes, the full moon means that high tide is only a little bit higher than normal, but what was normal on the night they stole the original?"

My stomach sank.

"Oh no," I said. "Don't tell me. It was not, in fact, high tide, nor was it a full moon when they did the original job."

Richa said, "According to historical data, the night would have been a half-moon, and while I do not know the exact time, presumably it was similarly late in the evening, and that means it would have been close to a low tide, or at the most, mid-tide, when they stole the original."

Time and tide.

For most of the job, it didn't matter, but the tunnel was ancient stone, sturdy, but not fully weatherproof. Its original use before the banker had transformed it into a secret entrance to the vault antechamber was not clear, but I suspected it had been a place for servants to move unnoticed, scurrying invisibly below the feet of the rich and powerful who lived in or visited the doge's palace. At the time, hundreds of years ago, it probably stayed dry, but then, slowly, it began to be a place that could flood. It was a space that had, the banker aside, been ignored and forgotten as the world changed, and this Saturday night, in the dark heart of February, it would almost have the effect of a wind tunnel.

Richa said that when Nando and Giovanni had shared the bundle with her, she had also asked if a thirty-something-year-old plan might require updates. She had also noticed that it might be unpleasantly exposed in February as opposed to the original summer wedding. Nando assured Richa it was no big deal, that Dad and I would only be in there for a few minutes while we waited for our opportunity to exit the tunnel. Easy for him to say. He wasn't the one who would have had to shiver his butt off in the winter air.

But this morning, Richa said, for some reason, she'd thought to check the water levels and realized there would need to be a change.

"I do not think it will be completely underwater, but with the tide, I do not think you can avoid getting wet in the tunnel," Richa said. "It will be a difficulty for you."

"Dry and cold is different than wet and cold. That's a real problem. I don't know what I'm going to do to fix it, but—"

"You aren't going to tell your father?"

I took out my phone and held it so Richa could see the text as I typed it: *We need to talk about the job.*

Almost immediately, Dad texted back: *Stop whining. It's fine.*

"There you go," I said. "He and Nando have it in their heads that everything should stay the same. Which is ridiculous. But there's not a lot I can do about it. I tried asking about alternate options when I was looking at the plan, and Dad made a dismissive remark about me not being able to fly."

"Fly? In the air?"

"See the seam in the stone there? Where the tunnel ends? Now look up."

She looked up at the third floor, where a Juliet balcony dangled above the canal. "You would not need the tunnel if you were able to get in that way?"

I shrugged. "Not that way. On the other side. Same place we access the tunnel, but instead of going under the turret and across through the tunnel, we go up the turret and cross through the air."

"You fly?"

"No. Zip line. Attach a rope from one turret to the other, if I can figure out how to make that work. It's not perfect, but everything else about the plan could stay the same *and* we could avoid getting hypothermia. Not like Dad will even listen. Nando too. It's like it *has* to be the way they did it." I did my Nando voice: "Can you not understand the poetry of doing it exactly the same way?" And then Dad's voice, gruff, annoyed: "If it was good enough for us thirty years ago, it's good enough for you now."

She laughed, and I said, "It's like they refuse to believe anything should ever be different. They have this weird idea that it should be the exact same job. It's like this entire thing is just a trip down memory lane for all of them. You know what Nando told me? He said, 'The moon waits for no man.' But the real saying is 'Time and tide wait for no man.' It means—"

"I know what it means," Richa said. "My father and mother spent many years trying to convince my grandparents it was time to allow them to update the restaurant."

"How'd that go?"

"I'm glad I was away at university."

We both laughed, and then we stood there, not talking, staring across the water at La Casa del Libretto. One of the narrow barges that plied the waterways of Venice arrowed its way down the canal, passing a smaller personal craft. The two men driving their respective boats exchanged lazy waves.

Richa's phone pinged. "Giovanni requires my presence. What will you do?"

"I don't know," I said. "Figure it out, I guess. What else can I do? It's not like I'm going to be able to get them to listen. It will be a lot easier if I fix the problem. I'm going to walk around for a bit, think, see what comes to me."

She started to speak, then changed her mind and pulled out a wad of notes from her purse—probably five hundred euros—and gave it to me. I asked if it was "walking-around money," which wasn't a joke she seemed to get, and she said it was in case I had any expenses and that she'd meet me later, back at Giovanni's palazzo.

"You going to need receipts?"

She pursed her lips, amused. "Make sure you have enough left over to buy me a drink later. You can tell me what solutions you have devised."

"Perhaps," I said.

A look flittered across her face, but she turned and left before I was able to decipher it. I watched her move briskly down the narrow walkway, cross the bridge, and disappear out of sight. She didn't look back.

I checked the time.

It was a beautiful watch.

I should have told Dad. He and Nando could be as dismissive as they wanted, but it didn't change the facts: We were going to be underwater in that tunnel. The plan was borked. Not to mention—forget about knee-deep or even chest-deep water in the middle of

February—we had other problems, like another team apparently working the job. But telling Dad would mean he'd throw a fit. He'd tell me I was a moron and here were fifty different reasons I didn't understand what I was talking about . . . I had to go to him with the alternative completely thought out.

53

I TRIED NOT TO THINK ABOUT my two main problems while I walked: how to get from one turret to the other, and what to do about Motorcycle Jacket and Beard. It wasn't any different than taking a shower or going for a run. By actively concentrating on other things, I let all those bits and pieces—Dad and Nando's intractability about the plan, the other team scoping out the sight—rattle around and bounce off each other. There was a certain kind of alchemy that occurred by *not* thinking, the time and tides of my brain doing the work for me.

In the meantime, while I was walking, I left a message with my usual weapons broker, Noor. Noor had a high-end car rental business that was an extremely profitable front to an arms business. I was hoping I could get a referral for somebody local to provide me with a pistol. It would have to wait, though. There was no chance Noor would be in before noon California time. I left a message saying I was on a family vacation in Italy, and I thought it would be fun to rent a sports car. Noor would know I meant I needed a pistol.

After I called Noor, while I continued walking, I called Ginny's care home. George was about to wrap up his shift, and he told me that there was nothing new. The tests the doctor had ordered for Ginny yesterday had gone off without incident, but there were no results yet. One of the surgeon's residents was going to stop by the care home this morning, and George said he thought they'd have the results by midday, but, he added, that wasn't the same as the doctor interpreting the results. As always, he said, they'd call if there was news.

As always, I felt a bit hollow when I hung up.

I thought about calling Dad again, but I knew it was pointless trying to get him to listen unless I had a different option ready. I could have called Helen and had her talk to him, but that felt like running to the teacher. Better to see if I could fix it on my own.

In the meantime, I played tourist. The last time I'd been to Venice before this, I'd met Ginny and the guy she was dating at the time. He was an absolute dick-bag who did some sort of data analysis so that the hedge fund he worked for could eke out an extra percentage point or two. I was dating a trust fund girl who was happy to have me as her kept man; I'd spent my last haul so fast that I needed to be kept. The four of us were supposed to spend a long weekend together in Venice, but by the end of the first night, I thought I was going to drown Ginny's boyfriend in the Grand Canal, and Ginny and my girlfriend had resorted to the impeccable politeness of two people who dislike each other intensely but have realized that it is for no particular reason other than the quirks of existence.

By the end of the second night in Venice, both Ginny and I were newly single, and we went out to a dance club and made friends with a group of German tourists. They ended up taking us to a little hole-in-the-wall jazz bar. The jazz bar was a cool place, and we were all out until the wee hours of the morning, one of those magical nights you never wanted to end, Venice at its best.

As long as I was wandering around Venice to clear my head, there was no reason not to try to find the jazz bar again. If I stumbled across it, I could drop a pin on my phone, and maybe after Richa and I had that drink she'd almost promised me—I wasn't counting last night—I could casually tell her I knew a tight little spot if she wanted a second drink.

I'd begun to shiver, so I walked at my "city" pace, rather than the more leisurely ramble I preferred when I was playing tourist. The shape of Venice is reminiscent of a fish, and I walked to the head and then the tail; despite the temperature, I warmed up quickly, and comfortable as long as I kept moving, though I did pop into a boutique to buy a pair of lined gloves. I walked for hours, but because I stayed outside of the main areas that would have been crowded with tourists even in the middle of a nuclear war—St. Mark's Square, the Rialto Bridge, and market area—particularly after the sun had set, the city had an oddly deserted feel.

I didn't want to have to fight with Dad and Nando about going in through the turret instead of the tunnel, so I came up with and dismissed a dozen half-assed solutions for the tunnel: self-enclosed balls, dry suits, stripping down to our skivvies and getting cold, spare tuxedoes, none of them workable. For a few minutes I even entertained the idea of asking Richa if she could come up with some sort of submarine before realizing exactly how stupid that "solution" was for our problem.

I wanted to bang my head against the wall. Dad was right. I was going to need wings to get the zip line from one turret to the other.

My phone pinged: Richa said that Giovanni had arranged for us all to attend an opera at Venice's most famous opera house, Teatro La Fenice, and wanted to know if I'd be joining.

I was tempted simply because Richa was asking, but I hadn't solved the problem with the job yet. I texted back that I was going to skip, and that I would see them all later, back at the palazzo.

I walked back to the square to check out La Casa del Libretto again.

There was a certain kind of bustle and energy to the evening, and as I drank a glass of wine and stared at the building, I casually checked out the tourists walking by, but there was no trace of the professionals from the other night.

I finished my wine and decided to go walk a little more.

I was frustrated. I should have been able to figure it out. There had to be a way to attach the zip line between the turrets. If I'd had wings, like Dad joked, it would have been a breeze, but if I had wings, I could just fly myself across and...

A drone. We could go up the opposite turret, and from there, I could use a drone to fly a rope across to the other turret. I was going to have to work out the technical part of it, but I didn't think that would be a problem.

I was delighted by myself, and then even more so, because almost immediately after the solution came to me, I stumbled on the jazz bar I'd been hoping to find. It was down a long, narrow street, barely wide enough to walk two abreast. It was almost purely residential, unless none of the other businesses had signs either. But in the window, shoved between the glass and the closed blinds, there was a record album cover: Chet Baker. I dropped a pin on the map on my phone, and then stepped inside: It was still the hidden gem I remembered, with low, warm-toned lights, maybe a half dozen tables, and a turntable behind the bar.

With everybody else out at the opera, I wasn't in any hurry, so I had a drink, and then a second, and around ten o'clock realized I'd never had dinner.

I set out from the jazz bar in search of something to eat, turning left from the narrow street, still pleased with myself for solving the turret problem, and thinking warm thoughts about bringing Richa to the jazz bar.

Ahead of me about thirty meters, a couple came out of a hotel.

They turned away from me, walking down the wide boulevard, oblivious to me following in their wake.

Because, suddenly, that's what I was doing: following. Not walking, not strolling, and certainly not rambling.

The couple in front of me wasn't a couple.

It was the team.

Beard and Motorcycle Jacket.

54

"PICK UP, PICK UP, PICK UP," I muttered, but Dad must have still been at the opera, because it went right to voicemail.

Neither Beard nor Motorcycle Jacket seemed to have their antenna up, but I was far enough back that I couldn't tell if they were truly unaware or if they were good enough pavement artists not to tip that they'd made me.

It had been an instinctual reaction to start tailing them. They were a threat I didn't understand, and the more I knew about them, the easier it was to make sure they didn't get in my way. The right thing to do would have been to let them go. I'd probably be able to pick them up again tomorrow at the hotel they'd come out of—it would be easier to tail them working in tandem with Dad and Helen—but there was a chance that wasn't where they were staying.

I could hear my dad complaining, "They were right there, and you let them go?"

At the corner, instead of crossing the canal, they turned. I took my time, not wanting to get too close, but when I followed around the bend, they were stopped and looking at a storefront only fifteen feet in front of me. Beard was saying something to the woman, and she laughed and said, "Not likely." Her Irish lilt was thick enough to cut the glass between them and the old-fashioned toy store they were peering at. If I wasn't following them, I would have stopped to look at the display myself: clapping monkeys, wooden trains, a spinning doll acrobat engaged in a continuous performance inside a brocaded hoop, three kites made of silk with swooping tails.

I kept walking, and I could feel them turn away from the window, now behind me. It was an impossible situation. Dad hadn't picked up, and even if everybody hadn't been at the opera, I couldn't risk calling or texting Helen or Paulie or even Richa now that they were behind me. I didn't even have Nando's number. Plus, while a forward follow is possible, one of those tricks of tradecraft that can be the difference between getting what you want and getting shot in the head, a single-person forward follow is nearly impossible in a labyrinthian city, particularly at night, and even more so since I had absolutely no idea where my quarry was going.

Wait. That wasn't true. I might not be certain, but I could take an educated guess as to where they were going. Same place I'd seen them last night: La Casa del Libretto.

If I was correct, Beard and Motorcycle Jacket would turn right, up ahead.

I turned left.

I felt like Orpheus as I forced myself not to look behind me, and finally, I gave up and peeked. They were out of sight.

I started running.

Over a bridge, right, cut through a small alley that led to another alley, over a different bridge, stop to check the map on my phone, then left, right, wrong way, turn around, check my phone, a few taunts from a group of teenagers making fun of my rush, over another bridge, and then I was back inside the *bacaro*, with a glass of wine in front of me by the time Beard and Motorcycle Jacket showed up in the square in front of La Casa del Libretto.

They popped into a different *bacaro* that was at the end of the line of the three trattorias, on the other side from where there'd been the night before.

I didn't have a great view of them inside the *bacaro*, but that was fine. I'd see them exit. I relaxed and ordered some *cicchetti*—bar snacks—to take the edge off my hunger.

I nursed a glass of wine and ate some crostini, and basically just chilled.

The only interesting thing that happened had nothing to do with Beard and Motorcycle Jacket: The kid that Giovanni had bought the joint from yesterday came into the square with a meandering stroll. He stopped outside, in front of where I was sitting, and lit up. He leaned against the window, his back to me, oblivious to everything around him. I noticed the designer brand of his jacket and decided that he was probably just a spoiled kid, smoking his way through a gap year tour of Europe underwritten by his wealthy parents.

As I was watching the kid get high—or, realistically, more high—I almost missed Motorcycle Jacket leaving.

I made a quick decision: because I only had to worry about the two of them, and because I knew where they'd come from, as long as Beard was settled in, it made more sense to follow the woman. Maybe I'd learn something new.

I threw back the last of my *ombra* of wine, peeled a twenty euro note from the roll Richa had given me, tucked it under my empty glass, and headed back into the early-night air, passing through the kid's haze of smoke as I started to tail Motorcycle Jacket again.

She didn't seem to be in any hurry, and her jacket made her easy to mark from a distance. I let forty or fifty meters open between us, far enough that in the darkness, if she'd looked back, I would have been a vague shape in the distance, not a man on her tail, but she didn't look back. I followed her for ten minutes as she walked leisurely through the Venice night. She didn't seem to be following any deliberate path, and I lost sight of her once or twice, having to pick up my pace to keep bird-dogging her.

I tried Dad again, thinking that by now the opera had to be over, but again it went to voicemail. I wasn't worried anymore, though. Beard was ensconced in the square, probably enjoying some *cicchetti* himself, and following one person from behind was wildly easier than trying to follow two people from the front.

Ahead of me, she turned again, into a rabbit warren alley, and as I followed, hurrying up my pace, I barely caught sight of her turning again.

When I popped the second corner, it was onto a walkway alongside a smaller canal. The walkway was about ten feet wide, littered with shadows, and completely deserted except for the woman: She was stopped, reading a flyer posted on the wall. Once again, I didn't have much choice other than to keep walking. Even though these pros hadn't impressed me with their tradecraft, if I came to a sudden halt, it would be as good as sending up a flare.

I decided this was as good of a time as any to break off my pursuit. I didn't want to push my luck too far—it had been a stroke of good fortune to have them step out in front of me in the first place—and I was certain I could find them again later. If they weren't in the square staking out La Casa del Libretto again this evening, I could pick them up at their hotel. Sometimes, you had to know when to walk away. There was a stone bridge over the canal past the woman, and I figured I'd walk by her, cross the bridge, and head back to Giovanni's palazzo in time for cocktail hour.

That's what I was thinking as I approached her, but when I got about ten feet away, she turned to face me, blocking the way.

I stopped.

Of course.

Beard was behind me.

I turned ninety degrees, so I could put my back to the wall, putting the woman on my left and Beard on my right.

I wished I had gun.

I'd been bouncing along blithely, convinced of my invisibility, like the absolute moron I was, but they'd made me at some point.

Probably at the toy store. When I'd bounced ahead to lay in wait in the square, I'd given them time to set the trap: the woman leading me into her spiderweb, the man behind me to make sure I was working alone. I'd been so confident of myself, so busy watching the woman in front of me, that I hadn't noticed that I'd gone from predator to prey.

Except, instead of showing me sharp teeth, the woman pulled a folded knife out of her pocket. She opened the blade with a snick, holding the matte black handle in a reverse grip, which either meant she'd watched too many movies or that she was planning on slicing me to pieces. She didn't look like a movie critic.

I *really* wished I had a gun.

To my right, Beard pulled out an expandable baton and gave it a quick swing to snap it open, the sound not too dissimilar from a shotgun being racked, and almost as unsettling as the woman locking her blade open.

I really, really, really wished I had a gun, but if there was anything to be thankful for, it was that they weren't working heavy either. I would have been happier if it was pure hand to hand, no knives or batons, but it could have been worse, and who said I got to be happy in this life?

Time to find out how professional these pros were.

55

BEARD TOOK A SHUFFLE STEP FORWARD. He led with his left foot and was holding the baton in his right hand, his left hand up in a defensive rather than attacking position, his fingers curled lightly rather than in a tight fist. The woman was a lefty, and she'd adopted a low, athletic crouch, leading with the knife but in no hurry.

I said, "Anybody want to try talking this out first?"

In my periphery, as I spoke, Motorcycle Jacket took a half step forward and then danced back again, while Beard stayed rock still.

Beard said, "You shouldn't have tried following us."

I wasn't an expert on Irish accents, but he sounded like he had marbles in his mouth.

I gave a theatrical sigh. "This is the part where I say something clever about how you're making a mistake, but then you go ahead and attack me anyway."

"Yeah?" the woman said, the tip of her knife pointed at me, "And then what happens?"

Beard said, "And then what happens is we dump his body in the canal."

"I doubt that's how the story goes," I said. "Might be a different ending."

Beard inched forward. The tip of the baton wavered.

I was going to put him down first. Even with the knife, the woman's smaller size meant she was my secondary target. There's a reason why professional fighters have weight classes, and I didn't want the guy's bulk to jam me up. As I took him down, I could peel the baton off him, use that to make her drop the blade, and then—

Beard came in high, swinging the baton with his full force. I managed to roll enough to catch it on the meat of my lats rather than my collarbone, where he'd been aiming. I kept spinning, even as I felt heat across the muscle group where he'd tagged me. I raised my right arm and then dropped it over his baton arm, catching him at the elbow.

I used my leverage to turn him into a shield from the woman's knife thrust. She pulled back, readying herself to come at me again. Beard tried to yank himself from my grip, but I had him locked: His elbow was pinned against mine. I latched my left hand on his wrist, making it impossible for him to swing the baton. If we'd been sparring, he would have tapped out.

But we weren't sparring, and his arm was straight and pinned.

I grunted with the effort of torquing it backward, snapping his bone.

He screamed. I let my hand slide from his wrist to the baton, pulling it from his grip. In one continuous motion, I swung the baton at him. I was aiming for the vulnerable spot behind his ear, a killing blow, but he turned his head barely in time. I caught him on the cheek instead. He staggered, going down to one knee, his broken arm flapping like a useless wing.

Instead of fighting my own momentum, I pushed off Beard and continued around until I was facing the woman.

She bobbed back and forth, weaving like a snake, the blade of her knife glinting in the moonlight as she looked for an opening.

I could hear the man trying to get up off the ground, and without even looking, I flicked the baton to my side. There was a thwap and another grunt from him.

The woman, thinking she had an opening, started to come at me, her knife held in a reverse grip now. But she was too slow to take advantage of it, and I whipped the baton back to position and stepped forward.

She'd been ready to come low, planning to swipe upward and open me up from belly to throat, but I had the advantage of reach with the baton. She aborted her attack, taking three quick shuffle steps backward and opening a space of about ten feet between us to regroup and reconsider her position.

I didn't give her the chance.

I came in fast and full of violence, the baton to her wrist making her drop the knife, and then my spinning elbow connecting with a crunch to her nose as her blade clattered to the ground.

She was a pro, though, and she kept fighting.

I barely dodged a knee between my legs, taking it hard on the thigh, but my shot to her face with my elbow left her disoriented enough that it was easy for me to slip behind her and put her in a chokehold.

I applied pressure to her carotid artery. After about ten seconds of her futilely trying to escape, she slumped into unconsciousness.

Beard was mewling on the ground, holding his ruined arm. In the moonlight, it was too dim to tell for sure, but he had that eyes-glazed-over look that made me think I'd given him a concussion.

I thought about just killing them—that was the only sure way to make sure they never bothered me again—but that would mean either dealing with the bodies or causing the Venice police to get all hot and bothered.

Instead, I broke the woman's arm as well, so they were a matched set of invalids.

Problem solved.

56

I LEFT BEARD AND MOTORCYCLE JACKET behind and began my walk back to Giovanni's palazzo.

I was shaking a bit from adrenaline, so I decided to check out La Casa del Libretto again. Even if I'd solved the problem of having another team working, I still had to nail down all the details of my zip-line concept.

After fifteen minutes of exploring around the outside, I thought I had it sorted out well enough. Even if I didn't exactly have every detail locked in, what was Dad going to do when I told him about the tunnel flooding? Raise his hand like Moses splitting the sea, perform a miracle to keep us dry?

Huh. That gave me an idea.

The MOSE project, or Modulo Sperimentale Elettromeccanico, a five- or six-billion-dollar moonshot project to stop the city of Venice from flooding. Heavily criticized as environmentally unsound and over budget, it was, essentially, a series of mobile floodgates that rested on the seafloor but that could be inflated with compressed air to stop the incoming tide. It was a giant wall that could be called upon at will to part the waters.

I wondered if Richa—or, rather Giovanni—had the juice to get Venice to activate it.

I texted Richa, to ask.

A long shot, but maybe the MOSE project could keep the tunnel dry?

But if not, the turret was the only way for us to get in.

With the adrenaline finally cleared out, I was suddenly hit with a wave of exhaustion. It had gotten late. It was time to go back to Giovanni's and get some sleep so I'd be ready for tomorrow. Though I thought I could manage a second wind if Richa happened to be waiting up for me...

I'd turned to leave the square when my phone rang. The number popped up with no caller ID information, but I recognized the area code: 310. Los Angeles. And before I could answer, the caller ID information filled in: Ginny's surgeon.

She started speaking, talking about the results from the tests she'd ordered, about what the care home was telling her, about Ginny's recovery. She rattled off the test results: The numbers were *good.* Don't pop the bubbly, but keep your fingers crossed, hope those angels keep watch over your sister.

The doctor hung up before I got the chance to ask where the angels were when Ginny was chucked off a sixth-floor balcony in Paris.

57

WHEN I GOT BACK TO THE PALAZZO, the lights were on downstairs, and for a wonderful few seconds, I thought that maybe Richa *was* waiting up for me.

It was Dad.

He was alone in the parlor. He was sitting on one of the plush chairs, watching the fire. He was drinking a glass of brown liquor, and he blinked with a slowness that made me wonder if I'd just missed getting to see him zonked out, asleep in front of the fireplace like an old man.

He saw me. "Where've you been all day? You missed your fitting."

"What fitting?"

"Tuxedos. For tomorrow." He looked at his watch. "Yep. The job's tomorrow, because it's still tonight."

"How was the opera?"

He sipped his drink with a deliberateness that made it clear he'd already had enough. He grunted. "Eh. Seen better. Nice dinner, though. Shame you missed the food. Giovanni's chef is pretty good. Where were you? Richa said there were a few wrinkles you were trying to iron out and that you were clearing your head? Speaking of wrinkles, she's got the tailor coming back for you in the morning. I like that one."

"You like the tailor?"

"No, dum-dum. Richa," he said cheerfully. "I told her you liked her."

"Dad!"

"Oh, get over yourself, Duke. She laughed. She thought it was cute. No, grab a drink and sit down. God, I forgot how funny Nando and Giovanni are together, and Helen and Paulie had this thing all night they were doing that Richa showed them. I don't know. Some internet dance, but I'll tell you, at least that opera was short."

It was fifty-fifty with him, but tonight he was a happy drunk. He continued. "We were back here"—he looked at his watch—"a while ago. But once Nando and Helen called it a night, the party was over. Except for me. Don't leave me hanging. I said grab a drink and sit down. Woof. I'm going to be hungover again tomorrow."

"You going to be sober in time for the job?" I asked.

"Relax," Dad said. "It's slice and bake. Come on. Have a drink."

I considered him for a second, then I looked over at the bar. The bottle was still out. A different whiskey from the night before, doubtlessly as expensive. An open bottle of wine too. There was a plate of cookies, and some fresh berries and melons neatly garnished with sprigs of mint. I snagged a cookie and popped it into my mouth. I brushed the powdered sugar from my fingertips off on my pant leg, and then took two of the sprigs of mint and chewed them to clear out the taste of the cookie. I picked up the bottle of wine and eyed Dad.

He was staring at the fire again, lost in thought. He took another sip of his drink. Another long, slow blink. An Italian pop song from the 1960s was playing quietly. I couldn't see the speakers, but it made the room feel even more out of time than it already did. The whole trip had felt that way for me.

I put the wine back down without pouring myself a glass and sat in the other chair. We were at forty-fives to each other, the perfect angle for a conversation where I didn't want to make eye contact.

We both watched the fire. We'd been sitting quietly for a minute or two when Filomena came in and asked if we needed anything. Dad thanked her, and Filomena said that if he needed anything,

anything at all, she would be waiting in the back room, to please come find her, and they stared at each other for long enough that I wasn't sure if I was supposed to make my exit.

When she finally broke eye contact with him and left the room, I figured he wasn't ever going to be in a better mood than he was right then, so I said, "Hey, Dad?"

"Uh-oh," he said lightly. "I know that voice. That's your 'I did something dumb and don't want to have to admit it' voice. What did you do this time?"

"Dad," I said.

"What was the name of that school in Korea? Not once, but twice," he said, laying out his thumb, "don't fight civilians," and index finger, "don't fight civilians."

"I said I was sorry. I've said I'm sorry like a million times since then, but also, Dad, you ever think about how many of those 'ho, ho, remember that time Duke acted like a baby?' stories occurred when I *was* a baby? I mean, not a baby, but you know, a kid, and it was age appropriate at the time. When you always bring those stories up, it's . . . it's embarrassing."

"What? You mean with Nando? You want to talk about babies, he's known you since you were born. What's there to be embarrassed about? Plus, I've known him longer than I've known you."

"Yeah. And now I'm working with all of you, and you treat me like I'm tech support. 'Oh, we have this awesome heist, except for this one teeny tiny almost totally insignificant part that literally could not be done without you, Duke.' "

"Give me a break, Duke. We did the job without you before."

"That's my point. You did it without me before, but that was a long time ago, Dad. The job won't work the way you have it lined up."

For the briefest instant, I wished I was back in that narrow street, my back against the wall, the canal in front of me, the man with the baton closing in on one side, the woman with a knife coming at me from the other, because that seemed much, much less scary to face than fury coming at me from my dad's stare.

I didn't say anything.

He didn't say anything, either, but his face started to untwist.

After a while, he took a sip, leaned back in his chair again, and considered his glass. There were still two fingers of booze in it. "I've been drinking too much."

"Helen said that's what happens when Nando's around."

He laughed. "He's always been a boozer. Helen described Nando to me once as a 'glass-half-full kind of guy.' As in, he's the kind of drinker who, no matter how often you top up his glass, it's almost immediately half empty again. It's good to see him, though. Been too long."

"I know you don't want to hear it," I said, "but the job's messy, and you guys have been acting like we're on vacation."

"We're just catching up. *I* haven't seen Nando since the last time *you* saw Nando."

"We're supposed to be working, Dad. Somebody's going to get hurt if we're not careful. And I don't mean Helen's pratfall. There's no such thing as a totally safe job. You know that."

He swirled his drink and stared at me. "*You* are telling *me* to be more careful? That *I* am not taking the job seriously enough?" His voice had gone rough, hard-edged. "Do I need to say your sister's name?"

"Dad. I'm talking about this job, okay. Things are—"

"How about you take responsibility," he challenged.

"I'm trying to," I said. "I'm trying to tell you, we've got—"

"You're telling me? Me? I *know* to be careful. I've *learned* to be careful," he said, leaning forward, emphasizing with the hand holding his drink, slopping a little out of the glass, which seemed to make him even angrier. He huffed, and then, aiming the words at me, carefully enunciated: “How about you being careful? Tell *me* to be careful? I know to be careful. Can’t protect her and it’s *my* fault? It’s *your* damn fault. You know it. I know it. Helen and Paulie and even Nando know it. Everybody knows it. Doesn’t matter whatever else you do; you can’t make up for it. It’s your fault.” He sagged back into his chair. “Your fault.”

58

FINALLY TELLING DAD THAT HE *needed* me on this job, that times had changed, and they could only pull off a repeat of the Venice Double with me helping had felt liberating.

Like I was flying.

But having him tell me, to my face, that what happened to Ginny was my fault?

That felt like the engines in my plane had suddenly cut out mid-flight: sudden silence in the aftermath, sudden terror. And then, after a wobble, settling into a glide, the question now whether we ended up in a fatal crash or if there was an open field up ahead for us to set the plane down.

And then Dad rubbed his face with his free hand and said, "Oh, I don't know. I've had too much to drink. You need to stop worrying. He's going to be fine. He's like Chemical Will."

I was confused. "Who?"

"Giovanni. Isn't that what this is all about? I know you don't like the idea of working with an amateur, but Giovanni, he's like Chemical Will. You know, he's not going to take a bullet for you, but you can trust him. And, come on, all he has to do is be a lookout and then close a door and lock it. No problem." He grinned at me. "Beside which, technically, Giovanni isn't an amateur."

"You're making a joke? He's not an amateur because it's Giovanni's *second* job?"

"Because it's his second job," he echoed with that drunk-dumb smile plastered on his face. "Even, I guess, if it's the first job a second time."

After a short interlude to get my temper back down, I gave back something at least approximating a smile.

That was as close as we were going to get to apologizing to each other, at least tonight.

I said, "I talked to Ginny's doctor. Right before I came back."

"And?"

"Nothing concrete, but she was positive," I said, deciding not to go into it while he was drunk. "Listen, can we please, please talk about tomorrow? It's not Giovanni, but we have to change some things for the job to work."

Dad stood up. "I need to go to bed. I should have stuck with the beer and wine." He looked at the glass he was holding as if he was having a private conversation with it.

"Dad?"

"Yeah?"

"Why didn't you say that in the first place?"

He stopped looking at his drink and looked at me. "What?"

"About Giovanni. Why didn't you tell me in the first place that it was going to be like the Chemical Will situation. I would have known what you meant."

Dad considered me, and then said, "Because I shouldn't have had to explain anything. I'm your dad. It should have been . . ." He gulped down half of what was left of his drink, coughed, and then said, "It should have been *enough.*"

It should have been enough that he said Giovanni was on the job. He should have been able to say it, and to have that be enough for me.

"But it's not," I said. "It used to be, Dad. But it's not enough anymore."

He walked over to the fireplace, took the poker, and gave a few half-hearted nudges at the fire. He hung the poker back up and said, "How bad is it?"

I looked at him. It took me a beat to realize he was finally listening. "The job? You mean, how bad are things with the job?"

"She said there was a problem you were working on. Richa said that. I told you she said that. Some wrinkles. Fine, if it's not about having Giovanni along, what's wrong with my plan? Why isn't it good enough for you? I'm telling you, it *worked*. And now you're telling me that *you* should take over the job?"

I hesitated.

"Jesus. What now?"

"Dad," I said. "Remember when Mom's parents came out to visit us in Los Angeles, and Granddad was already sick, but he wanted to rent a car, and Grandmom took you aside and told you that she didn't think it was a good idea to let him drive with me and Ginny in the car?"

"Yeah," he said warily, though it could have been the drink. "If you're talking about Nando, he couldn't drive for crap even when I first met him."

"No, I mean . . ."

"You mean *me*? I shouldn't be driving?"

"Don't freak out on me, okay? And, obviously, I don't mean driving. But you missed some things."

He stared at me, wobbling a little, gathering himself up, but then, instead of launching into a storm of invectives, he shook his head. He looked desperately sad, and I was at a loss.

Gently, I said, "I know you think everything's perfect, okay, but I've been out here, trying to fix problems, and—"

"What would Ginny say?" he asked. "If Ginny was here, what would she say?"

His voice was quiet, but he spoke clearly, the drunkenness shaken off at least for a few seconds. "Seriously. If Ginny was here, what would she say? She was always a better planner than you. She saw the whole field."

"That's not fair."

"Fair? Fair?" he blustered. "Because Paris worked out so well?"

"You think I blueprinted that job on my own? Of course she helped, Dad. Jesus. You think it was all *my* fault, don't you? You asked me what Ginny would say, well, if you want to talk fair, Ginny used to say sometimes that it wasn't fair, you know, how you treated us?"

"I've got to go to sleep," he said. The fight had gone out of him. "I'm too tired for this. We can talk about it in the morning. I know you don't like Giovanni being on the job, but he's good. He's solid."

"I know. I believe you. But I don't think it matters anyway."

"Oh god. Can we deal with this in the morning?"

I thought about Beard and Motorcycle Jacket on the ground, their matching broken arms, about the time and tides and the tunnel flooding, about all the ways Dad was dropping the ball. But none of it mattered. I could make the job work.

"Yeah. We're good. The morning's fine. I've got everything taken care of."

"Duke?"

"Yeah?"

He considered me, and then finished off his drink. "We're good, right?"

He answered his own question: "We're good. But I've got to stop trying to keep up with Nando," he said, placing his now-empty glass back down. He came over, patted me on the top of the head like I was a dog, and said, "You do okay sometimes."

He turned and walked out of the room. He turned toward the stairs, stopped, and then turned around in the other direction and stalked toward the back. I was about to call out to him, to redirect him, when I remembered what he had so clearly kept in mind when he'd done an about-face: Filomena was in the back room.

Infuriating how he could draw women like moths to a flame. But also, he looked so damned sad that for once, I was rooting for him.

I looked at my watch. It was early afternoon where Ginny was, closing in on midnight here, in Venice. I was exhausted. With the time zones, and being out in the cold all day, and with my concerns about the job tomorrow, I was ready for sleep. One way or another, we were going to be swapping out the Puccini score tomorrow, but it was going to be a busy day getting ready. My bed was calling for me.

Except, as I was about to get up and leave, Richa came in. She had changed for the opera, from a sweater, jeans, and boots into an emerald cocktail dress.

"Can I join you?" she said.

"Please," I said. "I'm wide awake."

59

"YOU JUST MISSED MY DAD," I said as she sat down in his vacated chair.

"I know. I was waiting for him to leave. I wanted to talk to you privately."

Oh.

She smiled and glanced at the floor.

I cleared my throat, but for once, I couldn't think of anything to say.

She said, "It won't work. Too many people would ask questions. It cannot happen."

Oh. Well. Okay. "I understand," I said. We were having fun, and there was clearly some chemistry that we both could recognize. Another time, another place maybe, that chemistry, that steam, would have popped the cork out the top of the bottle and we would have each made a few wishes, but she was working, and if we hooked up, there'd be gossip. I could see why she didn't want to make things messy at her job. I snorted. "I don't think that's going to stop Filomena with my dad, though."

She looked up at me. "What are you talking about?"

"Filomena? She made it pretty clear to my dad that she was... Wait. What are *you* talking about?"

"Your text about the MOSE project"—the giant seawall gates designed to protect Venice from flooding—"but what does the MOSE project have to do with Filomena?"

"Nothing," I said. "Forget it."

“Ah,” Richa said. “I understand now what you were saying. Filomena and your father. Yes. That does not surprise me. She has not been subtle about her interest in him.”

“And the MOSE project idea won’t work?”

“No.” She shook her head. “It was a smart idea, but even if we were not worried about drawing attention, I cannot simply raise my hand and make this happen in time. The MOSE gates cannot be operated simply because Giovanni asks.”

“That’s okay.”

“You are not worried about the water?”

“No. I mean, yeah. Hypothermia in a flooded tunnel sounds unappealing. But I’ve figured out how to get the zip line set up so we can go in through the turrets.”

I sketched out what I’d come up with and what hardware I needed. She asked a few pointed questions, but understood almost immediately, and agreed that everything for the task was easily obtainable, if not in Venice itself, then on the mainland. I told her I wanted to sleep on it, to make sure there wasn’t anything I was forgetting, and she laughed and said it was not as if she could send Fio or Bosco out to a store at midnight to shop for a drone and rope and harnesses for the zip line anyway, but for now to give her a list of everything I wanted, and she would ensure they went shopping first thing so that by the time I was ready to present the modified plan to my father and the crew, I had everything in hand. There would be no difficulty.

Despite talking about business, with the crackling fire having burned low, there was a sense of intimacy between us. I was about to compliment the necklace she had on—a deep blue sapphire providing striking contrast to her dress—when we heard a soft giggle from the hallway. We both turned in time to catch Dad and Filomena walking past the door of the parlor, headed toward the stairs together. They were engrossed with each other, oblivious to our presence in the parlor.

After they passed, Richa and I stared at each other, her eyes wide in amusement, and me shaking my head, chagrined. We waited several seconds, and then, unable to help herself, Richa covered her mouth with her hands to keep her laughter quiet, and then she said, "I am glad to see that it is not only Nando and Helen who have found Venice to be... inspiring."

"Please don't," I said, but I couldn't stop myself from laughing with her. "It's, you know, you don't want to think of your parents, your grandparents..."

Her smile turned wicked, and she said, "But this way, maybe all of them will be happy in the morning. In a good mood for you to explain how it is that you have learned to fly."

"Oh god. I don't want to think about them being all jolly."

She got serious. "But what of the man and the woman from last night? The professionals? What are you going to do about them?"

"It's taken care of," I said, not feeling the need to tell her about my little bout of excitement.

She considered me, appeared about to ask a question, and then shook her head and stood up. "It sounds as if there is nothing else to be done tonight, and now it is time to go upstairs to bed."

"I might need to add some more gear in the morning to my list for getting in through the turret, but I don't think it's anything that will be hard to get. Even if the stores were open right now anyway, it's probably good for me to sleep on it."

"Yes. It's time to go upstairs to bed," she said again.

I nodded, but I wasn't listening. I was thinking about attaching the zip line. Maybe I couldn't part the waters, but I'd figured out how to grow wings. Or, at least, that a drone could do it for me. And I was hopeful that, after our conversation tonight, Dad might listen.

It helped that I could present my solution neatly wrapped with a bow so there was nothing for him to complain about. I watched the fire again, the flame moving and shifting, thinking about the Juliet balcony high up the turret.

"Duke," she said.

"It's fine," I said. "I've got it worked out. Mostly. It's all stuff Fio or Bosco can pick up easily. My shopping list can wait until the morning," I said.

"Duke."

"Yeah."

"It is time to go upstairs to bed," she said for the third time.

60

I ROLLED OVER, REACHING OUT FOR RICHA, but I was alone in my room.

If there hadn't been the faint, familiar hint of vanilla and cinnamon on the other pillow, the same scent from the gym, I might have believed it was all a dream: the moonlight spilling through the window and over the sheets, Richa leading me across the room by the hand, kissing me, turning so that I could unzip the back of her dress.

It was half past eight in the morning, and I figured there was a reasonable chance, given the amount of booze that Dad—and I was assuming, by extension, everybody else—had put down the night before, that I was the first one up. Again. Well, not counting Richa, wherever she'd gone off to.

I put on clean workout gear and headed downstairs. Fio and Nicole were on duty. I was thrilled not to be greeted by Filomena; it was too early to handle *that* without a coffee. And then I realized there was a good chance the reason I didn't see her was because she was still upstairs, in bed with my dad.

I tried not to think about it, and asked Fio for an espresso. Nicole informed me that an early lunch would be served at eleven o'clock because Giovanni, Dad, and Paulie all had appointments at noon. Which suited me fine: I'd gotten a text back from Noor about my request for a "sports car." After breaking an arm each for Beard and Motorcycle Jacket, I didn't expect any additional problems, but as long as Noor had already arranged a pickup for me, I'd take the opportunity to make the pickup. Anyway, with the time change between Venice and Los Angeles, it was probably more hassle to cancel than to get the pistol.

Nicole continued, telling me that Richa had asked for me to be told that she would be back between ten and eleven o'clock, and would be happy to attend to any of my needs at that time. For half a second I thought Nicole was making an innuendo, and maybe she was, but if so, it was unintentional; Nicole seemed oblivious to what had happened between me and Richa the night before. She added that Richa had also asked her to inform me that if I texted her my requirements, she would forward them to Bosco, who was already on his way to procure the items I would need. He would also, as required, make an additional trip if there was anything I'd forgotten. Fio returned with my coffee, and at the same time, the tailor arrived to make up for my missed appointment yesterday.

I didn't bother to complain that nobody had even told me I was supposed to have a fitting yesterday. As I changed into the tuxedo, I wondered if this was the same tailor who had worked his magic on my mother's dress all those years ago. He was a gnome of a man, of indeterminate old age, but he was efficient with his chalk and his pins. The tuxedo fit decently off the rack—looking at the label, it was an expensive rack—and the tailor enthusiastically ensured me that it would be perfect in time for the gala this evening. I mentioned a few special requirements, and he nodded and said he could accommodate those without difficulty.

When he was done, I changed back into my shorts and T-shirt, and pounded through my workout in the exercise room. As I went through the motions, I played every aspect of the upcoming job through my head, looking for holes and finding almost none. For the first time since Dad had hustled me out of the bar in Florida, I was feeling like I had a solid grip on things. Sure, I'd have to figure out the Frankensafe in the middle of the job, but with Beard and Motorcycle Jacket out of the picture, and with the turret worked out, the Venice Double part two was ready to go; maybe it wasn't the exact revival Nando and Dad wanted out of the production, but with my updates, it was a show that we could perform.

I finished my workout at ten o'clock on the dot, with a few all-outs, and then, still gasping and dripping with sweat, I headed back to my room. I pushed my clothes into the corner of the bathroom and got into the shower. I had finished soaping up when I heard a noise from the other room, and then the click of my bathroom door shutting.

I was well prepared by the time Richa slipped into the shower with me and offered to soap my back.

We got clean, and then we got dirty, and then we got back in the shower so we could get clean again.

She slipped discreetly into the hallway, and I finished dressing; we were due downstairs.

When I came into the dining room, she was laughing with Dad, who had a big grin on his face. He didn't seem to be nursing a hangover, and clearly, his night had ended in a satisfactory manner. Nando was drinking a cup of coffee and showing Helen his phone. He seemed diminished somehow, but Helen's body language was one of affection; at least for today, they wouldn't have any difficulty playing a long-married couple.

Dad turned to talk to Paulie, who was sitting alone at the other end of the table, and Richa caught my eye. She didn't exactly wink, but it did remind me of what she'd said last night about how maybe Dad and the gang would be in a good mood this morning when I broke the news about the job's complications.

Filomena was apparently back on duty, because she was fussing with a spread on the sideboard: meats and cheeses and pastries and fruit. I did my best to greet her as if she and my dad hadn't spent the night in bed. I asked for a cappuccino since it was still the morning, and then spent some time filling my plate.

61

AS SOON AS I SAT DOWN AT THE TABLE, Paulie loudly said, "You get any sleep last night, Duke, or were you up all night too? Maybe tonight, you dirty birds"—she gestured lazily at the other side of the room—"can keep the noise down?"

I thought I was going to die of embarrassment.

And then, I *knew* I was going to die of embarrassment, because both Nando *and* Helen blushed, and at the exact same time, the coffee cup Filomena was carrying on a saucer rattled and she made eye contact with Dad, and *they* both blushed, and then Paulie cackled and said, "I was joking, but looks like me and my nephew here were the only two who didn't get laid last night."

I decided not to correct her, and seemingly oblivious to any connection between me and Richa, Dad said, "Paulie, play nice. You're jealous because you aren't a free agent."

As he spoke, Giovanni came in and asked what kind of free agent should Paulie be, exactly, which led to a whole round of bawdy jokes between the grown-ups, complete with a few allusions to what had happened between Paulie and Giovanni back in the day, and why, exactly, it was that her relationship to Uncle Charles was fine and dandy on that front, thank you very much, and then an *extremely* bawdy joke about how it was, exactly, Paulie had broken her arm.

I studiously avoided locking eyes with Richa again and concentrated on my plate, waiting for when the joking had died down, but the joviality still remained.

It was Richa, however, who ripped off the Band-Aid: "There is a difficulty with the plan, but Duke has a solution."

Both Helen and Paulie looked to my dad, waiting for him to explode, but it was Nando who seemed ready to try to wave me off. Except, this time, before Nando could start his whole condescending song and dance, Giovanni interrupted him.

"What is the difficulty, Richa?" he said.

I wasn't sure if I should be offended at how dismissive the grown-ups had previously been of me, or pleased that Giovanni took Richa seriously, but either way, they all listened quietly as Richa explained the problem with time and tides. When she finished, making a point of saying that I had offered several options to work within the parameters of the original plan—including my "brilliant" idea about using the sea gates from the MOSE project—and why none of the possible solutions were workable, she turned to me and suggested I tell them what I'd come up with.

Again, there was a moment of tension and hesitation, as Nando and Dad looked at each other, but to my surprise, instead of complaining or pushing past it, Dad said, without a single note of malice in his voice, "All right, we're listening."

It took most of my restraint to avoid going for a victory lap. Despite how drunk he'd been, he'd *heard* me last night. Maybe not entirely, but enough.

Graciously, I said, "Actually, Dad, you were the one who helped me figure out the answer. I totally understand why you guys went through the tunnel. It was a good plan. It *is* a good plan, but, you know, there's not much we can do about the water, and if it must be tonight, then it won't work with the tunnel."

"Like I said," Nando chipped in, "the moon waits for no man."

Helen glanced sharply at him, but she didn't say anything. I eyed Richa, who gave me a subtle nod, and decided to let it go too. Instead of being infuriated by his need to be right, I suddenly felt sorry for him. He seemed . . . old. It didn't matter anymore. All I wanted was to get this job over with. Maybe before I headed back to Florida, Richa and I could go somewhere for a few days, go to Tuscany or Florence. Maybe she'd take me to her family's restaurant.

I said, "Right. The moon waits for no man, and we were all focused on the tunnel. But it was Dad who helped me figure it out. Remember when he asked me if I could fly? Well, it turns out, there *is* a way to grow wings, only it didn't exist when you did the original job."

Even though Richa, Giovanni, Helen, Paulie, and Nando were listening, it was really a conversation between me and Dad. As I explained my plan—using the drone to attach a zip line from the accessible turret to the turret that led down to the same place we would have exited the tunnel in the original plan—he nodded, asking a question here and there. Even though he never came out and said it was a good solution, he did acknowledge that he thought it would work.

By the time I was finished, Paulie was checking her watch, Giovanni was looking at the door, and I was starting to get itchy. Neither Richa nor I had mentioned the specter of the other team staking out La Casa del Libretto, but since Dad and Paulie had their own appointment at noon—something touristy, believe it or not, even though we were in the middle of a job—and Giovanni had his own scheduled meeting completely unrelated to the Puccini score, I was saved from having to make excuses about my own appointment to pick up the pistol Noor had arranged for me.

As we gathered up to go, Nando suggested we all meet in the parlor at four to run a dress rehearsal, and that in the meantime, he might go take a nap.

He looked like he needed one.

62

RICHA WAS WAITING FOR ME AT THE FRONT DOOR.

I didn't want her to get upset about the pistol, so I said, "I've got something I need to take care of. By myself."

"Of course," she said, somewhat stiffly. "In fact, I am only here to confirm that your payment for the job was processed. Paulie provided your banking details for the wire, but I am simply doing my job."

Even I was smart enough to realize I'd screwed that up. After a quick check to make sure there was nobody around, I stepped close to her, putting my hands on her hips. I said, "Sorry. I didn't mean it like that. There are just some parts of this that you don't need to be involved in."

I kissed her. She kissed me back, and while I wouldn't have said there was no lingering stiffness, she had certainly relaxed, and she gave me an unexpected swat on my ass as I walked out.

I made a point of glancing back at her and rubbing my butt as if it had stung.

The look she gave me as she closed the door was almost enough to make me turn around.

Almost, because I was cutting it close with my timing.

After yesterday's miserable misting morning rain, today was Venice in glorious winter sunlight. Ten hours until our little escapade: The water in the canals sparkled, and tourists passed me unaware of the larceny in my heart.

While I walked, I pulled out my phone so I could finally find out what I was getting paid for the job. I ran a VPN and several bounce-backs, so I wasn't worried about security; I had all my own systems automated, and the information Paulie would have given Richa for wiring me my payment went to an account in the Caymans and was from there automatically transferred multiple times before ending up in a different offshore account, making the whole thing about as fireproof as you could get.

Paulie could be hard-nosed about business dealings, and she was a big believer in there being no such thing as a free lunch; even though I had managed to basically bankrupt myself in the aftermath of Ginny's accident—not working plus having a gambling problem wasn't the best combination—Paulie had insisted on keeping my setup squeaky clean, probably as much out of self-preservation as feeling like it was her duty as my aunt. Either way, I appreciated it. Nothing wrong with a big bag of cash, but it was sure a heck of a lot easier to get paid by wire.

When my account information finished loading, I almost fell into a canal.

Richa had wired me five million dollars. Five. Million. Dollars.

Holy crap.

I was for sure going to Vegas when this job was over. After, of course, I finished things up in Florida. Unless it conflicted with me dog-sitting for Meg, I thought, pleased to realize the idea didn't give me as much of a pang.

Five million dollars. Yeesh.

By the time I met up with Noor's contact to grab the pistol—even if, in the wake of my dismantling of Beard and Motorcycle Jacket it seemed unnecessary—I was feeling pretty darn pleased with myself.

63

YOU LEARN EARLY IN THIS kind of work to eat and sleep when you can. The house was quiet, so I went upstairs, took off my shoes, lay down, and closed my eyes. I was able to fall asleep quickly.

My alarm went off at 3:30, and I did some gentle stretching, working the kinks out. When I got downstairs, Bosco ushered me into the parlor and showed me his haul. I checked everything off against the list in my head and complimented him on a job well done. I was sitting on the floor, finishing setting everything up, when Dad arrived.

"Tuxedos are here," he said, glancing down at me. "Fio is hanging them up in our rooms. You know what Nando said to me yesterday, when I had my fitting? He couldn't believe we hadn't brought our own, and he said, 'What kind of a peasant travels without a tuxedo?' That guy. He never worked an honest day in his life." He shook his head, still in a good mood, and I wondered how exactly he'd spent the rest of his afternoon after he and Paulie had finished sightseeing, and then I realized there was a reasonable chance it had been in his room with Filomena, and I was glad I hadn't asked.

He hovered over me, looking at the drone and all the other gear I had spread out on the ground, and then gave an approving nod. Which was as close as I was likely to get to a "good job, Duke! Thanks for saving my ass and making this job a go!"

He sat down in one of the plush chairs, and then, unexpectedly, he laughed.

"What?"

"I don't know," he said. "When I was at Terminal Island"—the federal correctional institution where he'd served nearly two years of an eight-to-twelve before I'd managed to get him released with his record wiped clean—"I kept thinking, well, that's it. By the time I'm out, I'll be too old to work anything other than a straight con again, and in a few hours, I'm going to be riding a zip line across a courtyard while I'm wearing a tuxedo. Your mom would have thought it was hilarious—"

Neither one of us said anything for a second.

Finally, Dad said, "I wish Ginny was . . . I don't know. Sometimes it doesn't feel real."

Another second.

"Your mom would have liked that you got to be part of this, I guess. That's all I'm saying. I didn't know if I'd get to do this again. I'm looking forward to tonight. You?"

"It's a weird job. If I'm being honest, there was a part of me that thought you guys were putting me on."

"Putting you on?"

"You know what I mean."

"I don't."

"It's not like this is a normal job," I said.

"You complaining again? We're doing it the way you want to," he said, pointing at the gear on the floor. "What's the problem now?"

"There's no problem. I'm not complaining." I hated how defensive I sounded, how easily he could put me on my back foot. "I know what you mean about getting back to work."

He gave me a sharp look, and I wondered if he was thinking of the Paris Job, when I'd blown apart our lives, or the Volkov Job, when I'd started to sew the open wounds back shut. I was expecting another jab from him, but maybe when we'd talked last night, I'd gotten through to him in some way, because his eyes flickered, and then he said, "Okay. No problem. What do you mean you thought we were putting you on?"

"You know. Like a snipe hunt," I said, thinking of the old practical joke of sending a new camper out into the woods to look for a "snipe," and then pretending to be surprised when the camper can't find an animal that doesn't exist. I continued. "We've never done a job where we aren't stealing. Putting the original score back is, well, I mean I get why we're doing it, or rather why Giovanni wants us to do the job, but yeah. It sounds kind of like a snipe hunt, doesn't it?"

Nando walked in while I finished speaking, and a flash of alarm crossed his face. "A snipe hunt? What do you mean?"

64

"OH, IGNORE DUKE," DAD SAID TO NANDO, but it was cheerful and almost friendly. "Yeah, it's a weird job, Duke, but at least you're getting paid. Hey, Nando, remember that time you sent him to the hardware store for the long weight?"

I was ten, and we were in some stupid town in the UK for a month, Herkershire or Hepishire or Hempside or something like that, a bank job that Helen had wired up that had no place for me and Ginny. It was forty degrees and rained all day every day, and while Ginny seemed fine, I was losing my mind. In retrospect, some good ADHD meds would have gone a long way in my childhood, but I was driving even Nando nuts, and he sent me down to the village hardware store to get a pair of pliers, a roll of electrical tape, and a long weight. Of course, when I got to the store and ten-year-old me said I'd been sent for a long weight, the old guy working the till asked me how long the weight needed to be. I said I didn't know, but I wanted to get it right because with the weather, everybody was in a bad mood, and once I was home and dry, I didn't want to get sent back to the store for a different long weight. The guy gave me a stare then pointed to a bench, told me to settle in, and that if I made sure to stay in that spot, he'd make sure I got a nice long weight, one that would make the adults happy.

I sat on that bench for nearly an hour before I figured it out: a long *wait*, not a long weight.

Nando and Dad thought it was as funny at the time as they did now, both trying to outdo each other as they described the pure fury

I'd been in when I'd come storming back, and then, how all it took to calm me down was to send me back out, but this time with Ginny, to get ice cream. The anger shifted in me, and I started to laugh, too, and when Paulie came in, Dad told her I was being a goof about the job, and went through the whole story again, and then Paulie reminded him of the time their dad had sent the two of them to buy a bucket of striped paint, and how they'd been afraid to tell him they couldn't find one before figuring out he was screwing with them. The difference being that at that point in their childhood, their dad was a violently abusive raging alcoholic, and my dad can be... kind of a dick.

Helen and Giovanni came into the room together at the stroke of four, trailed by Nicole, as I was almost done setting everything up. I told Dad that I needed a couple more minutes before we started, and he nodded and got up and walked over to where Giovanni had settled in by the bar, talking with Paulie.

Helen took Nando off to the side, and the two of them were chatting quietly. She looked intent, if not worried, and Nando was clearly trying to explain himself to her. He kept shaking his head, and she kept prodding, but I couldn't make out what they were saying over the sound of Giovanni and Paulie chatting with Dad. All I could hope for was that the inevitable implosion in Helen and Nando's relationship would wait until after the job, but they were both professionals, and either way they'd see the job through. Nicole was busy making drinks, and asked me if I wanted anything, but I declined.

I was almost set, though I had plans to run through a few things, get a little practice with flying the drone, and then make sure everything was in place before we headed over to La Casa del Libretto. I snuck a few peeks as Nicole put together drinks. I was pleased to see that Dad was sticking to San Pellegrino. Nando, on the other hand, happily received an old fashioned, after nudging Nicole to go a bit heavier on the whiskey. I kept my displeasure hidden, but his role didn't require a lot more than appearing to be upset when Helen took her dive; he could do that as easily drunk as sober, and frankly, given his "glass half full" approach, maybe drunk was the only way he could operate. Plus, I thought, we weren't doing the job until ten, and he seemed to perk up when Nicole handed him his drink.

Finally, as they all made their way to the sitting area, Nicole left, closing the door behind her: This was an "operational only" meeting, and that meant even Richa was out. I thought it was a bit silly—at this point, what did it matter if Giovanni's staff sat in, given how much they already knew?—but it hadn't been my decision and it wasn't worth arguing over.

I finished neatening up the gear on the floor, and sat down on one of the loveseats, waiting for Dad to call us to order.

But he looked at me and said, "Well?"

Nando, Helen, Paulie, were also waiting. Giovanni, too, even though, with the new plan, he'd just be a member of the audience and not part of the team.

The world had tilted.

It was my show now.

65

THE EVENT STARTED AT THE appropriately European time of eight o'clock, and for that first cocktail hour, waiters would circulate with trays of prosciutto-wrapped melon balls, caviar-topped buckwheat blinis, and caprese skewers. Dinner was to be served at nine o'clock, with breaks between each course so that a veritable who's who of opera performers could entertain us with selections from Puccini. Sometime during dinner, Auldhilda was slotted to get onstage with an accompanying tenor who would sing "*Che gelida manina*" to her so that she could answer by singing "*Sì, mi chiamano Mimì*"—*Yes, they call me Mimì*—back to him. I was sure, when that happened, Giovanni and Nando and Helen and Dad and maybe even Aunt Paulie would swoon with the romance of the job. Richa told me that *Che gelida manina* and *Sì, mi chiamano Mimì* were saved for Auldhilda's appearance, but as dinner was served, we'd get a selection of Puccini with each course: black-truffle risotto followed by "Senza Mamma" from *Suor Angelica*; lobster thermidor with a side of "Un bel vedremo" from *Madame Butterfly*; wild mushroom and truffle polenta accompanied by "Signore, ascolta!" from *Turandot*; and finally, radicchio and arugula salad and "O mio babbino caro" from *Gianni Schicchi*. Not that I recognized or knew any of the songs, but Richa seemed to enjoy telling me what to expect.

She'd complimented me copiously when she'd come to my room and seen me in my tuxedo. With the floor-length black gown she was wearing, complete with a pearl choker and matching earrings, I think my eyes did that "awooga awooga!" thing from the cartoons.

We came dangerously close to being late meeting everybody else downstairs.

When we arrived at the event, close to 8:30 and fashionably late, the square in front of La Casa del Libretto was hopping. I felt like electricity was running through my veins, but in a good way, not like when I'd almost stopped my own heart trying to open the Nimsik. Even if this job was kindergarten level, I was excited. I'd felt the same way during the Volkov Job a few months ago, getting back to work for the first time after what happened to Ginny; I'd walked away from my entire life until I was walking the straight and narrow. As if going straight could make up for what happened with Ginny. I'd been fooling myself. This was what I was meant to do, and it felt good. Colors were brighter, lines sharper. I felt *alive.*

There was a red-carpet photo walk—which everybody but Giovanni skipped for the obvious reason that none of us were particularly interested in appearing in a "notable guests" article—and a few dozen autograph seekers who squealed with delight when a short, rotund, bearded man arrived, evidently a famous lyric tenor. He was the one slated to sing "*Che gelida manina*" to Auldhilda, and to await her response as she sang "*Sì, mi chiamano Mimì*" back to him.

I was concerned when Nando seemed to stumble on the steps, but Helen had her hand on his arm, and Giovanni and Richa were right behind him. From a distance, I could see Helen speaking and Nando shaking his head. Richa simply took Nando's other arm, but Giovanni couldn't stop himself from looking in our direction. Dad gave him a subtle head shake, and Giovanni seemed to gather himself.

"Probably better Giovanni's not part of the job anymore," Dad said.

"Now? You're saying that now? And what about Nando?"

"Nando will be fine." Without pointing or moving his head, he said, "You see the cops? A single by the door and a pair at three o'clock."

"Got 'em," I said. We were bringing up the back for this specific reason, to make sure there wasn't any security we were missing. The cop by the door was wearing a suit and overcoat that would have looked nice if he wasn't competing with the rich, opera-loving crowd wearing tuxedos and evening gowns covered by designer coats. The other two men were wearing *polizia* jackets and seemed bored.

"You clock the undercovers too? Absolutely useless."

They were off to the right and impossible to miss: They looked like a comedy duo and were hawkishly monitoring a scruffy backpacker who was watching the hoopla with his mouth agape despite the only threat he could possibly pose being that of body odor. For a tenth of a second, I thought I caught sight of Beard at the edge of the square, but then relaxed: It was just the stoner kid again, and he was clearly making his way to somewhere else. Besides which, Beard and Motorcycle Jacket were nothing to worry about anymore. I'd taken care of them easily enough on my own, and that was *before* they both had broken arms and I was sporting a pistol.

Inside, after we checked our coats, Dad broke off from me to find Paulie, who'd gone in ahead of the team for much the same reason Dad and I had brought up the rear. I spotted Nando sitting at a high-top next to Helen in the main banquet hall, encircled by a small scrum of Giovanni's acquaintances who they'd met at the club the day before. Helen was gesturing animatedly, and the group of Italians seemed entranced, showing that the prep work they'd done yesterday had paid off. But Nando seemed to be almost withdrawn. If we weren't in the middle of a job, I would have asked if he was doing okay, but Richa appeared at my elbow with a glass of sparkling water. She told me where to look for Giovanni, who was circulating, and of course, had a constant stream of well-wishers wanting to talk to him.

66

THANKFULLY, RICHA AND I WERE SPARED the hassle of having to be social. We left the main banquet hall and moved into one of the overflow rooms, which were crowded enough that we could be functionally invisible. My least favorite part about this entire plan was the "hiding in plain sight" aspect, even if there wasn't any other viable alternative. When I'd looked at Dad's bundle, my first thought had been to ask why we didn't do the old dress-up-as-caterers trick, except that only worked if the crew was large enough, and more importantly, unfamiliar enough with each other, that nobody asked questions, but Giovanni had nipped that in the bud; in fact, some of the waiters tonight had actually worked the same event three decades ago. We would have stuck out like sore thumbs if we'd tried to pass as waiters. Also, if I was being completely honest, I hated carrying a tray of canapes; I wasn't cut out for service work. If blending in meant hanging out with Richa while she was wearing an evening gown was the worst thing about Dad's plan, well, maybe it wasn't such a bad plan after all.

Before they started to serve dinner, during the first performance, I was able to snag Helen for a quick, whispered exchange; I asked a few pointed questions about Nando's health and ability to see the job through, but Helen assured me he'd be fine.

When it was time to be seated, Richa, Dad, Paulie, and I took a table near the back of the banquet hall. A couple who made Nando seem young and sprightly joined us, and Dad turned on the world's most charming party-guest con, chatting them up in Italian. In the unlikely event anybody asked any questions about us being here or intimated that they were suspicious of us—or, later, being gone from dinner for about fifteen minutes—they'd be sure to say that the questioner must be mistaken, such a delightful man! Dad could make small talk with the best of them when he wanted to. Paulie, as was her wont, spent most of her time critiquing the food, giving it a solid B minus, which was a high mark by her standards, and she was very pleasant when she asked me if I could cut her food for her because of her broken arm. It made me think of Beard and Motorcycle Jacket sharing a meal together with their matched set of broken arms: Who was going to cut *their* food?

Otherwise, it was just waiting. I wasn't hungry, I didn't want to drink, and the opera was lost on me; if Richa weren't there, I might have lost my mind with the waiting. But as we got closer and closer, I could feel myself start to come alive. By 9:55, I felt like I had electricity running through my veins. But in a good way, not like getting zapped by the Nimsik Elite.

As the waiters started to bring the next course, I saw a woman join Giovanni and Helen and Nando at their table, and even from a distance I knew it had to be Auldhilda: I hadn't seen the necklace that had been in the safe with the original Puccini score, but it was a showstopper, a big chunk of ice. It was an exquisite piece of jewelry, high seven figures retail, though after dealing with a fence, you would only be left with low seven. Still, between that and the jewelry other people at the event were wearing, I could see why Beard and Motorcycle Jacket had thought about making a move.

Auldhilda was a surprisingly small woman, not what I'd expected from a former professional opera singer, but she had the aura of somebody who commanded attention. She had that ageless look of a certain kind of woman that is much easier to achieve with unlimited resources and a dedicated stylist, one that says "rich" as much as it says "young," and I doubted she'd stay a widow for long. I suspected that if Helen wasn't there, friend or not of Giovanni's, Nando might have taken a swing at the ultimate con of landing Auldhilda.

Though, as I stood up to make my way out of the room, a glance at Nando made me second-guess myself; from a distance, he looked worn, a completely different man than the one I'd remembered from my childhood.

But that didn't matter anymore. It was time.

67

"SEE YOU IN A BIT," I SAID TO RICHA. I thought she might kiss me for luck, but she simply smiled.

I walked past the bathroom, then turned left. Dad was waiting for me. He nodded, and we continued down the corridor. At the end of the corridor, we turned again. If there'd been a staff member doing rounds, we would have asked him for directions to the toilets, followed him out, gone and washed our hands, and then come back. But there was nobody there. Helen had been right about the security: Fio, Bosco, and Alvise had studiously ignored me and Dad and Paulie all night, which was hilarious, because we were sitting with Richa, who they obviously knew, but it seemed to make them happy to pretend they didn't know us. The rest of the staff at La Casa del Libretto, including the caterers, seemed to assume we belonged there since we were dressed for it.

Dad and I walked to the opposite turret from the vault without seeing a single person.

The stairway up the turret we needed to access was across from the door with the padlock we would have opened—and which Giovanni would have had to lock behind us—if we'd been using the tunnel, which was almost certainly hip-deep in water right now.

I liked my way better.

I'd had the tailor make a couple of specific alterations to my jacket, including tailoring the back to mask the bulge of my holstered pistol, and adding a few interior pockets for me to hide some basic tools. Dad and I made our way up the stairs, and then, at the top of the turret, I took out a pick and a tension wrench, and waved them at the locked door leading out to the roof.

I opened the door, and then we stepped out onto the roof. We had to wait for our eyes to acclimatize to the darkness, but with the full moon, it didn't take long. I found the controller where I'd dropped it off.

Earlier, when I'd been organizing the gear for the job, one of the things I'd had to do was clone a second controller and headset for the drone. Then, after we were done with our pre-heist meeting, I packed the cloned controller and headset in one of the payload boxes—basically just plastic cases I could attach to the drone—flew it to La Casa del Libretto and did a quick drop-off.

Maybe somebody would have noticed a drone buzzing around, and I had no clue whether they were legal in Venice, but it had seemed unlikely that anybody would stumble across the box I'd released from the drone onto the roof: I'd had Fio spray-paint all the payload boxes the same color as the roof tiles. If I hadn't known exactly where I'd dropped it, even with the moonlight, I might have had trouble finding it myself.

I opened the box and powered up the spare headset and the cloned drone controller. I had a moment of panic when they didn't connect to the drone back at Giovanni's palazzo immediately, but after about fifteen seconds I was live.

The headset gave me a first-person view from the drone's perspective, and as I punched the drone into the air, even though I was locked in to the task, I was still able to enjoy the aerial tour of Venice at night. I flew the drone from Giovanni's palazzo, where I'd left it ready to go, to where Dad and I waited on the roof of La Casa del Libretto.

It took me three trips with the drone to bring over the additional payload boxes I'd prepared. The first box contained the original of the Puccini score; if we couldn't get that to us, then nothing else mattered. The additional two boxes had spare batteries, harnesses, hardware, and rope for setting up the zip line. I flew them from Giovanni's to La Casa del Libretto one box at a time.

I suppose I could have flown them all over earlier, or done it in fewer trips—the drone had a decent carrying capacity, with a nearly five-kilometer range and seventy-minute flight time—but this seemed like the least risky way of approaching it.

Once I'd finished the final drop, I landed the drone at our feet and shut down the rotors.

We had two different kinds of rope with us: a lightweight three-millimeter line and a heavier rope that could support our weight for the zip line.

Dad attached the three-millimeter line to the drone's catcher, a sort of remote-controlled claw, and I put on my harness. It was almost perfect timing. I'd just finished buckling when the bright lights coming through the glass parts of the courtyard roof dimmed: The performance was starting.

This was the part where you needed wings: We had to get the zip-line rope from this turret to the other turret, loop it back so we could secure it, zip-line across, and then undo the whole thing.

After that, it was down the stairs and we'd end up in front of the same secret door that we would have used if the tunnel hadn't been full of water.

"Ready?" I grabbed the remote and the headset again.

"One second," Dad said. Then he picked up the reel holding the three-millimeter line. He had to keep enough tension on it to keep it from sagging as it played out, but not so much that he impeded the flight of the drone. The line had a great weight-to-strength ratio, with a breaking point of four hundred foot-pounds, but it also weighed less than half a pound for a hundred feet of length. I was afraid that if I tried this with the heavier rope we were going to use for the zip line, the drag would have made it too hard to control the drone.

"Ready," Dad said.

I kept the drone at a modest speed, the rotors barely making any noise. It didn't have any lights on it, and there weren't any good vantage points for somebody to be looking down on us. With the houselights brought low because of the performer onstage, even with the full moon and the line trailing behind it, the drone was functionally invisible.

It was simple: I flew the drone across to the other turret, carefully maneuvered it all the way around the solid pillar I'd scoped out earlier, and then flew it back to where Dad and I were waiting.

At that point, I landed the drone, and Dad disconnected the three-millimeter so he was holding both ends as they looped around the pillar and back to us. I flew the drone back to the other side and landed it there so it would be waiting for us.

Then, I tied the end of the heavier zip-line rope to one end of the three-millimeter line, and Dad carefully started reeling it in until the stronger rope had made it all the way around. We tied off the zip line rope into a big loop, from one turret to the other, almost like a clothesline.

We needed to avoid having the zip line sag too much—otherwise we risked getting stuck halfway across!—so the next thing was for me to use some of the three-millimeter line to tighten everything up.

It was fussy, but not difficult.

While I was completing the rigging, Dad policed the area to make sure there was nothing left behind. He used carabiners to clip two payload boxes to each of our harnesses. I'd lost track of which one had the Puccini score, but it didn't matter.

I connected the zip liner, or trolly, which was just a metal frame with wheels that would, well, zip us across. Then I looked at Dad.

"You want to go first?" I asked. "Age before beauty?"

He eyed the trip. We were on the fourth floor, except it was a European fourth floor, which meant the fifth story of the building, because in America the ground floor was the first floor, but here, it went ground, one, two, three, four. The top of the cover to the atrium was still two stories beneath us at its peak: enough of a drop to give your stomach a little twirl. Plus, we were starting the zip line on the fourth floor, but we were getting off on the matched Juliet balcony to the canal side, which was on the third floor, and now that we were up here, I was realizing that the change in elevation was a bit steeper than I'd expected. The trip across was going to go quite a bit quicker than I'd planned for, but it was too late to change anything now.

Dad reached out and plucked at the rope like it was a guitar string. He looked back at me.

"You know what," he said, "if experience has taught me one thing, it's when to let somebody else show you how it's done."

I clipped in and stepped off into thin air.

68

I WAS MOVING FAST AND WAS halfway across when one of the Prusik knots I'd made from the three-millimeter line to tighten up the zip-line rope slipped on me.

A Prusik knot is just a friction hitch. It's commonly used in climbing and rescue work. They are normally bomb-proof, but whether it was the difference in size between the three-millimeter line and the zip-line rope itself, a difference in the material used to manufacture the two different ropes, or whether I'd just been sloppy, the effect was the same: a sudden lurch as the zip line sagged two feet lower.

There was enough of a drop from one turret to the other that I was already cruising, but the sudden slack seemed to shoot me forward, which would have been okay if the bounce hadn't spun me around at the same time.

I came screaming into the Juliet balcony. Backward.

I hit the stone pillar where the rope was attached with a violence that I had not expected. I smashed the same spot on the bottom of my shoulder blades where Beard had clipped me with his baton, knocking the wind out of myself, and also managed to bang my hip and elbow.

I looked across at Dad and . . . he hadn't even been watching. He was staring down at the glass roof over the courtyard, distracted by the thin sound of singing that we could hear from below.

I unclipped and did an inventory: I was going to be bruised, and it was going to take a few seconds for me to catch my breath, but it could have been a lot worse. I'd managed to avoid a head injury or something incapacitating.

Across the way, Dad seemed to have finally realized it was his turn, and he clipped in and got himself to the edge.

He looked at me, then down, then at me, then down again. He took a step back.

I tried not to move. It was like he was spooked. Maybe being in prison had done a number on him. Maybe he'd lost his nerve?

He seemed to gather himself and then stepped back onto the ledge. He must have had to talk himself into it, because it was a long, slow three-count before he finally launched himself.

He came in hot, though he didn't have to suffer the shock of the Prusik slipping midway, and he stayed aimed straight, his feet in front of him. I was able to catch him as he came in, and with his legs to help absorb the impact when he reached the pillar, he had a much gentler stop than I did.

"That wasn't so bad," he said cheerily.

I rubbed my hip where I'd smashed it into the stone and stretched a little to ease the kink in my back.

He didn't notice; he was already at work disassembling the setup.

Dad tied the three-millimeter line back onto the heavier rope, and then I cut the rope—careful to hold on to it so it didn't spring through my fingers—as we reversed the process. We brought the rope back, untied it, reattached the three-millimeter to the drone, and then flew the drone all the way around to unwind the line so we had everything over on the other side with us.

Once we were done, I swapped out the drone's battery with a spare from the payload boxes so it would be ready at the end of the job. Dad handed me the original score and then loaded everything else, including the cloned controller and headset back into the boxes.

There was no sign we'd ever been there.

Well, no sign except for the drone and the payload boxes with the zip-line gear, but I would take care of that later using the original controller I'd left back at Giovanni's.

Just as we finished, the houselights in the banquet hall came on as the singer's performance ended, signaling to us that it was time to hustle down the stairs and open the secret door to the vault anteroom.

Dad said, "Told you this was going to be easy."

I limped a little going down the stairs, my hip tight from the impact, my elbow throbbing, my back aching, but once again, Dad seemed oblivious.

When we got to the bottom, Dad pulled the rope, triggering the secret door: The wall slowly swung open in front of us and we stepped through it and into the vault anteroom.

The door leading to the cashier's cage and front desk was still closed, which was something I'd verified on my way in, but that was still one of those moments when the job could have turned sour.

Inside the anteroom, we could hear the murmur of the party going on, and even from where I was standing, right next to the turret shaft, the counterweight was barely audible over the crowd nose as the wall closed behind us.

Dad looked at me. "Well, let's get this finished. The only way out now is through."

The room had enough ambient light through the frosted glass in the door leading to the cashier's cage that we could see each other's expressions as well as the numbers on the vault door's dial.

After he'd dialed the two vaults the first time, way back in the day, after the job was over, he'd written down the combinations in the bundle. It was one of his habits to update the plan after the job was done, though I'd never understood why he bothered. And even though it would have been a breeze to open the vaults again—if he could dial them, they weren't going to be a problem for me—it was still amusing to watch how pleased he was that the old combination still worked.

He grinned at me, and then we stepped inside the first vault. Dad repeated his trick on the second vault door, trying the combination he'd figured out more than thirty years ago, and letting out a quiet snicker when that worked as well.

One wall inside the second vault had floor-to-ceiling shelving, packed tightly with neatly labeled boxes and bins holding the artifacts the docents at La Casa del Libretto had deemed to be less valuable but still worthy of vault storage. The Frankensafe took up most of the rest of the room, and eyeballing it, I thought it must have been a tight fit to get through the two vault doors. As it was, I figured, even with the second vault door closed, I'd only be able to open the Frankensafe maybe three-quarters of the way.

Dad was outside the second vault, I was inside.

He gave me the "okay" signal with his hand. I gave it back.

And then he shut me in.

Showtime.

69

AS SOON AS THE VAULT DOOR WAS CLOSED, all outside sound was cut off. I turned on the light switch, and the only thing I could hear as I looked at the safe was the unpleasant buzz of the fluorescent ceiling fixture. I'd been worried about what I'd find when I got in front of the Frankensafe.

I shouldn't have been.

It wasn't a monster at all.

The Frankensafe was a blank sheet of metal on the front, interrupted only by a single dial and the unlocker.

I reached out and gave the unlocker a nudge, in case the last person who'd opened the safe had accidently left it unlocked.

No such luck.

Then I gave the dial an exploratory spin.

I couldn't stop myself from laughing.

I had no clue where the door to the Frankensafe had come from—it was a different color of metal from the body, clearly swapped out at some undetermined date—but the dial was barely a step up from what you put on your locker in high school. It was the definition of a friendly lock. I didn't even have to put my ear against the door to hear it clicking!

Every click of the dial was like a finger snap, and when I passed the first correct number, it sounded like a cymbal crash.

For my own amusement, I timed how long it took for me to crack it: thirty-six seconds.

With my eyes closed.

The inside of the safe was half empty and neatly organized. The replica Puccini score was easy to spot, and I swapped it for the original that I'd taken out of the Nimsik at Auldhilda's, closed the safe up, and then stood there for a couple of minutes, killing time.

I didn't need to make Dad feel badly about how easy it all was for me.

70

BY THE TIME DAD LET ME OUT from the second vault, there wasn't anything to do other than wait for the next performance to start; when it was over and the houselights came back on again, that would be Helen's cue to pull her pratfall, Nando's cue to make a commotion, and we could enter stage right without anybody noticing.

In the half-light of the antechamber, I disassembled the frame holding the forged Puccini score and gave the pieces to Dad. He distributed them in his tuxedo jacket since my pockets were full of the tools I thought I might have needed with the Frankensafe.

What a joke: The click, click, clack would have been enough to guide a blind man.

With Dad putting the frame pieces in his jacket, all that was left for me was to deal with the Puccini score. Or, rather, the replica, because the actual, original score was now, finally, back in the safe, where it was supposed to be, so that it could be returned to the original owners, an old wrong set right.

I felt a little proud of myself.

I looked at the scrap of paper that was left over from disassembling the frame. We were standing by the exit, to the side of where the light leaked through the frosted glass on the door to the cashier's cage, and I could barely see what was written on the forgery. It didn't matter. I knew what was there: *Che gelida manina, se la lasci riscaldar.*

And I could hear it too! The next performance had started. The short, rotund, bearded tenor who had elicited murmurs of excitement from the crowd.

I couldn't decide if I wanted to start laughing or crying.

The whole thing was ridiculous and beautiful at the same time.

I folded the reproduction of the score in half, and then half again, then half again, and slipped the piece of paper into one of the inside pockets of my tuxedo jacket.

Che gelida manina, se la lasci riscaldar.

Auldhilda would be onstage with the tenor, as he sung to her, rapt with attention, but surely, she was thinking of her late husband, of Giancarlo.

Just as surely, Giovanni was in the audience, pleased with the grandeur of the gesture, thinking of his beloved lost brother, of history, of romance, of mistakes that could be fixed, and mistakes that could not be fixed.

Nando would be wearing that self-satisfied smirk of his, readying himself for his star turn.

And I didn't know whether it would be out of genuine rekindled love, or simple nostalgia, but I was sure Helen had taken Nando's hand in hers.

I heard a sharp breath from beside me.

Was Dad . . . Was he crying?

I closed my eyes. I thought of falling asleep in Mom's lap when I was little, of the warmth and the music and the way I felt safe in her arms.

For several minutes, we studiously ignored each other. The tenor finished. The applause was warm and generous, if not thunderous. As it started to die out, there was a fresh wave as Auldhilda took her place, an acknowledgment of her return to the stage for the first time since she married, or maybe just a thank-you for her and Giancarlo's generosity to La Casa del Libretto over the years, or simply a tribute to the memory of Giancarlo.

Dad leaned close, and I could see he'd gone from melancholy all the way back to delight with how the job was going: "I told you this was going to be a breeze."

"We're not done yet," I whispered back.

"Come on. Your trick with the drone was pretty good. Like I told you, easy. Nothing to worry about."

I'd been out there, dealing with Beard and Motorcycle Jacket, figuring out how to salvage a plan that had become unworkable because of the moon and tides, treating this like the job it was, while Dad and the rest of the adults were lost in a haze of what had been.

But Dad wasn't wrong either.

It all suddenly seemed so silly and harmless. So what if this was just a chance for Nando to relive his glory days, for all of them to rekindle a moment in history when things had felt like they were at their best? I wondered if I'd be filled with this kind of nostalgia at their age, but all I did was nod and whisper back, "Nothing to worry about."

The applause died out and Auldhilda started singing about her simple life and her job as an embroiderer.

Dad whispered, "All we have to do now is wait for the fat lady to finish singing."

He seemed pleased with his dumb joke despite Auldhilda's diminutive size. He turned and put his hand on the rope that would open the secret door for our exit.

I got myself ready.

71

THERE WASN'T MUCH TO IT. Once the song ended and the applause finished, after about thirty seconds to a minute—Helen and Nando would make the call on the timing depending on how they read the room—Helen would have her "medical emergency." Again, depending on how they read the room, it would involve a pratfall or an ease-down. Once the room was all aflutter, Dad would pull the rope, we'd slip through the doorway into the wings, and as the doorway closed behind us, we'd simply make our way off the stage as casually as possible, and head back to our table, and ta-da! Drinks all around to celebrate a job well done!

As I heard Auldhilda approach the end of the song, the trill of a flute cuing us up, we suddenly heard glass breaking, plates and silverware crashing to the ground, a woman screaming.

Dad and I looked at each other, perplexed.

"Helen went early," Dad said, no longer needing to keep his voice down.

With the smash of glass and plates, I thought Helen must have taken the table with her, or simply grabbed the tablecloth as she went down. I made a note to compliment her on her commitment to the bit, even if she did jump the gun. There was more shouting and a wave of people's voices, cries for help, everything we could have hoped for in terms of a distraction.

Dad gave me a "what are you going to do?" look and pulled the rope, releasing the catch on the secret door. There was a one- or two-second delay as the counterweight began to open the section of wall in front of us.

I wasn't feeling even a pang of stage fright as I went through the door into the wing of the stage. There was a younger woman in front of me, dressed as if she was one of the upcoming singers, but she was looking out from the edge of the curtain at the audience, her back to us, oblivious of Dad and me coming out from the vault antechamber.

The houselights had gone on, and I could see Auldhilda and the tenor standing onstage, looking lost, staring out into the audience. The timing might have been off, but Helen's distraction was serving its purpose nicely.

Dad came through, giving me a convivial smack on the back as he passed by. I winced—he'd caught me in the same spot I'd smashed into the pillar during my high-speed zip-line approach, the same spot that Beard had whacked with his baton—and then followed him, sparing only a single backward glance to watch the door slowly reverse directions.

We got an odd look from an old lady at one of the tables near the half stairs leading off the stage down to the banquet hall. I smiled at her and her odd look turned into a smile back.

There was a huge milling crowd of people by Giovanni's table, and plenty of people in the banquet hall were standing and looking; Helen's pratfall was like a spotlight, focusing the attention away from us. I noticed Fio and Bosco with their arms out, keeping people back, and I could see the back of Giovanni's head. Somebody shouted for an ambulance, and a husky middle-aged man was standing on a chair and calling out for a doctor.

Dad and I nonchalantly made our way along the edge of the room to the rear. When we got back to our table, it was empty. The older couple who had been sitting with us was gone, and I had no clue where Richa was, but a few seconds after we got there, Paulie sauntered up to the table and sat down with me and Dad.

"Did I imagine it, or did Helen go early?" she said.

"Didn't make any real difference," Dad said. "I'm assuming she had some reason for it."

"I kind of wish I'd been here the first time," I said. "I bet it was fun for her to throw a drink in Nando's face."

"Your mom saw it," Paulie said. "She said he was sputtering his apologies to Helen, pleading innocence. She said it was terrific, but this worked as well, I guess. Any problems on your end?"

Dad was in a jovial and generous mood. He acknowledged my contribution, saying it had worked well, though adding that the zip line was a bit faster than he'd expected—and that was with me helping to catch him!—and then laughing about how the combinations on both vault doors were the same as they'd been decades earlier.

Paulie asked me how my part was, and Dad answered for me: "Took longer than I expected. A couple of minutes. It would have been cutting it close if I had to do it, I think."

Not even, a couple of minutes, I thought, thirty-six seconds, but it would have been bragging to say it out loud. And it would have taken Dad at least ten minutes to open the Frankensafe, even with the loose dial. But I was distracted. The chatter on the other side of the room had pitched up once more, and I saw one of the staff members from La Casa del Libretto whisk through the doors carrying an automated external defibrillator kit. I thoughtlessly rubbed my wrist, where my new watch sat, covering the slight mark still left over from when I'd zapped myself with the Nimsik.

Dad stood up, looked to the front of the room, and sat back down. "Helen's really milking it."

Paulie dismissed him. "Oh, you know how Nando is. If there's a crowd, he'll ham it up, and he's playing the doting husband. He wants to make it look good. Here," she said, and flagged down a waiter who was passing by with a tray full of glasses of prosecco. We each took one, and then Paulie held up her glass: "To a job well done."

"Again," Dad said.

I said, "To the Venice Double part two," and then we clinked glasses.

The commotion in the room had calmed down to close to the normal hubbub. Any second now—certainly before the staff member tried to use the AED—Helen would make a full recovery and get back to her feet. She'd say it was low blood sugar or whatever excuse she had worked out, and that she wanted to sit for a few minutes, drink a little water, and once she was feeling better, she'd have her husband, yes, that's you dear, she'd say to Nando, escort her out, but she was fine, no need to worry.

"Well," I said, looking at my watch. "I've had enough opera for tonight. There's this jazz club Ginny and I stumbled upon the last time we were in Venice, and I found it again yesterday. How about, once Richa comes back to the table, we get out of here and go to that club instead of Giovanni's palazzo? It's cute. You guys will like it, and we can have Nando and Helen meet us there."

Paulie gave Dad a "whatever" indication, and Dad said sure, but he seemed distracted. He stood up again, looked, and then sat down again.

"What?" I said.

"I don't know."

Even Paulie seemed unsettled. A minute passed.

I said, "Should we…"

Two paramedics rushed through the main doors, wheeling a gurney, moving with contained haste.

I looked at Dad and then Paulie.

"Nothing we can do," Paulie said grimly. "Keep your distance. Keep your discipline."

Then, from across the room, as the paramedics got to Giovanni's table, I saw Richa part the crowd, headed in our direction.

Even before Richa got to our table, before she opened her mouth, before she said anything at all, I knew that it was Nando.

72

WE STAYED TO WATCH THE paramedics bring Nando out.

Helen walked alongside the gurney, her eyes never leaving her ex-husband. Giovanni trailed them, ashen faced, until Richa darted over from our table; she intercepted him and pulled him aside.

I started to get up to follow Nando, but Dad grabbed my arm and yanked me back into my seat. "Give it a minute," he said. "No need to call attention to us."

I only caught a passing glimpse of Nando's face. He had an oxygen mask on, and his eyes were closed. His thin hair was mussed, and there was a thick smear of blood near his temple, where he must have hit his head when he collapsed. I waited for Helen to acknowledge us, but she didn't look over at all.

There was a brief lull in the room after the paramedics went through the door with the gurney, and then the high chattering surge of people asking each other what happened, if the man was all right, did anybody know what was going on. The night's emcee bounded onto the stage, took the microphone, and apologized to the crowd for the inconvenience, and said that the next performance would begin in a few minutes, and then dessert would be served, followed by the grand finale.

To the side, Richa was still speaking earnestly to Giovanni; he went from shaking his head to nodding, and then turned back to his table. Richa seemed to gather herself, and then she came over to where Dad, Helen, and I were waiting.

Before any of us could say anything, she said, "Helen said that he had not been himself all evening, but she had no warning. She was getting herself ready for her part as Auldhilda sang, but before it was her time, Nando collapsed."

Dad asked a question, but I was thinking about how he'd been the last two days. The way he'd seemed to be full of life one instant, the vital, enthusiastic Nando I remembered from my childhood, and then the next, an old man, his age showing through. I thought about the thinness of the skin on the backs of his hands, the age spots, the slight cloudiness in his eyes. But I also thought about the way he smooth-talked Helen, how he brightened in her presence. I thought about the way his hands fluttered while he told stories, how even if he couldn't deal as smoothly as he used to, he'd managed to sneak a few false shuffles in while he'd played hearts with Dad, Helen, and Paulie on the train from Rome to Venice.

Paulie asked me a question. I nodded in agreement, though I couldn't have told you what she said. I closed my eyes and rested my head on my hands.

After an indeterminate length of time, I looked up again. Dad and Paulie were gone.

Richa reached out, taking one of my hands. "Duke?"

The houselights dimmed for the next performance, and I bounced up out of my seat. "I need to go outside."

As we went through the lobby, Richa steered me toward the front door and then broke off to stop at the coat check. I didn't wait for her. I walked out the doors of La Casa del Libretto and into the square.

Here and there, patrons from the event were making their way home, a few early departures from an event still in full swing despite what had just happened with Nando. The sky was winter-clear, the temperature hovering above zero, a gentle breeze carrying the mineral scent of salt water and the lagoon. The moon hung in the sky like a prop from a movie, silver and full and taunting me.

The moon waits for no man, I thought.

I heard the tap of Richa's heels behind me.

"Here is your jacket— Oh, oh," Richa said. "No, no, please, don't cry."

She kissed me gently, and then again, and gave me a moment before pulling back and looking at me. "Would you like to return to the palazzo? Giovanni will be meeting the rest of them at the hospital, but if you—"

"No," I said, gathering myself. "I'm okay. I'll be okay. Just… Can we walk a bit before we go to the hospital?"

"Of course," she said. She took my hand, and we headed out under the moonlight.

It wasn't even eleven o'clock, but it felt later. We strolled silently for several minutes, and then Richa's phone pinged, and she said, "Your father and Paulie have arrived at the hospital."

I snorted mirthlessly. "I'm so sick of hospitals."

She glanced at me, but she either didn't understand or understood well enough not to mention Ginny's name. Instead, she gave my hand a squeeze, and we turned, and then crossed a bridge over one of the smaller canals and then turned again.

We passed through a square fronted by a couple of crowded trattorias and *bacari*, obscenely alive with lights and noise and people unaware of anything other than a Saturday night in Venice. I was glad when it was behind us, though the chipper bleat of music followed us as we turned down a secluded alley illuminated only by moonlight.

Richa and I were halfway to the next corner when I heard them coming for me.

73

I'D THOUGHT, JUST FOR A HEARTBEAT, it was Beard and Motorcycle Jacket making a second attempt despite their broken arms and how thoroughly I'd dismantled them.

I was wrong.

It was the kid. The stoner on the bench who Giovanni had bought the joint from. The one I'd seen loitering in front of the *bacaro* the night before. He was joined by an older, harder-looking man with a scar on his cheek.

I'd made a critical error. I'd dismissed the kid as harmless, but the layers and the smell of pot smoke had been camouflage. I'd never even seen the other guy. But there was no way it was a coincidence: I'd pegged Beard and Motorcycle Jacket as a two-person team, but there'd been four of them.

These two wanted payback for what I'd done to their partners.

Scarface had a knife, and the kid was sporting a pair of brass knuckles.

They came at me and Richa with speed and malice.

I swept an arm out, pushing Richa behind me, against the wall. She gave a sharp cry as she bounced against the stone, but I was too busy to worry about it.

Even though Beard and Motorcycle Jacket had been pros, these two were better.

The older guy came first. I heard the tear of fabric as the knife swept across my body. I managed to pull back just enough to avoid contact with my flesh, but I barely had time to get out of the way of the kid's attempt to cave my skull in.

I ducked under the brass knuckles, barely registering the thump of him connecting with the wall.

I kicked out, catching the kid in the knee. His leg buckled, and I took the opening to shove Richa as hard as I could, pushing her away from the center of the action.

The guy with the scar swung his knife again, and I caught his wrist with my hands, but at the same time, the kid, with one knee on the ground, punched out. He caught my hip with his brass knuckles, right where I'd smashed it into the wall earlier.

It made me lose my grip on Scarface's wrist, but I was able to bring my knee up into the kid's chest, knocking him back onto his ass.

Scarface jabbed the knife at me, and I wasn't quite able to avoid it; I felt a bright hot sting near the top of my left shoulder.

But he was overextended, and it left him exposed enough that I could chop his throat.

In that moment, with the kid scrambling back to his feet, and Scarface recoiling from the blow I'd given him, I reached my hand behind my back and grasped for the pistol. I wrapped my fingers around the grip, just as Scarface recovered and came back at me.

I shot him in the face.

The sound echoed in the alley, but I could still hear Richa's gasp as she suddenly seemed to understand what was happening.

The kid stepped back, raising his hands, staring in horror at his partner's body, the pool of blood spilling out on the ground from the hole in the man's face.

"Please," Richa said.

I didn't take my eyes off the kid. The pistol didn't waver.

"Please, Duke," Richa said again. "Please."

I flicked the barrel down and shot the kid in the ankle.

Richa shrieked but almost immediately cut herself off. I spared a look back in time to see her covering her mouth with her hands. Her eyes were wide, and she looked like she was barely stopping herself from panicking.

The kid was curled up on the ground, gripping his ankle. The blood welling through his fingers and the blood leaking from his partner's dead body looked almost black in the night.

I could hear Richa softly sobbing, but there was nothing to worry about anymore. Scarface was dead, and the kid didn't have it in him to keep trying.

I reached back for Richa's hand with my free hand, and felt a twinge in my shoulder where Scarface had stabbed me. It hurt, but didn't seem to have an impact on my range of motion.

Just to be safe, I kept the kid covered with the pistol as I walked backward to the end of the alley with Richa. As soon as we turned the corner, I started walking briskly, almost dragging Richa behind me.

My last image of the kid was him still gripping his ankle, staring at his partner, rocking and keening in pain.

They should have left me alone.

74

UNLESS THE KID WAS A complete and utter moron, he'd avoid the hospital; show up with a gunshot wound and the police would have a whole bunch of questions for you. I had no clue if they had a local vet lined up—usually a doctor who had money problems and was willing to turn a blind eye to reporting requirements in exchange for a cash payment, but sometimes an actual veterinarian—but Beard and Motorcycle Jacket would have needed to see somebody after what I did to their arms. But if they weren't professional enough as a team to have a crooked doctor lined up, screw 'em.

They were lucky that three of them were still alive. If Richa hadn't been there, I would have killed the kid too.

I put the gun away, pleased at how good of a job the tailor had done with my request; it had been riding against the small of my back all night and nobody, not Richa, not Dad or Paulie, not Helen or Nando, had spotted it. I'd felt a bit silly about even carrying it, but since I'd already arranged the pickup through Noor, I had decided better safe than sorry.

Thankfully.

With the gun holstered, I let go of Richa's hand to explore under my jacket and feel my shoulder. When I brought my hand back out, there was a smear of blood on it.

"Duke," Richa said.

"It's not bad," I said. "I don't think I'll even need stitches." As long as I kept my black tuxedo jacket on to cover my bloodstained white shirt, I didn't think anybody would notice.

Richa didn't respond to that, and I looked at her fully for the first time since we'd been attacked. She was barely keeping it together. She'd probably never seen anybody get killed before.

"You need a second?" I asked.

She nodded, and I stopped walking. She sat down almost immediately on the lip of an empty fountain. I started to speak, but she shook her head this time, and I gave her some space.

I thought she might start crying, but she just stared at the ground.

I could hear shouting and sirens, but they were in the distance. It had only been a few minutes since the kid and Scarface had tried to jump us, but it felt like it had been longer. We'd gone back in the direction we'd come from, retracing our steps toward La Casa del Libretto, getting closer than I'd realized: Two couples dressed in formal wear walked past us, chatting gaily. One of them, a man in his late sixties, looked at Richa sitting on the lip of the fountain, and then at me, and gave me a little wink and a smile, as if he thought we were in the middle of a lovers' quarrel. Then they were gone, and it was the two of us again.

I poked around inside my jacket again, probing at the wound, but it didn't seem like anything serious. Between that, my hip, my elbow, and my back, I was going to be sore for a few days, but I'd gotten worse just sparring with Ginny.

After a few minutes, I put my hand on Richa's arm.

"Richa," I said quietly, "it's over."

She nodded, but she didn't look up. I sat down beside her.

"I'm sorry," I said. "You're going to be all right."

"Nobody was supposed to get hurt," she said. "Nando promised, or we never would have agreed to it."

I thought of all the times Nando had promised me something when I was a kid, and all the times he'd melted away, leaving without so much as a goodbye. "He makes a lot of promises," I said. "That's who he is. I don't think he can help himself."

"I told Giovanni, when Nando came and he told us he wanted to do the job as one last—"

Her phone pinged and she cut herself off. She looked at her screen and said, "It is Alvise. The final performance has ended, and he is escorting Giovanni to the hospital soon to meet the others." She stood up. "Come," she said, her voice almost back to its normal, confident self.

I wanted to ask her to finish her sentence, but I realized I had a good idea of what she was going to say.

Nando. One last hurrah.

It had been him the whole time. Not Giovanni, but Nando.

We walked side by side, neither one of us speaking, but as we approached the hospital, she took my hand.

We found Dad, Paulie, and Helen in a waiting room off the ICU. The hospital itself, like so many things in Venice, was a blend of old and new, but the waiting room had the bland sterility of hospital waiting rooms everywhere. Industrial furniture and the standard scent of despair.

Helen rose from her chair and hugged me, as if I was the one who needed comforting instead of her, but I kept my jacket on and the blood was hidden from sight. Dad looked grim, catching my eye over Helen's shoulder and giving a quick, rough shake of his head. Richa immediately set out to see if she could get any more information, while Paulie brought me up to speed. Not that there was much more to tell me than what I'd heard at the gala: Nando had been feeling poorly, though he'd pooh-poohed it to Helen, telling her he was fine, until, as Helen readied herself for her pratfall, he'd simply collapsed. His heart, a stroke, something else, we didn't know. Giovanni arrived only a few seconds before Richa returned, and that's when he told us: Nando had been dying the whole time.

Cancer.

I thought about how old Nando had looked in certain moments, the tiredness, the occasional coughing fit. I'd just chalked it up to old age.

Nando had made Giovanni swear not to tell us. Giovanni said that Nando didn't want us fussing over him, had sworn he was up for doing the job when Giovanni had called him about a repeat performance—I looked at Richa when Giovanni said that, but she didn't seem to realize she'd accidently told me the truth, that it was Nando who'd wanted the job to happen.

The truth, Giovanni said, was that Nando was already months past the date the doctor had given him.

Helen started crying, and Dad and Paulie went to her. Giovanni stood back up, hovering over Helen, a stark look of guilt on his face.

I looked at Richa. She wouldn't look back at me.

She'd known he was sick the whole time.

I left the room and stalked the halls of the hospital, trying to clear my head. I stopped in a bathroom and went into a stall to get a look at the wound on my shoulder. It had stopped bleeding. I could deal with it later.

When I got back to the waiting room, they were all sitting silently.

Finally, after nearly two hours at the hospital, a doctor came in: Nando was stable. But what a man in his condition was doing out at a party, he'd never understand. The doctor looked at the six of us and said it would not be a good idea for there to be any commotion, but if his wife would like to see him, that would be acceptable, but then, please, we would all need to leave. It was very late. Come during visiting hours.

I looked at my watch. It was past one o'clock in the morning already.

Dad gave Helen's hand a squeeze, and she left with the doctor. When she came back a few minutes later, she seemed both shaken and somehow sturdier.

"Time to go," she said.

75

FIO HAD BROUGHT ONE OF Giovanni's boats to pick us up at the hospital, and the motor was the only sound as we rode back to the palazzo. Dad and Helen sat near the front, his arm around her, sheltering Helen from the wind. Giovanni and Paulie sat next to each other, but even though they were almost touching, the distance between them was unmistakable. I could feel Paulie's anger coming off her in waves.

Richa stared at the water, but she held my hand. It was cold. Even though I couldn't decide how I felt about her and Giovanni hiding Nando's condition from us, I covered her hand with both of mine, trying to warm her.

At the palazzo, Giovanni disappeared into the parlor, closing the door behind him. Dad and Paulie escorted Helen up the stairs. I started to follow, but Dad looked back at me, and said, surprisingly gently, "The job's not done yet, Duke."

With everything that had happened since we'd come offstage, I'd forgotten.

As the three of them disappeared, Richa looked at me questioningly.

"The drone," I said.

She nodded, understanding. "I'll wait for you."

"It won't take long," I said.

I took the drone's controller and headset from where I'd stashed them, and then went outside. Once I'd brought back all four of the payload boxes, I powered everything down.

But then I realized I'd forgotten one more thing. I went inside and grabbed a fresh battery. Richa was sitting on the stairs, but she didn't say anything as I came in and then left again.

Outside, I got the drone set up to fly again. Then I pulled out my pistol. I could smell the gunpowder as I attached it to the catcher.

I wanted to be done, so I flew it hard, pushing the drone as far to the edge of its range as I dared. Then, when it was over an empty stretch of the lagoon, the first-person view of the headset showing me nothing but moonlight bouncing off the water, I triggered the release and waited for the splash.

Once the drone was back, I powered everything down again, grabbed the payload boxes, the drone, the controller, and the headset, and brought them all inside.

Richa stood up as I walked over to her. She took my hand, and we went up the stairs together.

We were careful with each other, slow, as if we had all the time in the world. She kissed my neck and unbuttoned my shirt. She took a sharp breath through her teeth when she saw the crusted blood from where Scarface had stabbed me. She went into the bathroom and came back with a damp washcloth. She gently washed the blood from my skin, and once it was clean, there was little more than a small, bright mark, about the size of a dime.

I'd gotten lucky.

She put the washcloth back in the bathroom, and then stood in front of me and turned so I could reach the zipper on her gown.

The zipper went down to below her hips, and the gown slipped off her body and she stepped out of it.

The lights were off, but the curtains were open. The full moon had traversed the sky, but still hung in the darkness as if it had been placed there to give us enough light to look at each other.

Then she kissed me again, softly, gently, and led me to the bed, and we made slow, delicate love to each other, and when we were done, she nestled against me, and I fell asleep to the soft purr of her breath against my neck.

76

I AWOKE INSTANTLY AT THE BUZZ of my phone vibrating.

The first hint of sunrise showed itself through the window, which meant it was a bit after seven. I sat up and snatched at my phone, half expecting to be alone in my bed again, but this time, Richa was still there.

There's not much that is scarier than an unexpected phone call at a time when the only news can be bad, but I'd been waiting for it, expecting it. If anything, I'd been surprised Nando was still alive when we'd gotten to the hospital.

But even before I looked at the screen, I realized it wouldn't be the Venice hospital, that they wouldn't be calling *me* about Nando.

Los Angeles.

Ginny's care home.

The phone buzzed a second time.

And then a third time.

Richa sat up, staring at me, her eyes wide, though she had no idea what was happening.

Quarter after seven in Venice. It was a bit after ten o'clock at night in California.

I forced myself to answer.

"Duke?"

It was George, and between the tiny, almost imperceptible lag that occurs when you talk to somebody six thousand miles away, and the noise in the background behind him—several other voices talking, yelling, a general commotion, yelling, talking, celebrating—he had to repeat himself twice before I understood.

Ginny had moved her foot. Twice.

Yes, he was sure. It was Nurse Crusty this time, and she'd come running to him, and he'd gone to check himself, and when he got to the room, he'd almost dismissed it as Nurse Crusty imagining things. "But, Duke, I saw it myself. She moved her foot. I mean, not much, but I couldn't miss it."

I hung up, and then I think it was a while before I stopped crying, and by then I was shivering, despite Richa sitting behind me, her body against mine, keeping me warm. She didn't say anything. She just held me.

A little after eight o'clock, I went to shower. When I came out, Richa was gone.

Downstairs, Helen, Dad, and Paulie were in the dining room, finishing breakfast.

Helen looked exhausted and yet somehow bright-eyed. Her hair was pulled back into a messy bun, and she was wearing a cable-knit cream sweater, but her voice was full of hope as she told me that Nando was stable.

I stood there, not saying anything, not sure what to say, and then I started sniffling.

They stared at me, and then, in an awkward jumble, I tried to tell them about the phone call from George, about Ginny moving her foot, and Helen was holding me, and Dad had turned away from the table so that all I could see was his back, and Paulie was on the phone with Uncle Charles, and then somehow we were all in the boat—Giovanni and Richa with us now, Nicole at the helm—headed to the hospital for visiting hours.

Dad and Helen sat at the front of the boat. He had his arm wrapped protectively around her, though I wasn't sure if it was the chill coming off the water or the world itself he was trying to keep at bay. Helen stared straight ahead, but Dad watched the buildings and tourists as we motored toward the hospital, a wry little grin on his face. I sat next to Paulie, who reached out once and absentmindedly patted my knee. Giovanni and Richa were at the back of the boat, huddled with their heads together, talking quietly enough that I couldn't snatch even the smallest piece of what they said over the sound of the boat. The trip to the hospital felt different in the morning sun than it had going home the night before under the light of the full moon. I looked back at Richa once, catching her eye, and she smiled, and I felt something like hope.

When we got to the hospital, Helen was ushered in first, and then, after a few minutes, she came back to bring us in.

Nando was enmeshed in a spiderweb of tubes and cables, a cannula under his nose providing him with oxygen, and a monitor tracking his vitals blessedly silenced behind him. It was a private room, and despite the hospital's odd blend of antiquity and modernity, the room itself could have easily been plucked from Cedars-Sinai.

His color was off, his skin sallow, the cut on his temple neatly covered with a small bandage that did little to hide the deep purple and black bruise from where he'd hit his head when he fell. The blanket was covering his chest but tucked under his arms. Nando looked like nothing more than an old man in a hospital bed. And yet, despite his obvious tiredness, despite his sickly pallor and bits of white stubble that had sprouted on his face overnight, despite his mussed hair and feebleness, he brightened as we came in.

We took turns greeting him, Dad hugging him first, pressing his head against Nando's shoulder, and then Paulie kissing him primly on the lips. When it was my turn, Nando smiled at me. He held me for a few seconds and whispered into my ear, "Well done, my boy, well done." His voice was a creaky rasp, but it had the warmth of the sun over a summer field when he spoke to me.

I was thankful that when I stood up, Giovanni took his turn, kissing Nando on both cheeks, and then it was Richa, who simply took his hand and gave him an adoring look. By the time Helen said, "Nando, Duke has some news," I almost had control of myself.

I told Nando about Ginny moving her foot. His eyes welled and his mouth fell open, and then he closed his eyes and raised his chin, and I saw the first thin rivulet of tears stream down his cheeks, and then he started chuckling, and there was some of the touch of majesty to him again as he raised his hand and said, "You must go."

I shook my head. "No, it's okay. I'll stay here until—"

Dad cut me off. "He's right. You should go, Duke. Catch the next flight. Go be with your sister. Call us if anything changes, but we'll stay here." Paulie looked at him sharply, but he either ignored her or didn't notice.

Nando started to protest that Dad and Paulie should go immediately to Ginny's side as well, but Dad shook his head. "It's fine. We'll stay for a few more days. Now why didn't you say anything about the cancer?"

It was an odd tableau: Helen had taken one of Nando's hands and was looking down at him as if he was a child. Nando had closed his eyes, the exhaustion breaking through what I realized was a front he was putting on for me. Dad stared in concern not at Nando, but at Helen, the woman who was going to be left behind, again. Paulie shook her head, though I didn't understand what it was she had wanted. Giovanni stood a bit off to the side, clearly unaccustomed to being anything other than the center of attention, but even he understood that it wasn't his moment.

And Richa. She looked at me, and I couldn't read the little twist at the corner of her mouth. She said, "I took the liberty of booking multiple flights. I would recommend you catch this first flight if you are able, as it is the best option, though that will mean leaving soon."

I took a deep breath. "I'd like to talk with Nando. Alone."

77

RICHA DIDN'T ASK ME WHAT I'D said to Nando, and I didn't offer.

We sat together near the bow of the boat, and then she accompanied me to the Piazzale Roma, where Bosco was waiting for us with a car. When we got to the airport, Richa told me to let Bosco deal with my luggage, and then she took me to a private lounge where we could wait for my flight to board.

When it was just the two of us, she said, "I had the staff get another suitcase for you. For your new clothes. I thought you'd want to take them with you."

"Thanks."

"I've never been to Los Angeles," she said.

"I'd like to show it to you. Maybe..."

"Perhaps," she said.

I didn't know if it was the simple awkwardness of leaving, or if the savage part of me I'd revealed to her last night when I'd protected us had finally sunk in: She'd seen me kill a man, and maybe she'd realized that if she hadn't been there, I would have killed the other man as well without thinking.

This had all been a game to her, but the blood had made it real.

And then it was time for me to leave, and she kissed me, and I looked out the window as we took off, watching the water and Venice disappear as I flew back to California, wondering whether "perhaps" meant soon, and what Dad would say to Helen when Nando's hands had gone cold, and if I would know the instant when Uncle Charles passed by, going the other direction from me, on his way to join Paulie, and if, while I was thousands of feet above the ground, flying, flying, flying, Ginny would open her eyes.

But most of all, I wondered which Nando was the real one. Maybe it didn't matter. Maybe what mattered is the life he'd invented for himself.

When I'd spoken alone with Nando, in the hospital room that morning, I'd told Nando what I figured out, and then I asked him to finally tell me the truth.

I could see him trying to come up with one last dodge, but he was all out of cons. Because it was Nando, even when he was telling the truth I knew it was still bent, but he meant it when he said that Ginny and I were family, and that he loved us. But when he said he was sorry for lying to me, we'd both smiled, knowing that wasn't even close to the truth.

He wasn't sorry. Not at all. Not for any piece of it. Oh, he was sorry that my mom wasn't here anymore, but hadn't it been worth it, this one, last grand gesture?

He couldn't help himself, he told me: It had been his idea from the beginning this time. The second time pulling the Venice Double. Not the first time, he insisted. That truly had been Giovanni, though of course Nando had fallen in love with the romance of the idea. And it had been such a perfect time in his life, those years when he and Helen were together, when my dad and my mom were part of the package, when Paulie was working in the field instead of being "management," so of course, when the doctor told him six months ago that his life was over, Nando wanted one last chance to return to the glory days.

This time, the second time for the Venice Double, he had stacked the deck. He'd convinced Giovanni of the necessity of fixing his mistake.

"That was not a lie, even if I was the one who explained to him why he should undo his mistake," Nando said. "Giovanni wanted to make it right. But..."

Nando gave a wry smile. "All I can say is that Auldhilda made things more complicated for us."

The rush had been intended—the urgency part of any con, and a way to avoid having any of us ask too many questions—but not everything went according to the plan, he said.

I knew he was thinking of me almost electrocuting myself with the Nimsik, and having to use the zip line instead of the tunnel, but that's not what I was thinking of: I thought of Beard and Motorcycle Jacket, the grating, snapping sound of breaking their arms, the echo of the gunshot when I put a hole in Scarface's head, the sharp sound of Richa's gasp, the way the stoner kid had grasped his ankle and moaned in pain and sorrow as I walked away, the twinge in my back, the bruise on my hip and elbow, the pinprick scab from the knife, how lucky I'd been that I'd avoided anything more serious.

"Still," he said, "it was fun, wasn't it?"

"It's been good to see you again," I said.

"Please do me this one last favor."

"Anything," I said.

"Please just let Helen and your father and Paulie believe this was all about the job, that it was something Giovanni wanted, and that this was not just an old man's desperate attempt to . . ."

He stopped. "I'm sorry. I should have been a better man. You deserved better than me, Duke. So did Helen. I'm sorry."

"You are who you are."

He closed his eyes for a long blink, and then he said, "I wish your mom had been here. I wish I'd been able to say goodbye to your sister."

He grasped my hand weakly, earnest, intent on making sure that I heard him: When Ginny came out of her coma, and he knew she would come out of her coma, I had to tell her that he loved her.

"She'll be okay," he said. "You'll see. You have to hold the faith, Duke."

"I'm sorry I have to go."

"You don't want to be here for this," he said. "I don't even want to be here for this. This isn't a clean way to die."

He laughed, and then started coughing, and the way it racked his body made it obvious how much he'd been hiding. When he finished, his eyes were wet again.

I started to speak, but he shook his head. "Don't worry. I'm not going to die on you. Not yet. Soon enough, though. But if you'll excuse me, I must close my eyes. I'm sorry it went sour at the end like this."

His voice was weak, and his eyes had a film on them. I'd been deluding myself this whole time: I'd seen his age, but I hadn't been able to tell myself the truth. He was a dying man. It was only a question of if he had minutes or hours or days left.

He said, "I wanted to finish the job and just... slip away. Your last memory of me a bright one. But it was a grand time, wasn't it? And you got paid. Giovanni did that for me, a favor. A grand time, one last grand gesture."

"Sure," I said. I squeezed his hand, barely able to get the words out: "It was all a grand gesture."

"You described my entire life, kiddo," he said, and even though I knew it was an illusion, in those few words, he seemed as alive as he'd ever been.

And then, he closed his eyes and drifted off to sleep.

I held his warm, papery hands in mine, waiting until his deep, even breathing told me he'd fallen asleep. Then, knowing that this time was truly the final time, I kissed him on the forehead, thanked him for sharing the Venice Double with me, his one last grand gesture in what had been a grand, grand life.

EPILOGUE

78

NANDO DIED FORTY-FIVE MINUTES after midnight, at the hospice in Rome where he'd asked to be taken after he was ready to leave the ICU. A week in the hospital, then three weeks in hospice.

It had been almost a full cycle of the moon since I'd helped Nando run the Venice Double as an encore. Because 12:45 in the morning in Rome was 7:45 at night in Florida, Nando died only a couple of minutes before Janus motored into the marina.

I'd spent my first week back in California in something like a hospital as well, and the last three at my own special sort of hospice. Which, I know, is a dark way to think about all of it, but if Ginny's care home was like a chill hospital, and if a hospice is a place where people go when they are focused on end-of-life care, what was I doing in Florida but waiting to provide Janus with some end-of-life care of his own?

I cannot, for the life of me, overstate how boring and terrifying it is at the same time to sit next to your sister slash best friend and wait to see if she's coming out of two-year-long coma, while at the same time waiting to get the news that the man who had been like a grandfather to you had passed from this life to the next.

Ever wait for an important text? Or email? Or whatever people who have real jobs rather than stealing shit for a living wait for? Like that, but times a bazillion, except instead of constantly checking my phone for a text or call about Nando, I was constantly looking *up* from my phone to check to see if my sister had moved.

Spoiler alert: she had not.

Nothing. Not a toe twitch, not a nose wiggle, and certainly not her sitting bolt upright and declaring, "Duke, my favorite brother, I am back!"

After a week of me keeping constant vigil, the night guy, George, every single person on the day shift at the care home, Daisy, Nurse Crusty, Ginny's normal doctor, her surgeon, Meg, and then Meg and her new partner, Theroux, together, and then Meg, Theroux, and their dog, Fanta, who was an adorable misshapen lump of a pup, and then Aunt Paulie and Dad, each calling separately from Italy while they were getting Nando settled in the hospice, they all suggested, in their own separate ways, that it might be a good thing if I took a break from the hospital.

Dad even said, surprisingly and a bit slyly, "You know how your sister is. She won't want you there when she wakes up. This way, she'll have a chance to practice looking like it's no big deal to wake up from a coma after two years."

"You mean, I'll come in, and she'll be sitting up in bed drinking a cup of coffee and texting Meg, and she'll look up and be like, "Hey."

"More like, 'Hey, I know it's been a while' "—his imitation of her was *terrible*—" 'but when did you get so *old*, Duke?' "

I thought of Nando in his hospital bed, the old man's regrets about how he'd lived his life, ending things with a desperate attempt to recapture a moment in time when he had been happy, when life had felt whole for him.

"I'm going to Florida," I said.

"By yourself?"

"You said that the staff told you, and I'm quoting you here, Dad, that it was a 'huge bummer' having me there, and it would be 'awesome' if I took a vacation."

"Duke?"

"Yeah?"

"Tell me when it's over."

79

AFTER HE HUNG UP, I SNUCK A LOOK in Ginny's bathroom mirror. I didn't think I looked any older—certainly not compared to my dad, let alone Nando—but I did need to get a proper haircut now that I had money again.

Because that was one bright side to all of this. The money Giovanni had paid me for this last lark of Nando's was real, even though so much else had been a lie.

Everything felt weird and elastic. I was home, but it didn't feel like it. I'd told Richa I wanted to show her Los Angeles, but now that I was here, I couldn't begin to imagine it. I don't mean a vacation. I knew exactly how that would go: She'd come for a week, and we'd both be electric with anticipation and when she landed, we would have that same genie-in-a-bottle experience.

I thought about the morning I'd met her. How it was chemistry that was impossible to miss. But I'd forgotten that when there's a genie in the bottle, you always have to ask yourself who's the one granting the wishes and who's holding the lamp. After a couple of days, we'd start talking about the future, and we'd have to start admitting that there wasn't one.

I knew she liked me, but she wouldn't be able to forget what she'd learned because of what happened in Venice: Once you step into the shadows, you find out what's in the dark. Sometimes for better, sometimes for worse, and Richa was somebody who preferred the light.

But I also wasn't sure if I could trust her again. She'd known Nando was sick the whole time. And maybe she hadn't known *all* the pieces of what Nando and Giovanni had been up to when they'd brought us all to Italy, but she'd known enough. She'd played me.

If she could look past who I was, could I look past that?

I didn't know the answer to that question.

But once I stepped off the plane in Florida, I knew I was committed to the idea that I wasn't going back to Los Angeles until I'd settled things up with Janus. Or Ginny woke up. Whichever came first.

In all honesty, the first couple of days back in Florida were relaxing. The heat wave had broken. It was still hot in Florida, but now it was California that was sweltering, and the Florida sun felt like a kiss in comparison.

I believed in sun protection and wearing a hat and generally not being a complete idiot who doesn't believe in science, but also, there's something about a sunny day and the sand and a beach when you need a break. I mean, I wasn't on a literal beach, but rather at that same, hollowed-out strip mall, spending morning in the coffee shop, lunch at the sandwich shop next door, and then to the rooftop bar after lunch. But the rooftop bar had a view of the marina and hence a view of some water, and it had beer, and I was on "vacation," and for a few days it was, as Nando would have said, grand.

I brought a laptop and a couple of books with me, popped in my headphones, and was even more invisible than when I'd been here with Dad. I screwed around online, I read three novels, three graphic novels, a collection of poetry written by a college friend's boyfriend who had won some prize and if I read the collection, he promised he'd explain it to me, and I also used my paycheck from the Venice Double to catch up on paying all my bills.

And.

Oh.

My.

God.

I was so bored, and I was so sick of drinking beer.

But also, I was frickin' rich. I thought about what Dad had said about Ginny waking up and immediately cracking a joke about me looking old. Yeah. I needed to take better care of myself. I could afford a decent haircut instead of the do-it-yourself I'd been resorting to for the last two years, and once I was back in Los Angeles, I was going to upgrade my wardrobe too.

I spent some time thinking about what I was going to do with my money, including a trip to Vegas—just because I was suddenly solvent, I didn't think Paulie was going to reverse her stricture about me laying a bet in her territory—but even fantasizing about what to do with a windfall can't make a long wait feel quick. By the fourth day, I told the waiter that I'd tip him fifty bucks an hour not to bring me beer. He looked at me and asked if I'd gotten fired and was too afraid to tell my wife, and if so, I'd be the third guy pulling the same trick this year, and it was better to confess right away because fifty bucks an hour was steep. I said, "Here's fifty bucks," and he took it and left me alone.

After a week, I was pretty sure I was losing my mind. Coffee shop. Restaurant. Bar. I got an ice cream one of the days, but I was so full of coffee that I couldn't even eat it. Every morning, I got up a little earlier so I could run farther, do a few more push-ups and pull-ups and sit-ups, fight against my own shadows for one more minute. I lost count of the days I'd been in Florida—I was keeping track by the phases of the moon—but it had to be seventeen, eighteen. I was waking up at quarter to four every morning. Most nights, during the rooftop bar's happy hour, I was chatted up by one woman or another, and most nights I gave up my vigil accompanied by a new companion.

80

AND THEN, AT 7:45 IN THE EVENING on the day before the first full moon in March—the unromantically named Worm Moon—as happy hour came to an end, in the gloaming, the sunset turning the water into copper and fire, Janus brought his boat into the marina.

I was going to Vegas for sure when this was done.

I felt like I'd laid my rent money on a thousand-to-one, and all I needed was my team to score one more basket and I'd collect. And right now, the ball was in the air, the buzzer's about to sound, and—

—and I nearly jumped out of my skin when my phone rang. I never had the ringer on. Why would somebody like me ever keep the ringer on? Can you imagine the scorn from my dad if my phone *rang* while I was on a job? But, of course, I'd had my ringer on for the past three weeks, because what if I got a call from Los Angeles?

I caught my breath, and then held my breath, because the caller ID showed a name: Richa.

I figured it would have been Dad or Helen or Paulie if Nando's time had come, so it had to mean she was calling to tell me she'd booked a flight out to see me in Los Angeles. Even though I knew how that would end, should I tell her to come? Should I tell her instead what I was doing in Florida?

"Duke," she said.

I cut her off.

"Give me a second," I said. I risked a look through my binoculars. The boat's angle had changed, and I could see a figure standing at the helm.

Janus.

Gotcha.

"Between you calling and what I just saw, this might be the best day of my life," I said.

"It's Nando," she said.

I couldn't figure out what hurt worse: Nando dying or that it was Richa calling? I'd been braced for it with Nando, but dead was dead. There was no card for him to pull from the bottom of the deck. I could forgive Helen for not calling, but Dad, Paulie? Instead, they asked their friend's employee to do it for them?

And even if it embarrassed me to admit it, it hurt that this was the first time since I'd left Venice that Richa had called me. We'd texted a few times, sure, but when she finally called, it wasn't because she wanted to see me, but because she was doing her job.

"When's the funeral?" I asked, though I realized I had no idea *where* the funeral would be. Nando claimed, most of the time, to be originally from Portugal, but who knew with Nando, and it wasn't like he had any relatives. That I knew of. Maybe Helen had—

"No funeral," Richa said. "He didn't want one."

"Oh."

"So there's no reason for you to come here."

"Got it," I said.

"No, Duke, that is not what I meant, I—"

"Don't worry," I said. "I understand. It wouldn't have worked anyway."

Silence from Richa.

Janus's boat moved smoothly and slowly down the canal, easing to the side for a larger boat passing in the other direction. He had a few hundred feet to go before having to make a 180-degree turn into the marina. I'd have an excellent view of the boat in its berth, but right now, in the twilight, Janus was an idea more than a real person. But I was still going to kill him.

"I'm sorry," she said.

"Yeah," I said. "Will you answer one question? Did you know from the beginning that Nando was dying, or was it already in motion when you figured it out?"

She was quiet for several seconds, and then, instead of answering my question, she said, "Nobody was supposed to get hurt."

"That's not how it worked out," I said, and then we said goodbye.

I watched Janus make the turn and then come into the marina. He was a fair hand with his boat, and once he'd made shore, he took the time to reset his mooring lines, making the boat secure. He was settling in for a few days.

I went back to my hotel, changed my clothes, and drove back to the marina. I would have preferred a new moon to a full moon. The Worm Moon was unpleasantly bright for skullduggery. Fortunately, the marina itself was shockingly poorly lit, with almost no security. Sitting in my rental car in a mostly dark, half-full parking lot, even with a full moon, comfortable in the coolness of the night, I could wait until I saw a good opportunity. Janus was a pro, so I had to be smart, but it wasn't the place I would have picked to moor my boat if I was a backstabbing, betraying, lying, cheating—

There he was. I was using a pair of birding binoculars I'd picked up at an outdoor supply store, along with a book on birds in case anybody wanted to know what I was doing with the binoculars at the strip mall. A bit harder to explain what I was looking at through my binoculars at night. In my rental car. Watching a marina. Yeah, okay, I looked suspicious even with the bird-watching guide, but unless Janus went window to window or I was dumb enough to push the panic button on the remote, he wouldn't notice me.

He opened his cabin door, looked right, left, tapped his hip to reassure himself, and then stepped out. He locked and closed the door behind him. He was carrying a full tote bag and had a towel slung over his shoulder. He was wearing flip-flops. Once he disappeared into the bathroom, I figured I had at least ten minutes.

81

I HAD MY PICKS ALREADY IN MY HAND as I walked up the dock. I could almost touch his boat when I tripped on an uncoiled raft of line. I stumbled, had to put my hands down to right myself, and accidentally dropped the entire set of picks.

They made a little plop, plop, plop sound as they hit the water.

I stood up, closed my eyes, started to do a breathing exercise, realized that was insane, opened my eyes, and *then* did a breathing exercise, keeping a watch out for an early return by Janus.

I examined the lock. I looked at the door. I pushed the door hard. It opened.

And that, folks, is why I get paid the big bucks.

It broke the latch, but that was okay. It was on the inside of the door. You couldn't see any damage from the outside. All I had to do was hold the door closed, and Janus wouldn't be able to tell anything was wrong until he'd already turned the key in the lock. So, I waited, one hand holding the door closed, the other holding my knife.

There was a pane of tinted glass on the door, and in the darkness of the cabin—Janus had been thoughtful enough to turn off the lights—it was like looking out from a one-way mirror. If I had to worry about being surprised, I would have done the smart thing, and held my pistol instead of my knife.

I saw Janus come out of the shoreside bathrooms, his tote bag slung over one shoulder, his towel wrapped around his neck.

I put the knife away.

I was going to strangle him.

When he came through the door, I let it swing open as if naturally. I wanted to wait until I was behind him.

And that's when my phone rang.

I still had the ringer on.

I chopped his throat, and he grasped at it with both hands, the air blowing out his mouth making him sound like a child who couldn't whistle. I kicked down on the outside of his right knee, the snap of the bone almost as loud as his scream would have been if I hadn't started with his throat. His leg collapsed in on itself, but he stumbled into the table and stayed upright. Which meant I didn't even have to bend over when I took his left arm, twisting it behind his back like a cop subduing a suspect, until it was only a ruined approximation of a limb, and then I did the same thing again with his right arm, turning it past the point of tolerance. When the second arm made that crackling sound, he managed to eke out a shrill chirp that was still too soft to cause alarm.

I took an end of the towel with each hand and tightened it enough that I wasn't going to have to worry about him making another sound.

The son of a bitch still tried to put up a fight with his only working limb, though. He kicked and kicked as I dragged him in front of the full-length mirror, using the towel around his neck as a lever as I slowly, slowly, slowly, slowly tightened the towel up, making him watch as I choked him to death. That shrill chirp was the last sound Janus ever made, unless you count the final few thumps of his heel against the floor.

Nobody in the marina seemed to have noticed anything amiss, so I took an hour and did a full sweep of the boat. In the fifty-eighth minute, I found the hidden compartment, hilariously enough, behind the full-length mirror. It was about three inches deep, or slightly deeper than the width of a US dollar bill. There were four stacks, which meant the compartment was about twenty-five inches across. And I was guessing about six feet top to bottom. It wasn't completely full, but it was pretty darn close, the four passports not taking up much space at all.

I did the math in my head. It helped that I knew how tall a stack was—one hundred bills in the same currency—and I was doing a down and dirty estimate, but there had to be at least sixteen thousand twenty-dollar bills in there. More than one and a quarter million dollars.

All I needed for this to be the greatest day of my life was for Ginny to wake up.

Crap. I'd forgotten about Nando.

Which made me remember about my phone ringing when Janus walked in.

There was a voicemail from Dad.

"Hey. Give me a call. Nando died. Helen's losing it." A sigh? A hesitation? "I love you."

I listened to it again. That was the only time I'd felt bad about not telling them, but Nando had made me promise to let them believe the beautiful lie of the job.

"Let them have it," Nando had said. "Nobody likes to think they got made a sucker. Besides, it's not entirely untrue, and it's part of the fun, isn't it?"

I looked at the money, and I started laughing.

I'd had a weird couple of months.

On the drive back to California, I stopped twice at hotels and took my chances on leaving the cash in the trunk of my rental car. I didn't want to risk flying with it, but for some reason, I couldn't get myself to carry it inside with me.

I did not get robbed.

It was stupid, but you know, like I said. A weird couple of months.

When I got back to town, it was one of those sweet spots that appears only by magic once in a blue moon, when Los Angeles traffic suddenly disappears, and you can go wherever you want without delay. I took advantage of it for a quick stop to see Ginny. Dad, Paulie, and Uncle Charles had just touched down from Italy and were there, blessed by the same traffic gods as I was on their way home from the airport.

Dad asked me if it was over, I said yeah, and nobody made a fuss about any of it. There was no fuss with Ginny either. No change. Nothing. Nada. Zip-a-roo. I had more than a million dollars in cash in my rental car, another five in my account. It was only four hours to Vegas...

Except, Meg called me and asked when I was getting back from Florida. I told her I had just gotten back to Los Angeles and was about to leave Ginny's care home.

We settled on nine o'clock, at a pizza place where the only reason we could get a seat, even at nine o'clock on a Tuesday, was because Meg's new partner, Theroux, owned the joint.

It was a temperate night, and we sat outside, the moon waning now. Because Meg was dating the owner, we were treated like royalty by the waitstaff, but it was the kind of night where it didn't matter anyway: Everything was perfect.

I would have been comfortable in a T-shirt and shorts or jeans and a blazer. I was wearing shorts and a button-down with my sleeves rolled up. Meg was wearing a sundress. Mostly, Meg and I talked about her nieces and training at the gym and surfing, and we made plans to tentatively try to surf together later in the week. All in all, a delightful night, made more so by my ability to tip using the money I'd looted from Janus's boat.

It was about 11:45 when we said good night.

It was only ten minutes to Ginny's care home, and not much out of my way, so I made another quick stop to see her instead of heading back to my apartment.

Nando would have wanted me to go. He would have wanted me to keep hoping.

But nothing had changed since that afternoon.

Today was not going to be the day Ginny opened her eyes.

Except, it was nearly the stroke of midnight, and in a few seconds, it would be tomorrow; there was always hope, I thought.

I fell asleep in the chair next to her bed.

82

I WOKE UP TO WHAT I THOUGHT was a frog being boiled alive, before realizing it was Ginny, trying to speak.

I opened my eyes *just* as she closed hers again.

I did *not* play it cool. I started screaming for help, and pressed the emergency button, and generally freaked out.

It was kind of embarrassing.

But when Ginny opened her eyes the second time, just as George came barreling in, followed by almost the full complement of staff on duty, I had stopped babbling incoherently.

Ginny tried to talk again, but it was the creak of a screen door in a horror movie.

Her swallow reflex had never been a problem, so George and the other nurses on duty, in consultation with both Ginny's doctor and surgeon, allowed Ginny a sip of water. But by the time that had been approved, Dad, Paulie, Uncle Charles, and Meg had all arrived at the care home, and even though it was the middle of the night, Jameel had come in with the girls, and somebody had Helen on video, so when Ginny did take another sip of water, and then got ready to speak, I think we all held our breath. Which meant that every single person in the room saw her look at me, and in the pin-drop silence, heard her say:

"What's wrong with your hair?"

THE END

ACKNOWLEDGMENTS

Thanks to my wife and children for their support, and particularly for their patience when I'm writing and lost in my own worlds.

I am incredibly lucky to have a great group of friends, and it's not something I take for granted. Thank you.

I want to thank my literary agent, Bill Clegg, and the entire gang at The Clegg Agency.

Thank you to my screen agent Anna DeRoy (no relation!) at WME.

At Union Square & Co., I would like to thank Claire Wachtel, Juliana Nador, and the crew at Union Square & Co.

ABOUT THE AUTHOR

Jesse DeRoy lives in New York with their family. They are a former consultant, rock-climbing instructor, and award-winning journalist. *Safecracker* was Jesse's first novel.

RAISING READERS

Books Build Bright Futures

Thank you for reading this book and for being a reader of books in general. We are so grateful to share being part of a community of readers with you, and we hope you will join us in passing our love of books on to the next generation of readers.

Did you know that reading for enjoyment is the single biggest predictor of a child's future happiness and success?

More than family circumstances, parents' educational background, or income, reading impacts a child's future academic performance, emotional well-being, communication skills, economic security, ambition, and happiness.

Studies show that kids reading for enjoyment in the US is in rapid decline:

- In 2012, 53% of 9-year-olds read almost every day. Just 10 years later, in 2022, the number had fallen to 39%.
- In 2012, 27% of 13-year-olds read for fun daily. By 2023, that number was just 14%.

Together, we can commit to **Raising Readers** and change this trend. How?

- Read to children in your life daily.
- Model reading as a fun activity.
- Reduce screen time.
- Start a family, school, or community book club.
- Visit bookstores and libraries regularly.
- Listen to audiobooks.
- Read the book before you see the movie.
- Encourage your child to read aloud to a pet or stuffed animal.
- Give books as gifts.
- Donate books to families and communities in need.

BOB1217

Books build bright futures, and **Raising Readers** is our shared responsibility.

For more information, visit **JoinRaisingReaders.com**

Sources: National Endowment for the Arts, National Assessment of Educational Progress, WorldBookDay.com, Nielsen BookData's 2023 "Understanding the Children's Book Consumer"